Helen A Leith
PO Box 1318
Castle Rock WA 98611-1318

MW00945142

SHADOWS
AND VEINS

Ken –
So good to
reconnect. This
is a work of fiction
but does follow the
trajectory of addiction,
and today is so good!
with love,
Jeanine

SHADOWS AND VEINS

One woman's journey into the dark world of methamphetamine

JEANINE E. BASSETT

iUniverse, Inc.
Bloomington

SHADOWS AND VEINS

This is a work of fiction. All of the characters, names, incidents, organizations, and dialogue in this novel are either the products of the author's imagination or are used fictitiously.

iUniverse books may be ordered through booksellers or by contacting:

iUniverse
1663 Liberty Drive
Bloomington, IN 47403
www.iuniverse.com
1-800-Authors (1-800-288-4677)

ISBN: 978-1-4620-6906-4 (sc)
ISBN: 978-1-4620-6908-8 (hc)
ISBN: 978-1-4620-6907-1 (ebk)

Printed in the United States of America

iUniverse rev. date: 05/12/2012

Contents

Acknowledgements

For a writing class in the spring of 1986, I wrote a short essay about a former boyfriend who had overdosed on heroin in my basement a year earlier. That essay, along with other episodes from my own bouts with addiction, rattled around in my soul for years. Often I could hear the whispers, "Tell them. Tell the stories." I decided to listen.

At first I wrote in earnest. Then, during a period of prolonged procrastination, I dreamt that Annette, my main character, sent me a text that asked, "Are you just going to leave me hanging here?" No. This is a story that I needed to tell. It is not my story, fact-by-fact, but a work of fiction that draws from my personal experience and my work in addictions treatment.

I acknowledge the support of the many who edited, read and gave feedback, listened to my on-going challenges with self-discipline, or simply asked, "So how *is* that book going anyway?" Amanda, Barbara, Karen, Barb B, Lady, Phillip, Jill, Jayna, my Trust the Process family, including Tabor & Greg, Jerry, Joel, Dan & Leslie, Catherine—you and so many others are appreciated and thanked. Also, I express sweet gratitude to my husband, Kyle, who helped to create the space whereby I could finish this project.

I offer special thanks to David Luckert, whose artist's viewpoint helped to expand and shape the tale, and to Jay LaPlante, my friend, confidant, mentor, cheer-leader, and part of the process when the idea was still a dream.

I dedicate this book to the memories of Richard and Michael.
Without the places where our stories intersected,
this one may not have been written.

Prologue

"Don't die in my fucking basement, damn you!"

Besides being strung out on heroin, Daniel was a speed cook, a clandestine chemist. Judging by the sound of water gurgling from the little room under the stairs, there was a batch of crystal methamphetamine in process at that very moment. If I called an ambulance and he lived, Daniel would go back to prison. I might go to prison. If I didn't, he might die, and then what? How long should I wait? What should I do? I shook him violently, as if movement alone would bring him to life.

Speed! Junkie lore holds that amphetamine can bring a person out of a heroin overdose if you act quickly enough. Zip. Zip. Zip-ity-do-dah, his friends called it. Crank. Crystal. Magic. Ruining my fucking life. Where in the hell was it?

Yanking open the bar drawer, I scanned the contents, looking for the cigar box that I knew held his stash. There it was, under the baggie of pot and a menu from the pizza place up the street. Without stopping to measure I mixed up a hit, blending the off-white sticky powder with a teaspoon of water from the jug of distilled on the floor. Grabbing the syringe that he'd just used, I drew up the liquid. No time to worry about whether or not the tip was barbed.

I'd never shot up anybody else before. Hell, I could barely do myself. I yanked his left arm straight and with shaking hands, jabbed the needle into the bulge that was his vein and drew back. A thin stream of dark red blood entered the rig. Good. I was in. But then his body shifted, ripping the needle out of his arm.

Shit! I tried again, made a clean entry just above the first and injected the contents before he could move. A lump appeared at the injection point, which meant that the needle had slipped again. I pulled out, then rubbed hard on the swollen spot, praying that enough speed had entered his bloodstream to jolt him to life.

He was pale, but the gray tinge was gone and he seemed to be breathing, whether from my ministrations or simply the passing of time.

Finally, finally he stirred, raised his head and mumbled incoherently. I knew that I needed to get him up and moving, but the emergency had passed. He'd lived thirty-nine years thus far and was apparently going to live at least one more day.

I was exhausted, though it had been less than ten minutes since I'd heard his moans from the kitchen. As I guided him up the narrow staircase I was aware that Daniel had almost died and that it didn't seem unusual. For just a moment, I wondered what in me had died to make that so.

It was the spring of 1985. In the following months I became obsessed with the thought that it would happen again, listening through closed bathroom doors, down staircases and around corners for the thump of him hitting the floor. The strain of keeping us both alive grew to be too much. I wasn't ready to face my own addiction to methamphetamine, but I knew that I didn't want a junkie in my house. I told Daniel that either the heroin had to go or he did.

Within a week he had moved out. Two years later I was clean and he was dead from an overdose when no one had been there to listen through the door.

What follows is my story. I am Annette.

Chapter One

"JAMIL, JAMIL," I whispered, kissing my boyfriend's naked back as he slept, tracing his pale brown shoulder blades with my lips. Soft black hair curled down his neck, sweaty from sleep and a pending hangover. I loved this man. How would I tell him about this latest betrayal? Jamil was Arab, and this American raised, backsliding Muslim man of mine had lots of Old World ideas, like "your girlfriend should not screw around."

It hadn't been my intention to hurt him. That regrettable evening had started out like many other Friday nights. Jamil had been away for a few weeks with the family export business, and Joanne and I had met downtown at Rodeo, the club du jour, for drinks.

It was a little after 9:00 when I'd arrived at the club where Joanne and I were weekend regulars. Jim, one of the bartenders, was the brother of an old school chum. I was grateful when the beefy bouncer glanced my way and nodded me up front past the line of girls bulging out of sparkly tube tops and the guys in polyester wide-collared shirts who ogled them. With a tilt of his head, he motioned toward the bar where I knew I'd find Joanne holding court. Enveloped by the familiar club aroma of cigarette smoke, liquor, and musk cologne that would permeate my wool coat for a week, I held my breath and dived in.

Intentionally late, and sober at the moment, I shrank in anticipation of the noisy crowd from the time I left my car until I got through the door. But there she was: my best friend. With a four-inch Afro and an hourglass figure showcased in a low-cut tulip-hemmed dress, Joanne was hard to miss in the mostly white crowd. She was drinking sloe gin and grenadine by the looks of it, smoking a menthol cigarette and telling one of her outlandish tales to a small group of adoring co-workers. The sea parted as I walked up and on to the empty stool she'd been saving just for me. Here I was comfortable. Here I was safe.

"Vodka-7. Bring me two," I yelled to Jim, adjusting the shoulder pads in my sweater while plugging one ear against the pulsing disco beat.

"What's going on?" I yelled to Joanne, scanning the crowd.

"Not much," she shouted back, and with a raise of her eyebrows directed my attention to a table of Middle Easterners.

"Oh shit," I yelled. "Is that the Opium Guy?"

The Opium Guy was Persian. I couldn't remember his name, but knew that he daringly wore a diamond in his left ear lobe and had a heart tattooed on the right cheek of his small, muscular ass. Joanne and I had met him and his cousin nearly a year ago at this same club. After going home alone for the three years I'd been with Jamil, we'd ended up at their place with these guys, smoking opium. We stayed most of the night, Joanne in the bedroom with the cousin and me on the living room floor with this one. As we'd headed out just before dawn, our friend, Charles, a good buddy of Joanne's husband, Anthony, had pulled into the apartment driveway. I thought about the painful conversation I'd had with Jamil once word got out as I threw back the second drink. That would never happen again. I hadn't even looked at another man since.

Joanne sashayed off to dance with one of her friends and I became one with the bar stool, studying the ice in my glass, doing my best to be invisible, a skill I'd perfected growing up when "be quiet or you'll upset your father," was the prime directive. I'd been in Joanne's shadow since she moved in down the street during seventh grade. Even when I traveled with Jamil, Joanne and I talked on the phone nearly every day. Unlike Jamil's sisters with their probing questions, she already knew me and my family. She never asked "why don't you talk more?" or "tell me about your parents."

"Bring me another," I yelled to Jim.

I turned as Joanne approached.

"Look who I found," she exclaimed, feigning surprise. "You remember Mehdi?"

"Hello," he crooned, "It's been a long time."

'Yes,' I smiled, looking everywhere but into his liquid brown eyes. He was still wearing the diamond stud. Smiling, he leaned in and moved my brunette hair in order to speak into my ear.

"Would you like to dance?" he asked, his softy accented voice as smooth as spun honey, his breath warm with the scent of Scotch.

I started to say, "no," but it was only a dance and I didn't want to be impolite. Rolling my eyes at Joanne, I inhaled a gulp from my fresh drink and followed him to the floor. Reaching back, he grabbed my hand as we swam upstream through the sweaty crowd.

It was too loud for conversation, though he tried. From the bits I could hear above the throbbing bass, I learned that he'd been living in California, had been looking for me at the clubs now that he was back in Portland, and was in a new apartment on the west side.

Primed with the perfect measure of vodka, I swayed to the beat, staying upright as a woman beside me danced into my left hip. I smiled at Mehdi without looking at him, focusing just past his shoulder. We danced for over an hour, with side trips to my drink and then one more. As the clock inched past midnight, the DJ played a slow song. I needed a break. Mehdi followed me back to the bar with his hand on the small of my back. It felt good to have him touch me. Joanne was on my stool.

As I turned to thank him, he leaned in, hand on my waist.

"Would you and your friend like to come over?"

The look that passed between us in a millisecond said that he wanted me, and for the first time that night I felt completely alive. I hesitated. My promise to Jamil to be faithful was the angel on one shoulder, but all that vodka and Mehdi's deep brown eyes were the devil on the other. He was so handsome. And he liked me. We wouldn't stay long.

"We got to go," Joanne interrupted as she slid off the stool and yanked me by the arm. "Come on, little darling, we're about to turn into pumpkins."

"Sorry," I said, reaching for a last swallow of my drink as I grabbed my coat. I didn't look back as Joanne pushed me towards the door and out into the damp September night.

"Never twice with the same guy, especially if you got caught the first time," she admonished as we held our coats closed against the autumn chill.

"He sure is cute," I giggled. "And I bet he had some opium."

"Screw that," she laughed. "We need to call Michael."

Michael. Michael was our cocaine dealer, with permanent stubble surrounding his tiny mustache, a thick black ponytail, and the most readily-available product in town. Yes. I needed the wake-up of cocaine, not an opium stupor. To heck with Mehdi.

Stopping at a phone a block away, I fished in the bottom of my purse and handed Joanne a shiny dime as she stepped into the booth.

"Hey Michael," Joanne said. "It's Joanne and Annette. Wondering if you could set us up?"

I wobbled on my platform shoes, stomach rolling in anticipation of what would soon be up my nose.

"Sure, sure. Yeah, we could meet you. Unless you'd consider a house call?"

What was she saying? Jamil didn't like me having men in the house when he was away and Joanne knew it. But I couldn't really tell her to un-invite him after she'd already hung up, and I really wanted some coke, so I kept my mouth shut as we weaved the remaining blocks to our vehicles.

"He can't stay once he drops off the stuff, okay?" I slurred, getting into the driver's seat.

"You worry too damn much," she answered. "Michael's alright. We'll have fun. You'll see. Now follow me and drive straight."

Crossing the river, I followed Joanne to the north-bound freeway, careful not to drive too slow, or too fast. Exiting right before the bridge to Washington, we wound our way to Jamil's riverside condo. Michael was waiting in the parking lot by the time we got there with a gram of powder tucked in his wallet and a guy named Ben beside him in the front seat.

Maybe it was because it was Friday night. Maybe it was Joanne's cleavage and her nasty laugh. Maybe it was the memory of Mehdi's hand on the small of my back. Whatever the source, the sexual energy that night was thicker than the fat lines of white powder we chopped out on the mirror. I sat cross-legged on the floor across the coffee table from Joanne, Michael and Ben on the leather couch. With each line of cocaine, my anxiety lessened. Joanne was right. Michael was an okay guy. After snorting a couple of hits that made my eyes sting, I looked up to see Ben's hand resting on Joanne's thigh. She winked at me. For an hour we drank and snorted and I watched Joanne flirt. I wasn't interested in either one of these guys, but she made it look so easy. She made everything look easy.

Hyper-alert, I marched to the kitchen for beer number three, returning as Joanne and Ben stumbled up the carpeted staircase. I shook my head and laughed as Michael stood up, smiled and nodded after them.

"Seems like they have the right idea," he said, reaching his hand towards mine.

I paused. This isn't where I imaged the evening would go. *Oh Jamil, where are you?*

"Sure," I mumbled, too embarrassed to say "no."

What am I doing? What in the hell am I doing? My stomach churned with each step towards the bedroom.

"Michael, maybe this isn't . . ."

"Oh baby," he whispered as he put his arms around me, not listening, moving into what felt rehearsed, like a scene from a grainy porno movie.

I took a deep breath and tried to get in to it, tried to get in to him, tried to be sexy.

"Suck my cock," he said gruffly when he didn't get an erection.

"Shit," I thought, moving down between his legs. If I were good enough, sexy enough, he wouldn't be in this position and neither would I. If I were smart enough, I'd be down on the couch, alone. Wired on cocaine and now woozy from drink, we flailed pitifully until we heard Joanne and Ben laughing as they walked down the stairs.

It's tough to make small talk when you've just had a guy's limp penis in your mouth and he's embarrassed and you're embarrassed and disgusted at yourself for being there in the first place, except it's your house so you're stuck. I said something like "a drink sounds good" and we dressed without looking at each other.

More lines flowed as we rejoined the party. The next thing I knew, the talk turned to swapping. Whoa. This was hitting close to my "never-ever" list. The next thing you know they'd want an all out orgy. I looked at Ben with his fuzzy brown hair and nose now red and raw from cocaine and shook my head no. He looked relieved, and excused himself as the morning sun began to illuminate the window shades. I didn't know that he meant to crash in the spare room, but that's where he went, leaving me to grind my teeth on the couch while Joanne and

Michael had at it in my bed. I tried not to listen to her laughter and his grunts. That's my girl, I thought with a grimace. Now just hurry and get him the hell out of my house.

I was still wide-awake when the guys left an hour later. After a shower, Joanne decided to sneak home and into bed without waking her husband, who might very well have been trying to sneak home on her. Alone at last, I sat on the couch with my head in my hands. Coming down off cocaine is bad on a good day and hideous on a day that you and your best friend have just been naked with the same guy in the bed you share with your boyfriend. The guilt followed me around like one of Jamil's round Arabian aunties long after the hangover had passed.

And here I was several weeks later, in that same bed, trying to decide how to tell the man I loved that I'd been unfaithful, again.

Jamil had been home for less than twenty-four hours. His work as the family's roving consultant, purchaser and guy-sent-to-check-things-out took him out of town a lot. I drank a lot. Not a good combination. I'd picked him up from the airport, waiting at the gate wearing his favorite dress under my winter coat, my attempts with the curling iron falling flatter with each departing passenger.

"Jamil! Jamil!"

He looked tired as he scanned the crowd; suit carrier draped over one shoulder, black hair askew from napping on the long flight from London via Seattle. He hugged me tight, and walked with his free arm around my shoulder as we made our way to Baggage Claim and then home. Dropping his bags as we got through the door, we made our way to the bedroom. Wound up from the time change, he rebounded and we stayed awake until 2:00am, drinking and talking about his trip.

I let him sleep well into the next day, greeting him with dinner in our king-sized bed, an artfully arranged display of homemade pizza, two cold beers, and a packet of cocaine that Joanne had dropped off.

With cocaine and a drink, we could talk about anything. It was as if he'd never left and would never leave again. But this was now the second time I'd been unfaithful since we'd moved in together. Should I tell him? How to tell him?

"I can accept the truth from you, Annette, as long as I don't hear it somewhere else first," Jamil had said after he heard about Mehdi from Anthony. And so I admitted that I'd had sex. Why lie at that point?

"Girl, you are a fool," Joanne had told me afterwards. "No man wants the truth about that stuff, no matter what he says. You just go on and have your fun and keep your big mouth shut."

But truth-serum cocaine wouldn't let me keep my big mouth shut. Jamil and I told each other the truth, even when it wasn't pretty. We were trying to have an honest relationship, unlike my secretive marriage, or his string of good-time girlfriends. And so, after a few lines of coke, I held my breath and told him about that terrible night with Michael and how sorry I was and how none of this would happen if he spent more time at home.

I'd crossed a huge line by bringing the guy into the bed we shared. I knew once I opened my mouth that there was no justification for what I'd done. Funny how things that seem reasonable in your head sound ridiculous once you start talking.

"I'm done, Annette," Jamil said, in clipped and precise English after I told him, a mixture of sadness, disgust and anger in his voice. "I can't keep coming home to hear that you've screwed around, or spend all my time away worrying about whether or not someone else is in my bed."

He didn't snort any more cocaine that night, going directly into the spare room and closing the door. I was still awake the next morning when he came out, washed his face, repacked his suitcase and left.

"But sweetie, can't we talk?" I pleaded, tongue searching my dry mouth for even a hint of saliva. "You know that I love you."

He looked at me with such revulsion that I crumbled.

"Love? What do you know about love?"

Following him outside, I held his arm, and then the car door, running alongside as he pulled out of the lot.

"Jamil! Jamil! Please don't go!"

Mike, one of the condo neighbors, looked out from his doorway as I watched the Porsche drive away. "You okay Annette?"

I waved and went back inside, collapsing on the couch into a ball, crying until I couldn't breathe. Dragging my feet up the stairs, I buried myself under the covers, tossing and turning and weeping until I finally slept.

I met Joanne two days later, recounting the story over a pitcher.

"Well, you look like shit," she said from behind enormous tortoiseshell sunglasses.

We were at an outside table downtown at Main Place at 2:00 in the afternoon, in the company of a few businessmen drinking a late lunch. Wearing sunglasses that matched Joanne's to camouflage my bloodshot eyes, I definitely looked and felt older than twenty-eight, and not in a good way. Looking in the mirror that morning had been tough. I'd always been told I was pretty, with a pair of dimples and thick hair that hung nearly to my waist, but my lifestyle was beginning to take a toll.

The waiter brought burgers and more beer. I winced as the fresh pitcher met the glass tabletop.

"I feel like shit, if it's any consolation," I replied, cutting my sandwich in half.

Lunch had sounded better than it now looked, but I needed something other than Pepto-Bismol and beer in my stomach. I forced a small bite.

"Well you were crazy to tell him. That's all I have to say," Joanne said, her chocolate brown fingers reaching over to grab a handful of fries off my plate.

"You'd better hope he gets over this," she continued, twisting an end of her newly corn rowed hair with her other hand, "or you'll be looking for a place to live *and* a job."

She was right. Some days I could barely drag myself out of bed by noon. How would I hold down a job?

"Oh by the way, speaking of work, Anthony says that your ex-husband, Mr. Eddie himself, got laid off from the plant last week. Maybe you two could get back together and go on food stamps!"

Joanne found this notion funnier than I ever would. Eddie. He called me a bitch the last time I saw him when I wouldn't loan him fifty dollars for a gambling debt. Fat chance I'd ever get back together with him.

I pushed my dish towards Joanne. "Finish these damn fries so we can get out of here."

I drove ten minutes to Jamil's little two-man office the next day, busying myself with mail, organizing his desk, doing my best to make myself indispensable. His new assistant, Tim, came in just as I was leaving.

"Oh, hey Annette. Where's Jamil? We had a meeting with the guy from the Reno project yesterday."

I didn't like Tim. He was a few years older than we were, with a small paunch and thinning blonde hair, and acted just slightly superior.

He managed the books, kept appointments with bankers and realtors, and tracked shipments of rice destined for Saudi Arabia. He was the one who was indispensable.

"He had to go to Detroit unexpectedly," I answered, avoiding his gaze.

"It drives me crazy when he doesn't let me know his schedule," Tim groused, picking up the empty coffee carafe to take down the hall to the communal kitchen.

"Me too," I whispered, waving as I left, glad he hadn't pressed for more details. I stopped at the grocery store for a bottle of the new "lite" wine and cracked it as soon as I got home. I missed Jamil, and I was furious at myself for messing up so badly. I'd been in self-destruct mode since I was a teenager and it wasn't getting any better. It was like everyone else had an instruction manual while I was off in the next room trying to figure life out on my own. I wasn't doing a very good job of it.

Plopping on the couch and putting my feet up, I thought about Eddie and our ill-fated marriage, and how hopeful I'd been when Jamil and I got together.

Chapter Two

EDDIE, THE CUTE, longhaired guy from freshman study hall who plied me with candy and cheap wine during high school, had turned out to be a lousy husband. I'd had my suspicions, but when the borrowed minister asked his questions in my Aunt Ruth's backyard on that hot September afternoon in 1973, I'd taken a deep breath and said "I do," knowing that what I really wanted was to get out of my parents' house.

I first noticed Eddie in class when I nearly tripped over my bellbottoms while climbing over his long legs on my way to the only empty seat in the room. I blushed as he turned to say "hello" from beneath shaggy brown bangs.

Joanne caught it all. She tugged on my long hair and passed a folded note from her desk behind me.

"Watch out. That's one of the Clem brothers."

I'd heard of them. The seven-strong Clem clan had gone to a different grade school, but their reputation was known to every incoming freshman within weeks. There were three of them left in school. They smoked and skipped class, and were rumored to sell mescaline and cross-tops in the lunchroom. One of the older brothers was in prison, and Eddie had already been suspended for walking into the building with a lit cigarette.

But, he seemed nice, and he was really cute with startling blue eyes barely visible beneath brown hair that hung well over his collar. I started to watch him slink through the long hallways, always at the edges, rarely talking to other kids. He made it a point to sit either in front of or behind me in study hall, even when there were other empty spots. Joanne just shook her head.

"Have you ever actually talked to the boy?" she asked as we stood in front of the bathroom mirror at her house several months into the school year.

"Not really. But he always says 'hi' and he smiles at me."

"Humph," she snorted, patting the tight curls of her Afro into what was already perfect form.

And then one day he reached from the seat behind me and laid a chocolate bar on my desk.

"Candy, little girl?"

I giggled, afraid to turn around.

"Thanks," I mumbled, sticking the bar into the pocket of my navy pea coat.

That day he followed me out of class and asked if I wanted to go outside for a cigarette.

"I don't smoke," I answered, looking at my feet.

He smiled, nodded, and walked down the stairs.

Joanne and I frequently spent lunch period in Grant Park adjacent to our high school, smoking pot in the boy's bathroom. After spending my lunch money in the basement cafeteria on a couple of sugar cookies, or a bag of chips to share, we'd stop by a noisy table of black guys at a back table. Joanne would shake hands with a fellow named Ronnie, handing him the dollar that her mother had given her that morning with strict orders to eat something nutritious. In return, he'd slip a couple of joints into her coat pocket and we'd head up the stairs of the 1920's era building and outside.

"Hurry up," Joanne said. "Let's see if the usual gang is out here. Anthony is supposed to be waiting for me."

She had come to school that Monday with Anthony's jade ring on her index finger and a barely visible hickey on her dark neck. Anthony was in my algebra class. He played junior varsity basketball and was the center of attention out by the gym or in the park, joking and laughing with kids from lots of different groups. Anthony didn't care if you were a sosh or a juicer, black or white. He didn't sell but always had a stash of good weed he was willing to share.

The park was lovely, with huge pines and oak, now autumn-hued. But we were only interested in getting high, and seeing who else was getting high. Walking up to the little brick structure marked "MEN," we slipped behind a tree, around the corner and in through the half-open door. Anthony, his friend, Charles, and a guy named Dante were standing by the grimy sink, already smoking.

"Hey, Annette, how about one of those master charges?" Charles asked.

I smiled. The guys said that I could blow a charge like a brother.

"Sure," I said, "with your joint," feeling a contact high from merely entering the brick enclosure.

Ignoring the filthy toilets in stalls with no doors, I took the partially smoked joint from Charles' ebony fingers and took a deep hit. Exhaling, I carefully placed the lit end in my mouth and held my lips tight around the joint just past the fire. I blew hard as he came close, sending a thick stream of smoke into his open mouth as he inhaled.

"Hey man!" I heard Anthony say. "Gents, make room for my other-brother. Y'all know Eddie—he went to Rigler; got a bunch of badass brothers. He's cool, for a white dude!"

Anthony and Charles laughed. Dante, about as silent as I usually was, grunted while Joanne said, "Yeah, everybody know who Eddie is."

I took the lit end of the joint out of my mouth and took a long draw, holding my breath as I silently counted to twenty.

"Move your peanut head out of the way, Charles, and let my friend in there."

Everyone but Charles snickered. He did look like a peanut, with a narrow face and tiny ears flat against his skull.

"I'm up," said Eddie, as he moved in front of me.

I put the joint back in my mouth, squeezed my eyes shut and blew. When I blinked, Eddie was staring back at me. My wind gave out before his did.

"I thought you said you didn't smoke," he said, walking with me back towards the building and the ringing bell.

"Cigarettes," I answered.

He became my boyfriend without much more of a conversation than that. We started hanging out at lunch and within a few months were making out in the backseat of his brother's Mustang at the drive-in theater. It was easy. I gathered that his family was as messed up as mine, so we didn't need to talk about what went on at home. We didn't need to talk much at all. Eddie was quiet, and cute, and didn't make any demands. And he thought I was pretty. That was enough reason to

12

scuttle quick through the kitchen on Fridays after dinner, two or three joints hidden in my bra.

"Annette! Where are you going?"

"Out with Joanne. I'll be back later," I'd lie, already through the door, knowing that Eddie would be at Wilshire Park waiting. Skipping the second step, I would scurry the quarter mile to our meeting place. If Eddie didn't have his brother's car, we'd hide in a favorite spot underneath an enormously ancient rhododendron where we could make out, and get high without having to share with the other kids who frequented the park.

All through high school, Joanne and I met before class in the south hall girl's bathroom, squeezing into a single stall. Waving vigorously to camouflage the smoke from her cigarette, we discussed our futures.

"It's set," she whispered, blowing smoke rings, "I'm going to marry Anthony the minute we graduate. "

"Does he know yet?" I'd giggle.

Chocolate brown Joanne would marry light-skinned Anthony with his almond-shaped eyes and they would have beautiful babies when she turned thirty. I'd marry Eddie and we'd be neighbors and get jobs and have parties, and no one could tell us what to do. It would be perfect.

Only it wasn't. We were just kids trying to behave like grown-ups. I got a job at an insurance company typing benefits checks after graduation, and Eddie got on at the steel plant where one of his brothers worked. We came home to a bottle of Bali Hai wine most nights, throwing parties at our place, with its green shag carpeting and avocado countertops, or down the street at Joanne and Anthony's with matching decor, nearly every weekend. We'd never talked much, but after being married a year or two about the only time Eddie talked to me was to tell me I was stupid, or that he wouldn't be back soon when he left to play cards with his buddies. He gambled away our bill money and slapped me once with the back of his hand when I questioned him about the rent.

We were only married for four years, and none of it was great, but it was that slap that did it. I didn't want the slammed-against-the-wall kind of marriage that my parents had. I'd talked with Joanne about my disintegrating marriage for months. She got annoyed with my deliberations.

"Either go or stay," she said, "but please knock off all this debate. If he's no good for you, then be done with it."

It wasn't as easy as she made it sound. I was scared. At night as I fell asleep curled on the far edge of our double-bed, I'd picture myself in a little house with a garden, and with more friends than just Joanne, and maybe classes at the community college. But I kept waking up next to Eddie when the alarm rang at 6:00, hung over and tired and too intimidated by the unknown to do anything differently. So I went to work and met Joanne for drinks, cleaned the apartment and waited: waited for Eddie to come home from an all-night card game, waited for the weekend, waited for my life to change.

Joanne and I noted the upcoming 4th of July with drinks at the dingy pub near work.

"To freedom," she toasted.

Reaching across the booth for the ashtray, she waved to the bartender for another pitcher of draft.

"You'll never guess who I ran into at Lloyd Center," she said, blowing smoke rings over my head.

"George Washington himself?" I asked.

"Please. It was Jamil. You know that cute Arab guy who's friends with your cousin Jeff."

I knew exactly who she meant. Jamil was Palestinian, relocated to Portland from Michigan. He'd slid into our lives at a New Year's Eve party a couple of years earlier with a group of Saudi students who smoked incessantly and had a way of saying "Hello. It is nice to meet you" that sounded like "You are the most beautiful woman in the world." He'd known Jeff at the community college, where most of the Arab students started their American education with English classes.

He and Jeff hung out in the commons before Jamil went on to the university and started showing up at our parties, winding in and out of our group alone or with a pretty girl on his arm. He was friendly and talkative, and from several long conversations I learned about life in the insular Arab community in Detroit, his travels to the Middle East and elsewhere, and his conflict with wanting the freedom that America promised while being obligated to do his elders bidding. He was funny, sometimes unintentionally, since English was his second language; his mispronunciations surfaced when he was drinking, which he found hilarious. He loved to discuss politics and told me he was addicted to the evening news and the *International Herald Tribune*. His eyes crinkled when he laughed, which was often. And unlike my husband, he seemed genuinely interested in what I had to say. I liked him.

Joanne flicked the ashes off her cigarette and raised her eyebrows at me. "He's having a party on the 4th of July. He invited me and you, and our respective husbands."

"He mentioned me? I mean, us?"

"Well yeah, what do you think? Jeff will probably be there too," she snorted, inhaling now off her second cigarette.

I giggled and took a long swallow of beer. A party. Something to look forward to. I hoped Eddie would say we could go.

Joanne winked. "We need to go shopping. You need some new clothes, girl."

Joanne had been telling me what to do since we were in grade school and I welcomed the direction. It felt like nobody was in charge at home. My father had left with another woman for the first time when I was eleven, and John was eight, after another detox that had gone bad too quickly. Nobody talked about it to us kids, but he'd roughed Mom up pretty badly before he moved out. I hated him for that, and for leaving. And, though it sounds odd even to me, I missed him. I missed his dry humor and the way he got excited listening to Dixieland jazz. I missed him tiptoeing up to the unheated second floor to turn on the space heater before Johnny and I woke up on cold winter mornings. I missed the times he sang old Big Band songs and danced me around the living room while I stood on his feet.

Mostly I was sad. I'd eavesdropped on Mom and Aunty Ruth's murmurs when they thought none of us kids were around, and listened to Mom crying at night after we'd gone to bed. She said he was sick and needed help. I wanted to ask what kind of sick and was he coming back and did he still love us? But instead of asking, I tried to be quiet, and did my best to blend into the woodwork so I would be one less thing to worry about. That left John in his room creating towns out of shoeboxes for his miniature cars, Mom on the phone in her room with the door closed, and me staring out my bedroom window at the empty street below. Then Dad did come home. The fights took up where they'd left off, and I hated him for coming back. I was more likely to find him passed out in his easy chair than to see him dancing in the living room after that. It had always been solemn, but after he started the routine of moving out and coming back, our house took on a dark pallor. Johnny went to his room. I escaped.

That's where Joanne came in. Her family had moved in down the block during the previous summer, four loud kids spilling on to the big covered porch, with barbeques and backyard sleepovers on hot evenings. Her parents, Joe and Momma Lea, joked with each other, and patted each other on the butt in the kitchen, and welcomed me like one of their own. I was still quiet, and tried to blend into their woodwork like I did at home, but at Joanne's it didn't matter because there were plenty of other people making all sorts of noise. Joanne, even at eleven, was outspoken and funny and daring. She had cute clothes and great ideas and even though I knew in my heart that I couldn't be like her, I could surely tuck under her wing and go along for the ride. Never mind that some of her ideas got us in trouble. The adrenaline of excitement when I hung out with Joanne made me feel alive like the somber mood at home never could. I continued to rely on her, even as we play-acted through our teenaged plans for marriage and life on our own.

Jamil lived in a new condominium development on the Columbia River. His party coincided with the huge fireworks display across the river in Vancouver, Washington. Joanne announced that we would go early and stay late. Eddie and Anthony, hunkered down in an all-day poker game, wanted no part of it.

"Why don't you just stay here?" Eddie asked, as he slapped a pair of aces and three Queens onto our kitchen table. "Give it up!" he shouted to the groans of the three other guys, only half engaged in conversation with me. His brother, Mike, Anthony and Charles, along with various guys who came and went carrying six-packs or a baggie of pot, spent much of each weekend playing cards, either in my kitchen or Joanne's. Frequently the wives and girlfriends came along and the women danced to old soul music in the living room while the guys gambled, but just as often it was simply the slapping of cards on the table that reminded me I had a husband.

"I'm not interested in watching you lose our rent money," I replied, earning a howl from the table.

"Let her go brother! She's gonna bring a curse on you talking like that," Anthony laughed. He didn't seem to care that Joanne wanted to go. As long as she eventually made it home, he and Joanne did whatever

16

they wanted to. Sometimes they seemed more like roommates than husband and wife.

"Go on then," Eddie said out loud while the guys got up for a beer, turning to me to whisper, "I'm only letting you go because I'm winning. Be home early."

Wiping sweaty palms on my new white shorts as we pulled up to Jamil's, I cautiously followed Joanne in through the living room and out to the deck. I didn't recognize anyone. Neither did Joanne, but she grabbed a beer from the cooler and ambled up to a couple dressed in matching star-spangled T-shirts. I helped myself to a tumbler of Annie Green Springs on ice and perched on a wooden bench, studiously watching activities in the marina below.

"Hello, Annette. How have you been?" Jamil stood above me, six foot two with skinny arms poking out of his University of Portland t-shirt, a plate of hamburger patties in one hand and a beer in the other.

"Come and help me to cook," he said, his accent indicating that he'd been drinking since before the party started.

I followed him to the smoking grill where he did most of the talking, only briefly asking about Eddie. I made myself busy going back and forth to the kitchen for garnish and buns, glad for the escape but equally glad to come back to assist. By the time the fireworks started, I'd had enough wine to talk to a few of the other guests, and just enough of a hamburger to keep me standing.

By 11:00, with the residual sulfur smell of choreographed bombs bursting in air, I found myself in Jamil's arms wondering why it had taken so long. After that initial conversation at the grill, we had circled around each other all evening, always in the same room, in the same conversations, catching each other's eye.

"I know you are a married woman and shouldn't be doing this, but I'd really like to kiss you," he said, outside on a grassy rise away from the party.

We did more than kiss as we made our way back to the condo, hiding from the other guests in his walk-in closet with our pants around our ankles. When it was over, I started to cry, knowing that I'd crossed a line. I wasn't happy with my husband, but this wasn't how I'd intended to show it.

I could hear Joanne call my name as she came up the stairs. Running my fingers through my hair and wiping my eyes, I squeaked out of the closet through the sliding door to the bathroom.

"What did you do, fall in? Let's go," she said, checking her own hair in the mirror without giving me a glance. "Sure as shit, those fools will still be playing cards when we get back."

Which they were. But suddenly it didn't matter so much. As drunk as I was riding home from Jamil's, I knew that the fights weren't going to get any better and Eddie wasn't going to stop gambling. The argument I'd been having with myself about staying or going was just about over.

Jamil called the day after the party to tell me he would be away from Portland for at least three months and that he hoped to see me when he returned. As Eddie walked into the room, I pretended it was a wrong number and hung up.

I talked to my brother, John, about getting a divorce, remembering when we were kids and hid in his room while our parents fought. Johnny had always been my best little buddy. At three years younger he was old enough to get stoned with, and young enough to boss around. I protected him, but he watched out for me too. Dad never hit either one of us, which we attributed to our early warning system. My bedroom window overlooked the driveway, while John's was over the den. If Dad stumbled with drink when he got out of the car, I'd scoot to Johnny's room where we'd listen through the vent for signs of a fight. If they started screaming, we'd either stow away in his closet and pretend we were on a submarine in silent-mode (Dive! Dive!) or climb down the trellis and head to our cousin's three blocks away.

"What are you doing here?" Marcie would ask through the screen door.

"Nothing," I'd say, clutching Johnny's hand in mine.

"Come on in. We're just having dinner."

No questions asked, Aunty Ruth, Dad's sister, set extra places between Marcie and the boys, Jeff and Richie. After dinner, which usually included some hue of Jell-O salad and an episode of *Gilligan's Island*, she would call Mom. "Your kids are here. You alright?"

Depending on the answer we'd either go home or sleep over, snuggled together on the trundle-bed in Marcie's room. That was a long time ago, but talking with John that afternoon about my marriage felt a little like hiding out at Aunty Ruth's.

"John," I said, as we guzzled cheap beer on our apartment's deck, "I'm thinking about leaving Eddie. I want to move back to my old room until I find an apartment."

"What's taken you so long?" he asked, telling me how hard it was to listen to Eddie belittle me. He came over a few days later with a copy of the Declaration of Independence and read it out loud as we shared a joint.

"This applies to people, too, sis. Not just governments."

I smiled at my brainy little brother. Firing up a second joint, we talked about the future and all that we hoped to do.

"I want to go to England, Johnny. All the history, and castles. And Ireland. Aren't we part Irish?"

Eddie pulled up, gunning the motor of his Chevy to announce his arrival. Climbing over the railing that bordered the parking lot, he situated himself on the chaise lounge and reached for the joint, taking a long draw.

"And what about Italy?" John said. "I have to see the Sistine Chapel. Remember that slide presentation that Mr. Middlesworth did each year?"

"And Greece!" we sang in unison.

Eddie, who'd had his eyes closed, spoke with derision. "What in the hell are you two talking about? People like us don't go to fucking Greece. We work our asses off and pay our bills, and if we're lucky, go to the beach for a week in the summer. Let me know when you have enough money to go see the god-damned queen. By then there will be a mortgage to pay, and kids who need braces."

Johnny's eyes met mine. "Well, Eddie, I guess no one really knows how it will all turn out." Stretching as he stood up, he continued, "I'd better get home to see what crazy craving my pregnant girlfriend has tonight. It's going to be awhile before we can afford even a weekend at the beach, working my ass off or not."

Eddie stayed on the chaise as I walked Johnny to his car.

"Let me know when you're ready, Sis," he said, giving me a peck on the cheek as he got into his truck that shimmied when he turned the ignition. I walked into the apartment through the front door without speaking to my husband.

As the tension at home elevated, I talked with Joanne several times a day.

"You *what!*" she'd exclaimed when I told her about Jamil. "Humph. I didn't know you had it in you. Go on then and leave that no-good husband of yours. But you probably better not count on Mr. Playboy for the long haul."

I knew that. I'd been telling myself that Jamil was just a fling since I'd pulled up my pants in his closet on the 4th of July. But I felt stronger somehow, knowing that he wanted to see me again. Part of me said that I should wait until he came back to Portland before leaving Eddie, but I knew that I needed to go, Jamil or not.

Mom was the final person I consulted, taking the bus there from work one Tuesday. I'd never learned how to drive. I hadn't needed to.

Dad wasn't home. A long-haul trucker, he was often gone for a week or more at a time. It was about the only peace Mom got, other than the times he'd moved out with some chippie he'd met on the road or at one of the bars he frequented.

"Do you ever wish he'd stay gone?" I asked her that evening.

Sitting across from me at the kitchen table, she looked over my shoulder towards the back door. Taking off her scarf, she undid one of the pin curls that framed her face, twirling her dyed chestnut hair into a ring.

"Your brother and Michelle are coming by for dinner. Do you want to stay?"

Sometimes I felt absolutely insane at that damned kitchen table, like I was talking to myself, like I was ten years old. I half-expected Jeff and Richie to be hiding under her chair. But even though it made me crazy, I was drawn to that kitchen table like a bee to honey, like my family to bourbon, like our women to absent men. It took me a long time to realize that this isn't what a family was supposed to look like: the women commiserating over highballs, telling stories instead of the truth. If I closed my eyes, I could still hear their voices:

"And there was Annette in her red plaid jumper, standing right where Bob left her, no closer to Santa's lap than she'd been when they got there!"

That's the way they told it, Mom and Aunty Ruth, throaty laughter floating above the cigarette haze that colored all of their conversations, ice seductively tinkling in golden tumblers. That's the way they told it, about how I was too shy, or too dumb to move up in the line of other little kids waiting to see Santa at the Elks Lodge that long ago December morning while Dad moseyed over to the bar for a quick one. That's how they told it on a Saturday afternoon or a Friday evening after working through the ritual progression of our history: grandma's painful death from lung cancer, mother's miscarriage before I was born, the time Jeff and Richie jumped off the roof and landed on their heads, and wasn't it funny the time that Annette didn't get to sit on Santa's lap because she let the other kids walk in front of her?

No, I wanted to say. No, it wasn't funny. I didn't know what to do and where was Dad and I was only five and it wasn't funny if you were me. But I kept my mouth shut. I was good at keeping my mouth shut.

Instead, while little Johnny snuggled safely on Mom's lap, my three cousins and I hovered in the doorway, slithered under the table, hung over the backs of chairs or laid flat out on the kitchen floor, intoxicated by the sweet scent of Channel No. 5 mixed with lipstick and bourbon and cigarette smoke, entranced with the laughter and the clink of ice against glass, the strike of the match ("Let me! I'll light it!"). We were both enchanted and repulsed by the never-ending, often repeated stories of who we were, about the fractures in the bones that were our family. Grandpa was there most weekends, and sometimes the neighbors from across the street, but always Mom and Aunty Ruth. Dad wasn't around much back then either, and rarely spoke directly to us, but if there he'd growl, "Get these kids out of here. They don't need to hear this crap."

And as our mothers shooed us away with the same motion they used to wave the blue smoke out of our young faces, Gramps would reach deep into his right front pocket and pull out a small stack of shiny quarters, distributing one each to our outstretched hands.

"Get lost, you varmints," he'd say.

I'd been doing my best to get lost ever since.

"No, Mom, I can't stay for dinner. I need to get going. But I wanted to ask if I could come home for a while. I'm thinking about leaving Eddie."

She looked at me, down at the growing pile of bobby pins on the table, then back to me. "When did this start? What will you do?"

I didn't answer. I was sort of hoping that she'd tell me.

She looked back towards the door, took a deep breath and faced me.

"Oh, Annette. I just want you to be happy, whether you stay married or not. You know I've always liked Eddie, but he's a lot like Dad. Your father is a good man, and he loves all of us. It's the drinking. He's a good man when he's sober."

I snorted. "Yeah, but he's not sober often enough. And I'm talking about me and Eddie, not Dad."

"I know. I know," she said, looking in a small mirror as she drew her tightly wound curls into waves. "I just wonder if you need to be more patient with him."

More patient. If patient meant waiting, I was already more patient than anyone should be. I waited to see if our checks would bounce. I waited for him to come home for dinner, wrapping his plate when he didn't. I waited for him to finish when he woke me up for sex that had become essentially a solitary act. I waited to have a conversation, to talk about our dreams, to feel married.

Dad had told Mom that I was too young to get married in the first place and I hated to prove him right, but in he came through the back door as if on cue. Sober at the moment, he had the itchy look around his eyes that said he was headed for a bender.

"Have you given the guy a chance?" he asked after Mom told him why I was there.

Crying, I answered, "Yeah, Dad. I've given him a chance." I left out the part about Eddie hitting me, and the rent money, and me having sex with someone else. *Please just believe me,* I thought. *Please let me come home.*

His jaw clenched. "You can stay two weeks. Anything beyond that and you pay rent. This isn't a motel."

I left as John and a very pregnant Michelle pulled into the driveway. Trudging the four tree-lined blocks to the bus stop, I listened to the clanking of dinner dishes though open windows and screen doors and wished I could walk in to someone else's life, even if just for an evening. I looked up to a honk. Joanne's dad rolled down his car window and slowed as he drove past.

"Hey, Annette!" Joe's voice boomed. "When are we going to see you? You know Momma Lea misses you."

I waved. "Soon."

Eddie left the apartment a week later on a hot end-of-July Saturday morning, wearing aviator sunglasses and toting a six-pack of beer under one arm.

"We've got a card game starting at Anthony's. I won't be home until late."

I stood in the front door, shielding my eyes from the sun with my hand.

"I won't be here when you get back, Eddie. I'm leaving. I'm going back to Mom's."

He turned back towards me shaking his head.

"Leaving? What are you talking about? You aren't going anywhere. You aren't ever going anywhere."

I shook my head back at him, though my insides were in knots. "I'm done, Eddie. I don't want to fight anymore. I want something different for my life."

"You stupid bitch. What do you know about different? You don't know shit. Is this about all that 'going to Spain' bullshit that you and John were yammering about?"

I couldn't believe that he was any happier than I was. "No Eddie, this isn't about going to Spain or England, or any of that stuff. It's about both of us being miserable."

He slapped the hood of the car with his free hand. I flinched and took a step backwards, glancing at the other apartments. A curtain was pulled aside and then dropped in one of the upstairs units, but no one came outside.

"You'd better be here when I get home," he growled. Slamming the car door, he gunned the Chevelle as he sped out of the complex and onto the busy street that would take him directly to Anthony and Joanne's.

Closing the door, I sat on the couch and pulled my cat, Whiskers, to my lap. Maybe Eddie was right. Maybe my aspirations were too high. Maybe people like us *didn't* go to Europe. Maybe I wasn't supposed to be happy. Maybe I should be more patient, like Mom said. Maybe if I tried harder. But, thirty minutes later, John, Marcie and Joanne arrived with a stack of boxes. Three hours later I was at my parent's house, in my old bedroom, sobbing. Two weeks later I was in a ratty little apartment that looked like I felt inside.

Furnished with my childhood bedroom set, a couch from my brother's basement, and Marcie's discarded dinette, the apartment felt familiar but never like home. With a chipped tile in the tub and dingy vinyl in the kitchen, it wasn't nearly as nice as where Eddie now lived alone. I walked to and from work, talked on the phone with Mom and Marcie, and got stoned with my brother, passing time until the weekend when I went out with Joanne and drank too much. Twice in those first few months I brought guys home, because I could and it was late and I was lonely. I was enjoying my freedom, I told myself. It was just fun, I said to the mirror. I'd never been alone before.

I thought about going to the community college. I even called Jeff to ask about his classes. It sounded complicated, with placement tests and credit hours and majors. I put enrolling on my list of "to-do someday," along with that trip to Ireland.

Getting off the bus a few blocks early, I stopped at the convenience store most evenings for a bottle of Spanada or a six-pack, going home to a frozen dinner and a sitcom. Joanne convinced me that I needed to learn to drive, so for five weeks I was picked up by a middle-aged fellow from a local driving school who took me on the freeway, drove with me through the neighborhoods and taught me to parallel park. Going for my driving exam was terrifying. Maybe I was making a mistake. Maybe I should wait. Riding the bus wasn't so bad, I told myself.

After I passed my test, Dad took me to buy a car with the money I'd saved.

"Where's my skypiece?" he asked, referencing his favorite cap. He joked when he was sober, and today he was sober. Sometimes that was the only way I knew.

"Always buy a Chevy or a Ford," he said. "Even in the middle of nowhere you can find someone who knows how to fix them."

I couldn't imagine why I'd ever be in the middle of nowhere. The beach was as far from home as I'd ever been. But I took Dad's advice and bought a silver Nova, not too used, that looked like it could go a long way if it needed to. I kept walking to work, and Joanne drove her car when we went out downtown, but with that car in my parking space and my evening bottle of wine I felt like I was becoming more real, more grown-up, even though Joanne and I hadn't talked about this part when we'd made our plans for the future.

John was propped up against the concrete wall next to my apartment one Monday after work. He'd heard about me puking in the rose bushes while leaving a party at Richie's that weekend.

Depositing his lanky frame on the couch, he reached into his jacket and pulled out the cough-drop tin that held his stash.

"So you know Dad is an alcoholic, right?" he asked as he licked the edges of his freshly rolled joint before lighting up.

"No kidding? Was it the first detox or the last one that tipped you off?" I said, striking a match.

He inhaled, "Uncle Wally was too, you know. It seems like it runs in our family."

"Uncle Wally isn't a blood relative. What are you getting at?"

John held the joint for a minute before passing it to me.

"I'm kind of worried about you, Sis. From what I hear, you're hammered every weekend, and sometimes during the week."

"So getting stoned is better?" I asked, my voice raising an octave. "I'm not sure that it's any of your business how I spend my free time. I'm single, and for the first time in my life I don't have to answer to anybody. Not Eddie, not Mom and Dad, and certainly not you."

He winced just slightly, which I pretended not to notice. "Don't worry about it. Just checking in with my big sister after hearing the family gossip."

After a long toke, he stubbed out the joint and placed it tenderly in with the rest of his weed. "I'll catch up with you later. Come see Michelle and the baby this weekend?"

I'd held the baby once in the hospital, but she made me nervous. John was making me nervous. Now that he was a father, did he think he was some sort of expert on drinking? On *my* drinking in particular?

But I thought about our conversation in the following days, even when I was trying not to. Especially when I was trying not to. "Hammered every weekend," he'd said. Was it really every weekend? Doing a quick inventory, I reluctantly realized he was right. I would quit, or at least slow down.

I rode the bus straight home after work for the next three weeks, drinking herbal tea with my evening TV, avoiding Joanne on the weekends. "You're what?" she'd asked, when I told her I wasn't drinking. "Whatever for?" I even went jogging, huffing my way slowly around a five-block course. I'd show him.

But in the third week I noticed the same look in my eyes that I'd seen so often in my father's, that look that said a drink was in my immediate future; a look that said, "I'm really uncomfortable and I know what will make it better." I danced around that thought for another week without acknowledging it, adding extra honey to my chamomile tea, an extra block to my morning jog, a second piece of chocolate cake at the office birthday party. I lasted until Saturday evening when the prospect of staring at my four walls one more night seemed absolutely unbearable. Being sober was boring. Being sober was killing me. I called Joanne and it was if I'd seen her the night before.

"I'll pick you up at 8:00," she said, and did. I didn't drink at Rodeo, but by the time we got to the Keyhole I was so proud of my self that I had a double.

Jamil called from Michigan as that year's autumn gave way to winter rains. He'd been in the Middle East, and Malaysia, and had tried calling once but Eddie answered, so he'd hung up. He got my number from Information after learning from Jeff that I was on my own. He'd be back in Portland the next week. Would I meet him for a drink?

I spotted him before he saw me in the darkened bar, sporting a new moustache and goatee, wearing a denim sports coat. He leaned over and kissed my cheek, taking my hand as he simultaneously reached into his pocket for a cigarette.

"I've been thinking of you," he said, "wondering if you're alright."

"I've been thinking about you too," I stammered.

I was weeping, turning my head when the waitress came for our order.

"Hey, hey. It's okay. Let's get out of here and go have a nice dinner."

I spent the night with him and hadn't left since. Dad told Mom that I was going from the frying pan to the fire. I didn't know what he meant. Jamil was different. This time would be different.

Chapter Three

JAMIL WAS ABLE to uncharacteristically stay in Portland for nearly five solid months after that first night together, mainly by avoiding the telephone. I hadn't yet met his family but spent a fair amount of time with his brothers on the phone.

"Darn, you just missed him."

"He should be at the office by now."

"I'll have him call you."

He did call his mother once a week because she understood the dilemma he had with the family business, and agreed to stay mum on his whereabouts in exchange for knowing he was all right. He was her baby, and the only son to be raised in the States. She knew how much he disliked being told what to do.

Jamil's family was in the import/export business, mainly shipping rice from the U.S. and electronics from Japan to clients in Saudi Arabia, along with helping the Saudi employers keep a steady workforce of Muslim Malaysians. There was also real estate, both in the U.S. and Europe. Jamil's father had died when he was a boy. His uncle, the family patriarch after their father's death, had suffered a heart attack the previous year, which resulted in a double-bypass and instructions to scale back on work. Since Jamil was the youngest, and the only son without a wife and children, he was most frequently tapped to do the traveling that Uncle used to do. But because he was the least experienced, he wasn't quite trusted so had a very short leash. So, he was sent to Sacramento to look at an office building for sale, or Kuala Lumpur to interview potential warehouse workers, or Stuttgart, Arkansas to examine rice fields, reporting back to his elders via phone calls at all hours, from one time zone to another.

"I wish I could just run away and become a garbage man," Jamil said, beer and ever-present cigarette in hand as we watched the evening news. "I could come and go as I pleased, and work would be over when I came home."

Instead, we escaped into a cocktail haze every night, either at home or the nearby hotel disco. After two months of driving me to work while we were still buzzed from the night before, he asked that I quit my job. It wasn't the best job, but I'd been promoted from typing benefits checks to processing the claims, and I'd been talked to about working my way up to the assistant supervisor. Even hung over, I was a good worker. It was *my* job, which had nothing to do with Eddie being a jerk, or Dad's drinking, or the fact that I didn't see my baby brother so much anymore.

I held on to that job for two more months. Two more months of saying to Jamil, "I can't go with you because I have to work," two more months of going into the bathroom stall to throw up the previous night's booze, two more months of hanging on to my wobblingly fragile independence.

Finally, I gave notice, though the decision felt a little more like giving up than the celebration the girls at work made it out to be. "I'd give anything to be able to stay home," they'd said. "Lucky you." I wasn't sure.

I'd given up my apartment three weeks after Jamil had returned to Portland, storing the box filled with my childhood dolls and four cartons of books in that same walk-in closet that I'd first seen on the 4th of July. Setting up my deceased grandmother's stand-up desk in that huge closet under the skylight, I attempted to create a space that was mine in a tiny corner of his home, a space that seemed to get tinier after I left my job. Sometimes when he was still asleep, I'd sit at the desk and write in my diary, leaving out the parts about feeling lost.

I rode in an airplane for the first time that winter, flying to Los Angeles for a long weekend. We drove around Westwood Village in a Volkswagen Bug with an Iraqi friend, smoking a joint while singing along to Van Morrison at the top of our lungs. I wanted to stay in that car, laughing and singing and getting high, but we ended up at a Lebanese restaurant with a group of twelve. Jamil had said that an Arab would starve without a piece of bread in his right hand for scooping up food. I surreptitiously watched the others for clues on how to tackle the various dishes without a glob of hummus landing in my lap. The men sitting at our end of the long table teased me, while the women simply smiled and continued talking to each other. It would be a few years before I picked up enough Arabic to follow a conversation. For now I just sat quietly.

Joanne hung out with us nearly every weekend. She introduced us to Michael, who kept us supplied in the white powder whenever we called. At that point we were all new to cocaine and could make a single gram stretch an entire evening. Anthony played both sides of the fence, still involved in marathon poker games with Eddie, but coming to the clubs with us on occasion, especially with the promise of a line or two.

We celebrated Thanksgiving at Marcie's and Christmas at my parent's house, but other than the few hours Jamil spent not answering the phone at his strip mall office, we were together. We stayed up until the wee hours of the morning, playing old records or watching movies on the Beta-Max, and slept far too long into the day. I told myself that this schedule was only temporary.

Jamil took me to Las Vegas for the New Year where we welcomed 1982 wearing party hats with a table of strangers at the hotel casino event. As in Los Angeles, I watched those around me for clues on how to proceed with dinner. I didn't want to do anything to remind Jamil that before we got together I'd only ever been out for pizza or Chinese.

The telephone rang as we tumbled in from the grocery store one rainy February evening, arms full of paper bags and six-packs. Jamil reached into the fridge for a cold beer as I lunged for the phone.

"Is Jamil there?" a heavily accented voice asked.

"Is this Khalid? No. I'm sorry, you just missed him."

"I am at your airport. He needs to pick me up."

Able to hear the conversation, Jamil sat at the kitchen table with his head in his hands.

"Tell him I'll be there in twenty minutes," he said. "Outside Baggage Claim on the lower level."

Lighting a cigarette as he reached for his keys, he turned towards me with a sad smile. "It looks like our honeymoon is over."

Khalid stayed only two nights. That first night, they argued, in Arabic. I sat apart, listening to the inflection of their words, recognizing

29

terms of endearment that Jamil seemed to be directing my way. Khalid merely raised his eyebrows, as if to say "silly boy."

Well into the conversation, well into the bottle of scotch, Jamil played a cassette of Arabic love songs and began to dance, slowly shaking his hips as he snapped his fingers to the beat.

Khalid laughed. "Men don't belly dance, little brother."

"Yes they do, but only when no one is watching," Jamil roared as Khalid stood and joined him.

At the end of the song, they collapsed into each other's arms, crying.

"Our father loved to dance," Khalid said as he looked my direction, patting Jamil on the back.

Little was said the next day, but Jamil's suitcase came out of the closet. Family ties were strong, and while he could be one of the gang with me and our friends, Jamil the youngest son had obligations to uphold. On day three they flew to Detroit.

"I'll be home soon," Jamil said at the departure gate, holding my hands. I moved to hug and kiss him goodbye, but a slight shake of his head let me know that Khalid was watching and would not approve.

After the intensity of those first months, filling my time was a challenge. I once again considered taking a class at the community college. I even went to the campus one morning but drove away without getting out of the car. I wasn't sure where to go, or even what to ask. I reasoned that it made no sense to start something that I might not be able to finish if Jamil came home or asked me to meet him somewhere. That's what I told myself anyway.

"So what's it like being a lady of leisure?" Joanne asked at our second lunch date in one week.

I swirled a french fry through the dollop of ketchup on my plate.

"It's okay. Well, actually, I'm kind of bored," I replied. I made out to my mother and brother that all was well, but I couldn't hide the truth from Joanne. "We really love each other," I went on, "but I guess I didn't realize what it would really be like when he was away."

Joanne laughed. "So you're living for the weekends, just like I do, except your weekends are months apart."

We made plans to hit the clubs that Saturday.

"What about Anthony?" I asked.

"Anthony and Charles are going to the dog races. I've got all the time in the world."

No, I wanted to say, I'm the one with all the time in the world, but I kept my mouth shut. Who in their right mind would complain about not having to work?

Several months later I flew to meet the family in Livonia, a suburb of Detroit, with its large, heavily Palestinian, Arab population. It felt like another country, a Middle-Eastern county, where men wore traditional long white gowns, called thobes, on the street outside the Arabic markets and his family sat on the living room floor smoking jirac, a sweet smelling tobacco paste, out of a hookah.

I had dressed conservatively, like Jamil directed, in a long sleeved blouse and slacks. He described his family as liberal, meaning that the women didn't wear the hijab and were educated, but they didn't wear short skirts or drink alcohol either.

He held my hand as the plane landed.

"If you sit with your legs crossed, remember that it is an insult to have the bottom of your foot pointed at anyone," he said. "And it is probably best that you don't have a drink in my mother's home, even if my brothers insist. And don't tell them yet that you've quit your job. Or that you're divorced."

It was not reassuring to realize that he was as nervous as I was. I downed the last of my white wine as the landing announcement came on, cramming two sticks of gum into my mouth.

The cab deposited us outside a split-level with a tidy yard. A couple of olive-skinned boys who looked to be about twelve came bounding out of the house.

"Uncle! Uncle! Welcome home," they cried, taking our suitcases after reaching to kiss him on both cheeks. Shyly glancing my way they said, "Hello," with a slight nod of their heads before dragging our heavy gear up the cement stairs.

More kisses greeted Jamil at the doorway as his brothers, Khalid and Sammy, slapped him on the back and kissed both cheeks. He'd only been in Portland for two weeks, but they acted as if he'd been gone for a year.

"Welcome home, little brother. Annette, it is nice to see you again," Khalid said, reaching to shake my hand. "Our mother is in the kitchen, Jamil. You had better be hungry."

What I really wanted was a bathroom and a nap but felt myself being swept along to the steamy kitchen full of chattering women who fell on Jamil when they noticed him in the doorway.

"My son. My baby. You are here," his mother exclaimed as he bent low to kiss her cheeks.

"Welcome to our home," she said to me in heavily accented English, extending her hand, but then reaching up to kiss both my cheeks.

Jamil's sisters-in-law and aunties, four of them, crowded around, first him and then me. I really had to pee. I really wanted out of that kitchen.

I was able to excuse myself in the flurry. A young niece stood sentinel outside the bathroom door and steered me immediately back to the women. I scanned the fragrant kitchen for Jamil before realizing that the men were in an adjoining room. Scooting onto a stool out of the way, I inhaled the aroma of cumin and cardamom mixed with onion and garlic, windows foggy with condensation. The women spoke in Arabic, interspersed with English phrases, occasionally smiling towards me. As the meal preparations slowed, Fosiah, Sammy's wife, wiped her hands on a dishtowel and stood near me.

"It is nice to meet you, Annette. Jamil has never brought a girlfriend home from Portland before."

The other women giggled,

"Tell us about yourself," she continued. "Where are you from? What does your family do?"

That was a loaded question. My father was on a jag and hadn't been home for a week

"My father died when I was young," I lied. "My mother works for an accountant and my younger brother works in a warehouse. I grew up in Portland."

"I visited Portland once. It is a lovely city," she answered. "I am very sorry about your father. Our husbands, too, lost their father."

The other women clucked their tongues and turned back to the stove and kitchen table overflowing with dishes.

"Can I help set the table?" I volunteered as a way of changing the subject. Along with the niece, I carted plates and drinking glasses to the dining room.

Dinner was a raucous affair, with mother, two brothers and their wives, and the two elderly aunties around a long table, the children having been sent to the living room carrying plates heaped with food. Jamil and I sat near his mother. He grabbed my hand under the table and squeezed tight.

I silently recited Jamil's earlier instructions as I watched the others for clues on how to proceed: remembering the group in Los Angeles, I only used my right hand for eating; scooped with the hot pita bread, not a fork; took small bites because the hostess will insist that you eat until you burst. But it wasn't just the customs or the language that made me feel like an outsider. The interactions at this table were nothing like the silent family dinners at my house, or at Aunty Ruth's where the twins were likely to get their ears boxed for making each other choke with laughter. Jamil's family talked over and under each other, laughing and raising their voices to be heard. It felt like Joanne's kitchen, with Momma Lea bringing dish after dish to her hungry brood. And just like at Joanne's, I wanted to be invisible. But I wasn't any more invisible here than at my house or Joanne's, so I smiled and nodded and plotted my getaway.

Helping to clear the table when the meal was finally over, I passed on the thick coffee in tiny porcelain cups that was offered. As the men chased the children out of the living room so they could smoke and converse, I was finally able to escape, pleading weariness from the day of travel.

"Of course, of course," said his mother, who insisted that I call her "Oomi" like her children did. "It is Arabic for 'mother,'" she explained, again kissing me on both cheeks as she showed me to my room.

I closed the door and sat on the narrow single bed, covered with a pink quilted spread and frilly pillows. I had no idea where Jamil would be sleeping, but it wasn't here.

Jamil's family were polite, superficially friendly, but I got the feeling that they considered me temporary, even on my second and third visits, and when I joined the summer excursions to London to visit Nadim, the eldest brother. But his mother taught me to cook Jamil's favorite dishes and told me she was glad that I made her baby happy.

Our life in the next few years settled into a routine of absence. Jamil was in Portland one month, gone two; home two months, gone one. I traveled with him sometimes, visiting rice farms in Arkansas or Louisiana, or vacationing in Paris, but spent most of my time at home alone. Even with my weekly stops at the office, I felt useless and bored.

I thought about my old job, and my apartment, wondering if I'd given them up too soon. I spent less time at my little desk and more time sleeping until noon, waiting for my hangovers to evaporate, waiting for Jamil to come home. Mom was busy with Dad, who'd been in and out of detox twice in a six-month period. John had married Michelle and kicked out all the roommates so that they could raise little Lizzie in peace. That left Joanne, and our frequent lunch dates, and those Saturday nights at the downtown clubs.

I was so lonely when Jamil was away. It wasn't like I said "I'm going to go out and get in trouble." Like with Mehdi, and now Michael, it just sort of happened. Jamil would be away on business and I'd get wasted and at "last call for alcohol" the guy Joanne or I had danced with would casually walk over and ask if we wanted to come with him and his buddy to smoke a bowl, or do some lines. Usually I ended up at home, alone, in an hour or so but two guys was two too many. I couldn't really blame Joanne, though I think Jamil did. He wanted me to stay home and stay sober when he was away.

Jamil finally phoned from his mother's house two weeks after my painful disclosure about that night with Michael and Ben. I could picture him in the living room, barefoot and wearing his soft cotton thobe, his short, round mother and his equally short and round aunties hovering nearby. I know they wanted Jamil to settle down with a nice Arab girl, and I stood in the way of a suitable match.

Jamil always said, "No arranged marriages for me," unlike the two brothers who were married to cousins. By his view, being brought up in the States conveyed extra privilege to do what he wanted. But arranged or no, I was certain he was being introduced to any number of doe-eyed beauties who would gladly bear his children.

We talked about our relationship in several long phone calls from his mother's kitchen to ours. It felt like he had begun to accept my apologies and understand that I hadn't meant to hurt him as we talked about how we could spend more time together. I felt a wave of relief when he started to tease me.

"Is that Khalid?" I asked, hearing one of his brothers in the background. "What is he saying?"

"He's saying I wouldn't have any troubles if I married a nice Muslim girl," Jamil laughed, making a joke, but also making a point. Everyone, Jamil included, seemed to forget that I had converted to Islam a year

34

earlier, while on an extended family holiday in Hawaii. Apparently no one took it seriously.

Leading up to that decision, I took it very seriously. Jamil and I talked about religion and God for hours, especially when we'd been snorting coke. At the time I didn't see the inconsistency in that. In our long conversations, Jamil helped me to see the beauty in the faith, and the difference between customs and the religion. Life under Islam seemed well defined. I believed in God and I liked the idea of structure. What scared me, of course, was the part about not drinking alcohol, but almost all the Muslim men I'd met, and a few of the women drank, so I pushed that part out of my mind.

That's where the double-standard came in. As we prepared to go to the mosque the morning I converted, Khalid's wife, Siham, let me know that I would now be expected to abstain, and to dress more modestly. She said it nicely, as in "You've been hanging around with the men, acting like one of the guys, but now you will be able to join the company of our women." But it felt like an order, like she was handing me a tiny box to squeeze into. Spending time with the women hadn't been a part of the long, fascinating discussions I'd had with Jamil about the faith and converting. On the drive to the mosque, in the backseat between Jamil's sisters-in law, I realized that I wanted to convert to a philosophy while the family was expecting me to convert to the customs.

We pulled up to a non-descript building and entered a large, bright room. A Filipino woman, her smile made even wider by the covering that framed her broad face, led us down a hall to another bright room. The Imam was waiting for us, kneeling on a pillow in the middle of the empty space. With Fosiah and Siham on either side, I knelt in front of him and folded my hands in my lap, hoping that no one would notice their trembling.

The worst part of the whole experience was that I knew I was damned from the beginning. Jamil and I had been up most of the night snorting expensive Hawaiian cocaine and drinking rum, a pre-celebration of sorts. I was barely sober and certain that everyone could smell the stale liquor that I smelled on myself. It wasn't that I didn't believe. I just believed more at 3:00 in the morning when Jamil and I were exploring what life and God and religion all meant. I could recite the Five Pillars of Islam: allegiance to the One God, prayer, fasting, alms to the poor, and pilgrimage to Mecca, and could express my reasons for converting. But I knew that God knew I was under the influence so it was all a sham, no matter my intention.

The Imam, an Asian man, was no fool. As I knelt before him, battling with my borrowed headscarf, he softly mentioned that it was not a good thing to convert simply because of a relationship. Fosiah squirmed beside me and closed her eyes.

"Oh no," I told him sincerely, "I am doing this because I believe in my heart."

He nodded once and we proceeded. I left the mosque twenty minutes later with a certificate that declared my conversion and my new Islamic name, Noor Jehan.

I did believe in my heart. I wanted to embrace the faith, but the structure I craved didn't come with the certificate. I did cut down on the drinking in the weeks following my ceremony, praying five times a day as I faced east towards Mecca. And then it decreased to three times a day, and then none. Within a month I reverted to reciting the Lord's Prayer before I fell asleep, like my mother had taught me, but even that felt more like insurance than belief. I had always looked to Joanne, and then Eddie and now Jamil to prop me up, to make me feel like I belonged in the world. With the conversion I'd hoped that religion could do it. I was wrong.

The family never believed that I converted for any other reason than to snare Jamil. I'm not sure what Jamil thought, but I always hoped that God knew the truth, which was that I desperately wanted something to believe in. I just didn't know how to make that work.

Chapter Four

AFTER SEVERAL MORE entangled conversations, Jamil came home from his self-imposed exile in Michigan without a wife, and with a renewed resolve from me to be the kind of woman he deserved. We bought a new mattress for the despoiled bed, and stopped calling Michael for cocaine. Jamil went to his office during the day, then stayed up half the night, Scotch in one hand, cigarette in the other, on the phone with business connections in Saudi Arabia and Detroit. I passed out to late-night talk shows with a vodka-7 on the nightstand, wishing Jamil would come to bed, silently waiting for the next trip to take him away. I had a childhood fantasy of how life was supposed to look and it involved the man going off to work each morning and coming home at night to a waiting dinner, not disappearing for months at a time like my Dad.

I did try to make a life for myself, but Jamil's schedule made that difficult. That was my excuse anyway. The one time I'd gotten up the nerve to sign up for an evening poetry writing class at the nearby grade school I got a call to meet him in Hong Kong, which was exciting, but meant that I missed two weeks of class and simply didn't go back. I felt paralyzed and spent my days drifting around the house waiting for the phone to ring. I accomplished the household chores, met Joanne for lunch, or stopped in at Mom's. I read *Time* magazine, and *Glamour*, and shopped through the mail. Night was the worst. I had always been afraid of the dark, and we lived along the river where it was often noisy with the sound of the wind rattling sailboats in the moorage below. I'd make a tall, strong drink, or take a bottle of cheap wine upstairs to the bedroom where we had a little fridge that I kept stocked with snacks.

With the television on for company, I poured through catalogs, placing telephone orders for lingerie or knick-knacks in a blackout, wondering at the boxes that arrived weeks later. Jamil would call from Jeddah or Singapore or Tokyo and we'd say,

"I miss you so much."

"What time is it there?"

"Next year will be better."

That October we escaped on a real vacation. No business, just the two of us in Italy. Like much of our time together, it was mostly lovely, though our arguments had become more frequent.

We started in Venice. I was so hung over that the obligatory tourist gondola ride was torture, but we enjoyed ourselves toasting with tall glasses of beer in the Plaza San Marco and wandering the narrow streets. Laughing at the pigeons that surrounded us in the plaza, I had to pinch myself, this middle-class kid from northeast Portland walking hand in hand with my lover in Italy.

Jamil rented a car and we headed south towards Florence, stopping at sights along the way as we littered the backseat with candy bar wrappers and empty cans of Coke. We got into a fight at the Leaning Tower of Pisa. I was hung over, again, and became queasy and dizzy walking up the tight, narrow spiral staircase of the Tower. But instead of saying, "I feel sick," I snapped at Jamil and put a damper on what should've been a perfect memory. As the cutting words came out of my mouth, I thought, "Oh, just shut up." Instead, I harped at some inconsequential thing and Jamil stopped talking to me. I spent the rest of the day trying to be sweet and cute so he'd forgive me. It would've been easier if I'd just kept my mouth shut.

In Florence we celebrated my twenty-ninth birthday. It was strange not being home with my family. I'd never missed a celebration until now. Jamil tried to make it up to me. His brothers sent flowers and telexes to our hotel with "best wishes," and we ate dinner in a quiet restaurant. He told corny jokes as he chain-smoked, choosing an expensive wine and tiny quail eggs for our appetizer. The evening was lovely, though I couldn't stop thinking of my brother with his annual birthday poem, and blowing out the candles while the boys sang off-key, Aunt Ruth and Mom toasting with highballs.

But how could I complain? We were in glorious Italy, visiting places I'd only read about. No one else in my family had traveled further east than Denver. I counted the hours backwards and phoned home every few days.

"Mom? It's me. I saw the statue of David today. It's incredible. Yeah, I miss you too. What's going on there?"

From Florence we traveled by train to Rome. After two weeks, the constant noise and crowds were wearing, and I was exhausted navigating in a foreign language. My crankiness continued, and I felt queasy much of the time. I blamed it on the food, but maybe it was because we started drinking at noon and then continued well into the night.

On our last full day in Italy we ate lunch in a charming café a few blocks from the hotel. We'd slept until noon, so it was actually breakfast, a breakfast of red wine and antipasto and pasta and veal scaloppini. How could the locals eat like this and stay so thin and gorgeous? I was bloated, and nauseous, and my pants were too tight and I really just wanted a bowl of cereal and why in the hell was Jamil looking at that blonde?

"If you'd rather be with her, go ahead and change tables," I said, a sharp edge to my voice.

"Annette, please."

My name used to sound like silk coming from his mouth. Now it was staccato, an accusation. He placed his knife and fork on the plate as he shook his head.

"Why is it always me? I'm not the one ogling every woman in the place," I replied, thinking, shut up Annette, just shut up.

The waiter, who'd been about to refill our glasses, discreetly stepped back.

"Could we have the check, please?" Jamil asked in an overly polite voice that I heard as "please excuse my drunken American girlfriend."

I turned three shades of crimson.

"Oh, sweetie, I'm so sorry. I didn't mean it. I'm just tired."

He looked through me, as if at an empty chair. We sat in silence until the bill was taken care of, me shoving linguini around my plate, swallowing the last of the wine.

Jamil stood, moved to pull out my chair with the utmost formality, and turned to walk out. I followed, stumbling slightly on the step up to the door.

He walked at a brisk pace, just ahead of me.

"Jamil, slow down. I can't keep up," I pleaded, trying not to jostle any of the passersby.

He turned the corner, and for a moment I lost him in the afternoon bustle. I didn't know the way back to the hotel. I glanced at a pasticceria that looked vaguely familiar, white frosted cakes ornately reaching for the ceiling next to various flavors of biscotti, and there was the macelleria, the butcher in his bloody apron pulling a slab of beef out of the case. The Colosseum should be close by, on my left, which meant that the hotel was near.

There he was. I nearly ran to catch up, my breath coming in short gasps.

"Jamil, don't leave me. Please."

He didn't speak but slowed his pace. Two more turns and we reached the hotel.

"Well, it'll be good to get packed and organized," I said as the elevator door closed, avoiding my image in the smoky mirror.

When we reached the suite, Jamil went straight for the mini bar, grabbed a beer and turned on the television, loud. A re-run of *Bonanza* came on, dubbed in Italian.

Two could play this game. With a flourish, I snatched the bottle of vodka and a soda off the small desk we were using as a bar and headed towards the bedroom. Mixing myself a stiff drink, I chugged half, then dumped both suitcases onto the bed. We were headed to Cyprus. Maybe things would be better there.

The suitcases occupied me for one more drink. After finishing the packing, I poked my head out the door.

"Jamil? Is everything okay?" I asked, in a tiny voice.

After a pause, he replied, "No. How can you even ask that?" sitting upright in the same position I'd left him in an hour before, ever-present ashtray by his side.

At that moment, a Trail Blazer game recorded from a few weeks earlier came on, again dubbed in Italian. I broke down and threw myself on Jamil's lap.

"I just want us to be home. To have a regular life," I sobbed.

He held me, and for a second I thought I saw his eyes tear up too. I know that he wanted to be in Portland and that as long as he worked for his family that wasn't going to happen. And as much as we wanted to pretend otherwise, he would be working for them for as long as he lived.

We held each other in silence, and then Jamil told me how it was becoming hard to come home because he was afraid of what I'd have to report about my dalliances.

"You know I've never been unfaithful to you, Annette. I keep my word, but you don't."

By my reasoning, if he were home more, I wouldn't be going out, and if I didn't go out, I wouldn't make mistakes. He didn't see it that way. He thought it had to do with my drinking.

"Why can't you stop with just one or two? Or just not drink when I'm away?"

"What about you?" I asked, trying to keep my voice level. "Why is it fine that you drink all the time?"

It was a sorry attempt at turning the tables. Part of me knew he was right. It was the same conversation I'd had with John several years earlier. Deep inside I knew that I drank too much, but it wasn't like I could just turn the stuff off and on. I wasn't like Nadim's wife, who just had a single glass of wine with dinner, or the Michigan wives who didn't drink at all. Drinking was a game, our hobby. We'd even picked up a clock in Vegas that had nothing but "5's," on the face. "It's always 5:00 somewhere!" was our favorite toast.

We talked in circles for another hour, having moved from beer and vodka to Grand Marnier, finally agreeing that our lives were hard and that things would get better next year. That's when Jamil would miraculously find freedom from his family's rule, I'd start at the community college, and we'd live happily ever after. After a room service snack, we made sloppy, drunken love and passed out.

I woke to the annoying jangle of the phone.

"Good morning, sir," I could hear in accented English from my side of the bed. "This is your wake-up call as requested."

I so wanted to sleep, but there was a plane to catch. Jamil reached for a cigarette and the phone, calling for breakfast while I made my way to the bathroom and the Pepto-Bismol.

At least the luggage was organized. After forcing down a few bites of lukewarm oatmeal, definitely not an Italian specialty, and a glass of milk, I slumped on the couch wearing sunglasses. Jamil looked a little tight around the eyes, but he was up and moving, ordering a cab, calling the desk to arrange checkout. I marveled at his capacity to function.

The doorman situated us in the back seat of the cab, graciously accepting the folded bill that Jamil discreetly placed in his hand. I closed my eyes as the driver careened through Rome traffic, my face pointed toward the window I'd opened just a crack. *Don't let me get sick. Don't let me get sick.*

"Are you alright?" Jamil asked, from his corner of the back seat as he reached to take my hand.

I smiled, eyes still closed. "I will be, once I get a drink."

I squeezed his hand back and repeated my mantra: *Don't let me get sick. Don't let me get sick.*

We reached the airport with little time to spare, standing in line for check-in while nervously watching the clock, then moved in what felt like slow motion through security and down the long corridors to our gate. I wanted the hell out of Italy and I needed a drink, bad. Finally, finally our Cypress Air flight called for first class passengers and we boarded. I settled in the window seat and leaned my head against the pane, clutching the little in-case-you-get-sick bag. After a queasy take-off, our dark-haired steward, wearing a shirt belted to resemble a toga, brought us each a double Bloody Mary, which helped my mood and my stomach considerably. We were served feta cheese and olives with our drinks. If this was the Cypriot menu, I would like Limassol.

From the airline magazine I learned that Limassol is situated on the southern coast of Greek-speaking Cyprus. Intending to sightsee during the cab ride to our seaside hotel, I passed out against Jamil's shoulder, drowsy from the three drinks we'd had on the flight. After checking in, we both collapsed onto the bed and slept, leaving luggage and exploration for later.

Rousing ourselves for a late lunch of dolmathes and more feta, and a bottle of wine, we marveled at how quiet and slow-paced Cyprus seemed compared to frenetic Rome. We walked the beach with little intent. Gentle waves lapped the shore, barely making a sound, and we held hands while watching a group of small children build a sandcastle. Our life would get better next year. I could tell.

A thin and energetic Indian realtor came by the next day to take us to an apartment building a few miles down the beach. He smiled a lot and shook his head back and forth as he talked, describing the virtues of the location. Jamil's brother, Sammy, had recently bought a flat in the building, since they all spent so much time in the area. Jamil walked me through it, and the vacant apartment next to it.

"What do you think, Annette?" he asked, surveying the panoramic view of the sparkling Mediterranean. "You could stay here part of the year when I'm working in Saudi Arabia or Bahrain, and I'd come over on weekends."

I smiled and squeezed his hand. I smiled again over grilled baby octopus at a dingy seaside café while he and the real estate man talked about airport accessibility, and the mild Mediterranean winters. I nodded in agreement.

The idea of living in Limassol sounded exotic. Never mind being a tourist in Italy, imagine this kid from northeast Portland living in Cyprus. It was the answer to my insistence that we spend more time together. But I wouldn't know anyone. What would I do during the week when he was working? I didn't speak the language. I'd be so far from home. This isn't what I'm imagined when John and I had talked about seeing the world. But Jamil was wildly enthusiastic so I kept my mouth shut.

He wouldn't be back in Portland again until December, so we spent a few clingy I'll-love-you-forever nights and long lie-ins in the morning before he headed on to Saudi Arabia and Malaysia. From the little slice of the seaside that we saw, Cyprus did seem like a magical place, with the gentle sea and the promise of time together. Maybe it would be okay.

I traveled home via London in order to break up the long journey and visit Jamil's brother, part of his on-going effort to ingratiate me to his family. Nadim and his British wife, Kate, lived in Kensington in a beautiful home where the upper floors tilted just a bit from bomb damage in the last World War. I had visited twice before but never alone.

Theirs seemed such a civil life, one that I know Jamil wanted to imitate. Kate was a petite blonde; funny, smart and fashionable. She attended cooking classes, had learned Arabic and ate like a bird. I ate pizza with my hands and laughed too loud and the only Arabic phrases I knew were curses. But I could go drink for drink with Nadim.

I found myself thinking about my brother as I tucked myself into the bed that seemed like an after-thought in the tiny room crammed with toys, boxes and an extra wardrobe. John would love London. I would love to be here with him, instead of trembling in my loafers each time I left the house on my own. I'd taken a cab to the British Museum and had sweated through six levels of Harrod's, but was so self-consciously nervous that it was tough to enjoy myself. I knew I was pathetic, and I tried to push myself, but it was usually easier to simply stay in and offer to help with lunch.

Jamil and I resumed our three-times-a-day phone routine while I was in London, making plans for the coming year. I counted hours ahead to call and wake him up and we'd pretend that I was next to him. He'd check in midday and then phoned when I was going to bed. I was sleeping in a tiny bedroom on the fourth floor of his brother's house, trying to stay out of the way, and Jamil was in a hotel in Jeddah, but our future was filled with promise.

Nadim ribbed me unmercifully. "What is this? We can't go to dinner until my baby brother calls?"

Nadim could be difficult. With the build of a Sumo wrestler, he carried a great deal of clout in the family business since he was such a ruthless negotiator. Whether it was real estate or a shipment of rice that Jamil had arranged, you knew that the best deal was made if Nadim was at the helm. That ruthlessness seeped into his family life. His four children were perfectly behaved, and not because the nanny was strict. And he was a drinker, just like Jamil and me. Jamil sometimes resented Nadim's power, but he and I got along well.

At afternoon tea, the children would shyly tell me about their day in an English accent just tinted with Arabic, before being swept off by the Filipino nanny for a bath. Nadim would roar in from the office for a gin and tonic, and we'd head out in a flurry for dinner with their friends at his favorite Indian restaurant on Fulham Road or the newest Vietnamese place. Kate silently guided me as to which fork to use, and made sure to at least attempt to include me in their conversations. I smiled a lot, and nodded, and counted the hours ahead to Jeddah, or backwards to Portland, imagining next week, next month and next year.

Nadim hired a limo on my departure day and we barreled down the M1 towards Heathrow drinking champagne at 10:00 in the morning. He and Kate dropped me at the curb with a flutter of kisses on both cheeks and my empty promise to call when I arrived home. After getting my passport stamped and winding through the vast Duty Free shop without making a purchase, I settled into my window seat on the plane and stared at the clouds as we followed the day west.

After going through customs in Chicago, I shuffled listlessly up and down the concourse near my gate, stopping at a noisy bar for a drink. I was tired, from the inside out, tired and lonely and scared of Jamil's plan for the apartment in Limassol, scared of the tiny knot in my gut that didn't yet have words, but if it did might've whispered, "This isn't working." I asked for another beer and stared at the television above the bartender's head. It would be another five hours before I'd be in Portland, but the thought of calling a cab to ferry me to the empty condo brought tears to my eyes. I wanted to see smiling faces at the gate. I wanted to be welcomed home.

Finding a pay phone, I called collect, my wallet full of British pounds.

"Mom? Hi. It's me. I'm in Chicago. Will you come pick me up when I get there? Please?"

I asked her to invite Joanne and gave her the details of my arrival, doing my best to sound cheerful.

"Yes, I can't wait to see you too. It will be fun."

Finally re-boarding, I dozed the remaining hours scrunched up against the window with just the tiny airline pillow between me and a stiff neck. As we neared Portland, I climbed over the sleeping Japanese man in the aisle seat and unsteadily made my way to the bathroom. Forcing a smile into the mirror, I washed my hands and face. I was fine, really.

They were there as I stepped off the plane: Mom and Joanne, bright-eyed from cocktails in the airport lounge, enjoying the excuse for an outing. I nearly wept at the sight of my mother, graying hair recently permed, wearing a collared sweatshirt decorated with jack-o-lanterns; ubiquitous beige shoulder bag clutched under one arm. Joanne was wrapped tight in her scarlet trench coat, wearing the biggest smile I'd seen in weeks.

'Welcome home, honey," Mom cried out as she reached to hug me.

We made our way to Baggage Claim, Mom chattering on about Lizzie, John's little girl. I walked with my arm around her shoulder, while Joanne pranced ahead with my bag chanting, "I see London, I see France. No wait, I see Italy!"

From Joanne's back seat, I shared tales of Italy and Cyprus, leaving out the part about the arguments and that Jamil wanted me to live in Limassol. As painful as much of my childhood had been, I loved it that my parents lived ten minutes away in the house I grew up in. Aunty Ruth was still three blocks over, with the same picnic table in the breakfast nook, the boys' initials carved on the bench. I knew who I was there. I knew how to act in my mother's kitchen, on my cousin's porch. What would it be like to be twenty hours away? What if something happened to Dad and I needed to get home quickly? What about Christmas and the annual gathering? I'd have to be home in December. And in October for my birthday. And for the Fourth of July. I didn't want to move to Cypress. Not even part time.

I took my place on the front seat as we Mom off, promising to see her in the coming days. Pulling away, Joanne produced a white packet from her purse and waved it in front of me as she drove.

"A welcome-home present," she said mischievously.

Turning up the heat as we made our way into the condo, I let my bags drop as I ran up the stairs for our paraphernalia, right where I'd left it in Jamil's sock drawer.

We fell naturally into our ritual, settling on to the couch. I chopped the coke on the mirror using a single-edged razor blade. Joanne examined the few bills in her wallet, picking the cleanest in order to shape a snorting straw.

"Oh wait!" I exclaimed in my best British accent. "Let's use the currency of the realm!"

She took the pound sterling that I offered, rolled it once and then again tighter so that only a sliver of the Queen's face remained.

"You first, my traveling friend," she said, handing me the bill, mimicking my accent.

I took a deep breath and blew out, then leaned over the mirror with the rolled bill in one nostril. Holding the other closed tight, I inhaled hard. Switching sides, I snorted another line before handing the bill back to her.

"Whew! Good stuff," I said, swallowing against the residual coke that coated the back of my throat while the chemical electricity coursed through my body. I didn't ask where she'd gotten it.

After a few more lines, I started talking, telling Joanne about the fights interspersed with the sweetness and how I wished Jamil and I could simply stay in Portland together. Joanne offered sympathy. She didn't want me to move either. She talked about her job and her husband, and the friend from high school she'd recently run in to. I was home.

We stayed up the rest of that night and well into the next morning, Joanne calling in sick to work and letting Anthony know she was babysitting me. She left some time after noon, some time after the coke ran out. Wired but wiped out, I stumbled up the stairs and tripped over the suitcase now sprawled open on the bedroom floor, clothes half in and half out after my search for souvenirs. Packing was fun, organizing and making things fit in anticipation of a good time. Unpacking sucked.

Jamil phoned. I did my best to sound chipper and sober.

"What time is it with you?" I asked, from that nether world of jet lag and no sleep.

"Midnight," he replied, his own words slightly thick with drink. "Are you being good?"

"Baby, I've only been home twenty-four hours, and I'm way too tired to get into any trouble." I forced a laugh. Snorting cocaine at home with my best friend wasn't trouble. Not today it wasn't.

"God, I miss you," he said and I tried not to cry. "Get some sleep and I'll call you tomorrow."

My intention was to stay awake until a reasonable evening hour, in an attempt to acclimate to the correct time zone, but all the stimulants in the world couldn't overcome the exhaustion of jet lag combined with the cocaine let-down. I got into bed before nightfall and was out within minutes.

It was barely dark when I came to. Or was it barely light? The clock read 6:30. I had no idea whether it was morning or night, or what day it was. I was not a stranger to disoriented self-loathing and found myself, once again, feeling like my skin didn't fit, cringing with regret for what was undone as much as for what I'd done. Staggering to the bathroom, I avoided myself in the mirror even while splashing my face with cold water. Leaning in the doorway, I rested my head against the frame.

"This has got to stop," I said out loud. "I can't keep doing this." Wasted days and lost weekends were the norm; sometimes it was lost weeks. I had to figure out a way to wrest control of my life. My days were empty, hollow, punctuated by bits of superficial glamour. I was lost and alone and felt out of place nearly everywhere. I couldn't talk to Joanne about this stuff; she breezed through life. Certainly not my mother. And what could I possibly say to Jamil? I love you but I can't live this way? No. I would figure it out. I would make it work.

Turning on the bedroom television, I recognized the cute evening weather guy. God, it was still Tuesday. I'd only been asleep for a few hours. It was going to be a long night.

Hungry, I headed to the kitchen, leaving off the lights. A whole chicken and half a quart of pecan praline ice cream huddled in the freezer, a jar of pickles, some hot sauce, and a smelly yogurt that had expired ten days earlier in the fridge. Spooning ice cream from the carton, I glanced through the pile of mail on the dining room table that Tim had dropped off. Opening the side door, I stood breathing in the damp scent of rain soaked grass. I resolved to get my shit together. I knew that cocaine was not working for me. I wondered what was next.

Chapter Five

WHAT WAS NEXT turned out to be a good-looking speed cook named Daniel, who stuck a needle in my arm within half an hour of meeting him.

It had been two weeks since I'd returned to Portland. After that welcome-home coke binge, I'd gone six days without drinking, thinking that I could lose a few pounds in the process of self-improvement. I wasn't overweight. At five foot six and 130 pounds I was fine, but I'd always liked the sound of 125. Life would be great if I weighed 125. Then I could stop thinking about my weight and focus my attention on more important things, like the Arabic class I wanted to take, or finishing my photo albums.

On the seventh day, I celebrated my resolve with a bottle of "lite" wine, which mostly tasted like water. On the sixth day I had a few vodka-7's, figuring that there were fewer calories with the booze and diet pop than in a whole bottle of the diet wine. And if I could continue to limit myself to three drinks a night, which I could, I'd still be able to study for the class. I hadn't actually signed up yet, but I would next term. At this point I was laying the groundwork for the perfect life.

I stopped by my folks' house on a Saturday. Mom only worked part time in the winter months, until tax season hit after the first of the year when she was at the office six days a week. I joined her at the kitchen table after making myself a cup of tea, pulling out the packet of vacation photos I'd just picked up.

She put down the crossword puzzle with a smile.

"Look, here we are in front of the Spanish Steps in Rome. A nice German man took the picture for us."

I went through the whole trip, skipping the frowning shot of me in front of the Leaning Tower, and the one where I was asleep in the car. I came to a picture of Jamil on the beach in Cyprus, followed by one of me with Nadim and Kate's children in London. My eyes watered as I handed them to Mom.

"What's wrong, honey?" she asked.

"Nothing really. I just miss Jamil," I said. Mom thought that my life was exciting. I couldn't tell her that it was a mess and I was lonely and drank too much and now what do I do? I finished my tea and the photo descriptions, ambling home to the empty condo via an unnecessary stop at the grocery store for milk and an early poinsettia for the coffee table. The phone rang as I walked in.

It was Joanne.

"Annette, I'm coming over. I've just tried something and, sister, you are in for a treat."

"What are you talking about?" I asked.

We didn't talk specifics about drugs on the phone, so I answered my own question with, "Oh never mind. I'm here. Come on over." I did not want any cocaine. I don't care how good she said it was.

The doorbell rang an hour later. I looked through the peephole to see Joanne's grinning face smiling up at me.

"Woman, what are you going on about?" I asked as I opened the door.

As she stepped in, Michael and a guy I didn't know moved into view.

"Whoa," I said. "Joanne, are you trying to get me killed?"

"It's alright," she said, and under her breath, "Trust me, he won't stay long. Now let me in and I'll tell you what we've got."

My gut churned as I stepped back from the doorway so they could enter. Michael meant cocaine, and even the thought of cocaine had my stomach bubbling as if I'd just snorted half a gram of the baby laxative that he used as a cut. Michael also meant trouble with a capital "T." I had no intention of ever taking my clothes off with anyone other than Jamil, and certainly not with this weasel, but if Jamil even suspected that Michael had been in our house again, our relationship was dead.

But Jamil was in Malaysia and we'd already talked this morning and no neighbors were in the driveway, and it would only be a few minutes anyway.

"Come in. Hurry. Whose car did you drive?"

"Mine," replied Joanne. "Quit being so paranoid."

I took a deep breath as I closed the door behind them.

"Okay, okay. What've you got?"

I ushered them into the kitchen, fully prepared to explain that I no longer used cocaine.

"Hey Annette," Michael said, as he made himself comfortable at the round, wood laminate table. "Sorry about all the shit that came down."

Damn Joanne for telling him.

"It's handled," I said without looking his direction. "So what's up?"

"Annette, please meet Daniel," Joanne said with a mocking formality. "He is about to change your life."

"I don't know that my life needs changing," I answered, getting more confused and angry by the second. "What in the hell are you talking about?"

"Speed, my dear. Amphetamine. The elixir of the gods." She laughed and exchanged knowing glances with the two men.

I'd done my share of cross tops in high school, and we'd gotten a hold of some pharmaceuticals a few years earlier. That stuff was great. I was definitely interested.

"Well, actually," Joanne said, sounding nervous for the first time, "This is methamphetamine. Crystal. It's not a pill. You inject it."

"Are you crazy? You want me to stick a needle in my arm?"

"Hey, I've got plenty of buyers who want this stuff. I don't need any hassle," said Daniel in a deeply melodic voice.

For the first time, I really looked at the guy. He was slight, about five foot nine and built like a streamlined semi. Despite the weather, he wore only a white T-shirt tucked into his jeans, the sleeves taut against his biceps, chest muscles clearly discernable through the thin fabric. He had a tousled mass of brown curls that could only be described as cherubic, which contrasted with chiseled cheekbones and brown glinting eyes. Only later did I learn that the muscles and the fading tan were courtesy of a minimum-security prison in southern California where he'd just spent two years for the manufacture of a controlled substance. Apparently the feds hadn't changed his habits, but he sure looked good.

His head was slightly lowered so that he was looking up at me, a slight frown playing at the corners of his mouth. I did not want to give this man any hassles.

"Joanne, come talk to me," I said, looking at Daniel, while steering her towards the main floor bathroom and a closed door. "Michael, there is beer in the fridge. Amuse yourself."

I slid the door closed. Joanne sat on the toilet while I leaned back against the sink, our knees almost touching in the tiny space.

"Are you out of your mind?" I hissed. "What on earth are you thinking?"

Needles meant drug addicts, Times Square, shooting galleries. I didn't know any addicts, had never seen any addicts, and didn't like the idea that my best friend was suggesting that I become one.

"Oh, calm down," she whispered back. "It's not that big a deal. It's like snorting, only faster," she explained, licking her left forefinger and rubbing at a small darkened spot on her right arm, as if she could make it go away.

"When did you do it?" I asked, searching her face for signs of intoxication. Other than talking a little fast, she seemed normal, though now I noticed that her pupils were the size of saucers.

"A couple of hours ago," she said, "and last night at about 10:00."

She explained how she'd met Michael to get some coke. He wasn't holding, so had her drive him to some woman's house in outer-southeast. She had to wait in the car for twenty minutes until he came out and told her there was no coke, but there was a guy there with some speed and was she game?

"And you know me, I'm game for just about anything at least twice, or until I get caught," she said, muffling a giggle.

"Weren't you scared?" I asked.

"Just a little, at first," she replied, her voice rising to just above a whisper. "But it didn't really hurt, and the feeling is unbelievable. Me and Michael got it on in the back seat of the car, and then I went home and cleaned my entire house while Anthony was out all night playing cards with your ex-husband. I called Michael again first thing this morning. This stuff is great."

I tried to erase the image of Joanne and Michael having sex in her back seat as I considered the possibilities. I could use a little extra energy, especially if I was going to take that class. I'd loved the pills I'd had before and could see why it might be beneficial to hurry the dose along. Joanne described an immediate euphoria and then all that energy. I could use some euphoria.

I took a deep breath. I was game for just about anything too if it involved the promise of feeling good.

"Okay, I'll try it."

"She's in," Joanne said, opening the slider and rounding the corner back to the kitchen. "Set it up, my friend."

Michael chuckled, but I certainly didn't want him to be the one coming at me with anything sharp and pointy.

"I'll go with the maestro," I said, indicating Daniel. I watched him take a quarter baggy filled with a chunky, yellowish powder from his the front pocket of his jeans. I was used to snow white cocaine that disappeared in a humid room, but now watched as Daniel took a syringe from Michael's jacket, removed the round plastic cap, put some speed in it and asked for some distilled water.

I had some. I used it for my contact lenses.

"Bring some rubbing alcohol too, and a cotton ball," Joanne called after me as I headed upstairs. "And a cotton swab."

It seemed medicinal, not such a big deal like Joanne said. I gathered the supplies upstairs and returned to find Daniel in the little bathroom, paraphernalia on the counter next to the sink. I stood in the doorway to watch as he used a needle to put a small amount of the distilled water into the bottle cap with the speed and swirled it around until it liquefied. He then took a fresh syringe and quickly pulled off the skinny orange tip that protected the actual point. Taking a small bit of cotton from the swab, Daniel rolled a tiny, hard ball and dropped it into the cap.

He then began to draw the speed mixture into the syringe through the cotton ball, explaining that this filtered out any impurities. He held the syringe upright, tapping it with his finger as a small air bubble rose to the top. He pressed slightly on the plunger to expel the air, followed by a single drop of liquid.

"Do you want to do this, or shall I?" he asked, looking me dead in the eye.

"Oh for God's sake," Joanne said, walking to the door with a piece of rubber in her hand. "She's never done this before. You do it."

Joanne sat me on the closed toilet, then reached onto the counter for the rubbing alcohol and cotton ball and cleaned my inner arm while half in and half out of the john. I felt like I was at the doctor's office. The rubber, which turned out to be surgical tubing, got tied around my bicep.

"Make a fist," Daniel said as he ran two fingers over the crook of my arm.

"First time my foot," he said, looking at me suspiciously.

I looked at what he was feeling. Oh God. I was a member of the Gallon Club at the Red Cross. He thought those marks were from drugs.

"I give blood at the Red Cross," I said.

"Not any more you don't," he chuckled as he crouched down and brought the needle to my arm.

Oh shit. This was really happening. What if I died? What if I became an addict and started selling my ass on Williams and Russell, or wherever it was women sold their stuff these days? What if it hurt? I squeezed my eyes shut.

Ouch. It did hurt a little. Oh shit. I can't look.

"Here we go," he said. "Don't move"

I opened my eyes as he drew back on the plunger and watched as a thin stream of blood entered the chamber.

"We're in," he said softly. He loosened the tie and then slowly pushed down on the plunger sending the thick liquid into my vein.

Ah, well, I don't feel a thing, I thought with relief, and then BLAM! I had to breathe out through my mouth as a rush of heat hit my lungs and spread throughout my body and out my crotch. Jesus God, was I having an orgasm? I felt dizzy and light and heavy at the same time. The pure physical sensation was more amazing than anything I'd ever experienced.

"Are you alright?" Joanne asked, from somewhere far away.

I opened my eyes to see her, Daniel and Michael grinning at me like Cheshire cats. I must've been grinning back, because Joanne laughed and said, "What did I tell you?"

"Man," was all I could say. "Man, oh man." My eyes were closed as I felt every inch of my body tingle.

"Daniel makes this stuff, doll face," said Joanne, as she gathered the accoutrements.

"Made it? You made this stuff?" I asked, from somewhere outside of my head.

What did I know? Cocaine came from plants in Columbia and got stepped on twelve times before I ever saw it, and the only speed I knew about was pills.

"I didn't make this batch," Daniel said now standing outside the doorway. He offered a condensed version of the recipe for making dope: a little of this, a little of that, some stuff called "prope," ammonia and a bunch of stuff I didn't follow.

"It's a crazy mad-scientist scene," said Michael. "Bubbling vials and wild-haired guys."

"Something like that," Daniel smiled.

As my head cleared, I was full of questions, but Daniel demurred. It was then that Joanne took me aside and told me that he'd recently been released from prison for making the stuff. This was way more than I'd expected when I answered her phone call.

Daniel mentioned that I could go through Michael to get to him if decided I wanted more of the speed. I bit my tongue. I didn't want to go through Michael for anything but would deal with those details at another time. They left as quickly as they'd arrived. With a wink over her left shoulder, Joanne said she'd call me later.

By later I had cleaned the two-story, three-bedroom condo from top to bottom, including closets and the kitchen junk drawer. As I took a toothbrush to the tub grout, I said out loud, "I could do this stuff every day." Of course the spices wouldn't need alphabetizing every day, but imagine what I could get done. I felt like I had died and gone to heaven and realized that I'd likely been a few grains short of methamphetamine my entire life. It had taken twenty-nine years, but I had found my drug of choice.

I stayed up all that night and into the next day, organizing and reorganizing, talking to Joanne on the phone, and my mother, and Marcie. I felt great. And thinner. I wasn't hungry at all, but Joanne had told me to drink water so I wouldn't get dehydrated. I had beer instead.

Jamil called and was pleased that I was home, and that I was getting so much done.

"Okay, Miss Industrious, "he said, from somewhere in the previous day. "You can shine my shoes while you're at it."

Now there was an idea. I was going to be the best woman ever. Jamil would never again regret loving me. I figured he might like to try this stuff too, but I'd wait to tell him about it in person.

I slept like a dead person Sunday evening and well into Monday. I felt fine getting up. There was no hangover like I was used to with coke and booze. I was hungry as hell, and a little groggy, but that was a small price to pay for the great feeling I'd had.

I looked closely at myself in the bathroom mirror, searching for an outward sign of what I'd just experienced. But, it was just me staring back. My hair needed combing, but there was nothing to suggest how different I felt inside, like I was in on a secret that no one else knew, like I was connected to some bigger truth. I liked it.

Proceeding downstairs, I poured a bowl of cereal, pleased with the sparkling kitchen. I finished two bowls while flipping through one of my mother's discarded ladies magazines.

After eating, I wandered around the condo. There really wasn't anything to do. The place was cleaner than it had ever been. I could go to the store, but I didn't need anything. I could go see my Mom, but we'd talked for an hour the day before and I didn't have much else to say. I felt emptier and emptier as I moved from room to room, staring at the river from the bedroom window, picking up the stapler on the desk in the office, running my fingers along the mantle in the living room. That took up twenty minutes.

I could call Joanne. Just to see how her day was going. Just to say "hi." I wondered if she'd talked to Michael. Not that it mattered. I was just calling to say "hi."

I called and arranged to meet her for a drink after work. The minutes and hours clicked by with painful slowness. The house felt like a jail when only hours before it had been a fascinating project.

I spent over an hour getting ready, killing time. My third shower in twenty-four hours was anticlimactic. When I was high, the shower washed away the sweat generated by my frantic house cleaning. Every drop that hit my sensitized body was an electric current of pleasure. Today it felt flat. Yesterday I felt everything. Today I felt nothing.

I stood under the spray, my mind playing in circles, like an old 45 that skipped at the best part. I thought of my grocery list and tried to count backwards to what time it was in Malaysia. I thought about the empty apartment in Cyprus and the call Jamil had asked me to make to a decorator we knew. With all the internal chatter I could muster, I tried to erase the image of Daniel at my kitchen table, Daniel stroking my inner arm, Daniel breathing out with me like a birthing coach after he'd shot me up.

I was waiting when Joanne walked into the stale-smelling lounge. She looked like I felt—empty.

"I ordered a pitcher," I said, as she slid into the booth across from me.

"A gallon couldn't fix what ails me," she shot back, taking a Salem out of its pack. "It took everything I had to get through this day without calling Michael," she said, packing the cigarette against the tabletop.

"Are you really having an affair?" I asked.

She lit her cigarette and inhaled deeply, blowing the smoke up and over my head.

"Well, I don't know that you'd call it an 'affair,' but we've been lovers since that night at your place. It's the speed I'm talking about," she replied, looking at me as if I were an imbecile.

I marveled at how she did it. I had a one nighter or two and it nearly cost me my man. Joanne had full-blown affairs and Anthony was none the wiser.

"How does that work, exactly?" I once asked.

"Don't ask any questions—that's my arrangement with my husband," she'd said. "He goes his way and I go mine."

"But do you love him?" I'd wondered.

She thought about it for a minute and said, "Look, we have history together, and our families are close, and neither of us takes life too seriously. That's enough for me at this point in my life."

I let it drop. Love seemed like an inconvenience to Joanne. It's what made me feel so guilty when I "had my fun," as she called it. Love was what made me tell Jamil the truth and hope it would make things better instead of worse. But, I'd never known Joanne to get crazy about a man. Not her husband, not her one-night-stands. Maybe hers was the better way.

She continued to take deep drags off the cigarette, absentmindedly running her finger around the rim of her glass.

"Let me tell you something," she said, lowering her voice a notch as she looked around the nearly empty bar. "You have not lived until you have had sex on speed. I mean, Michael was fine before, but good Lord, you would not believe, you would not *believe* what it's like."

I stared at her with a fair amount of skepticism.

She looked me in the eye and tried to stifle a giggle. "I'm not kidding, Annette. This is no joke."

After shaking my head, I started to laugh too. How crazy was this? The sex I'd find out about when my own man came home. But sex or no sex, I wanted more crystal.

"So when do we call him again?" I asked, when our laughter died down, doing my best to sound casual.

"We? What's this 'we' business?" she asked. "You got a mouse in your pocket?"

She lit another cigarette as I refilled our glasses.

"*We* need to be careful with this stuff, sugar pie," she said, in a voice that sounded like she knew everything. "You know that Daniel is a criminal and he runs with criminals. This is a different operation than our favorite low-life cocaine dealer, who, at the moment, is our connection. Besides, I do have a husband and a job to go to every day. I can get away with staying up and out all night on the weekends, but not when I have to work."

I wasn't about to call Michael myself, so folded myself back into the leather seat. Joanne would come around, but not if I pushed her.

We nursed our pitcher for another hour before she had to leave. We didn't talk about the speed, but it was like a silent third at the table.

As we walked to the parking lot, I said, "So what's it going to be?"

"It's going to be Friday night, unless you call Michael yourself, for yourself," Joanne said as she climbed into her car.

I sighed and waved as she pulled away. Friday. It was going to be a long week.

I called Joanne on Wednesday. "I think you should call him today," I said, "to give him time to make the connect."

I could hear her typing.

"'Make the connect.' Listen to you," she replied, not missing a keystroke. "You've been watching too much T.V."

But connect she did, and on Friday we met for drinks. Joanne worked in the personnel department of a big department store at the mall, which meant that she got a discount on clothes. She strolled in that evening in a clingy black jersey dress with a wide belt, and black boots. She was busty and hippy, and used both to her advantage.

"Damn," I said, looking her up and down. "Michael's already hot for you. What are you trying to do, burn the poor boy?"

"Always make 'em want more, "she laughed. "Don't tell anybody, but I'm not wearing any panties."

Oh Lord, I thought. She's planning to have sex with her boyfriend in my house, her boyfriend who isn't allowed in my house.

"So what would you do if I said you couldn't come over?" I asked.

"Well in the first place, you wouldn't. And in the second place, the back seat of the Impala works just fine."

"Oh, you are nasty," I said. It had been a long time since I'd had sex in the back seat of a car.

"Nasty and happy," she said with a wink. "So here's the scoop."

Michael had talked to Daniel last night. Daniel was staying at an ex-girlfriend's house and she had strict rules about drugs. He had to wait until she went to work this morning to start making his calls. He and Michael would hook up this evening and meet us at my place at 10:00.

I got butterflies in my stomach just thinking about 10:00. I realized later that anticipation is a good part of the high. There's the planning to get high, the getting high, and the being high. And with any luck and forethought, there isn't too much space between the being high and the next plan. Because, of course, there was also the coming down: the trying to pretend you're not coming down, the actual coming down and the feeling like shit.

Two women that Joanne knew from work joined us at the bar, so we shot the breeze over a pitcher. I had a hard time making small talk anytime, but it was even more excruciating with the clock behind the bar ticking like a slow drip on a faucet. Have you seen that new show? Yeah. Yeah. So and so is sucking up to the boss. Oh, look at the time.

Saying our farewells, we left the bar, getting back to the condo after 9:00, almost giddy as we stumbled through the door.

"Alright baby. Bring it on, because I am ready," Joanne said as she checked her hair in the hall mirror. "Girl, have you got a toothbrush?"

"Have I got a toothbrush? Of course I have a fucking toothbrush. What you really want to know is if I have an extra, brand-new toothbrush that I can give to you, because I'm surely not letting you brush with mine," I laughed, running up the stairs two at a time to grab one from the linen closet.

We put old Motown on the stereo and sang along with Smokey, toasting "to Friday night" clinking our beer bottles, watching the clock. 9:25. 9:37. 9:53.

10:00 came and went. 10:20. Okay, it's all right. Call Michael. No, give him some time. You don't want to jinx the deal. God I wished we had a number for Daniel. What on earth were they doing?

At 10:45, Joanne called Michael's house and promptly hung up when his girlfriend answered.

"Shit. It was little Miss Shelly."

"Cut her some slack," I said. "Would you want to live with the guy?"

"No, no. I'm happy with this arrangement just the way it is," Joanne replied, taking off her boots.

We turned on the television for the 11:00 news, jumping at every sound on the street.

"This is bullshit," Joanne said as the clock inched towards midnight. "Pure bullshit."

I agreed, feeling like a balloon with a slow leak. Feet up on the coffee table, fresh beers in hand, we pretended to watch TV.

Joanne dozed. The phone rang as I walked into the bedroom for a blanket. I caught it on the first ring.

"Hello?" I said.

The crackling on the line let me know it was Jamil calling internationally.

"Hey baby. How are you?"

"Sleepy," I lied. "You woke me up."

We talked for just a few minutes, me feigning drowsiness. I didn't want to tie up the phone.

"Call me tomorrow. I love you," and he was gone.

Jamil, Jamil. I loved him so much. He would not approve of what I was doing. Not at all. I told myself that I'd just use speed a few more times and then not while he was home. That was three weeks from now. We were going on a Caribbean cruise for New Year's. That would be a good break.

I went back downstairs and covered Joanne. "Who was that?" she mumbled.

"Jamil. Go back to sleep," I said as I squeezed on the opposite end of the couch, pushing her feet so she'd make room.

I dozed too, waking to a tap, tap, tap on the front door. I looked at the clock on the mantle. 2:40. Jesus.

"Joanne. Wake up. They're here," I said, giving her a jostle as I moved towards the door.

"Just a minute," I said, running my fingers through my hair, and my tongue over my fuzzy teeth.

I opened the door and hurriedly whisked Michael and Daniel inside. At this hour there was no one in the parking lot.

"You are aware of what time it is?" Joanne asked, smoothing out her dress as she regarded Michael with a look that said "don't mess with me any more than you already have."

"We got held up over in south east," Michael replied, glancing nervously between Joanne and Daniel. He didn't acknowledge me.

We moved towards the kitchen while Joanne went to the bathroom. Michael followed, leaving Daniel and me alone. Until this point, he hadn't said anything. He now looked at me with a smile and said "hello," in that voice that could melt ice, as if it were noon on Tuesday and we'd run into each other at the library.

"Hi," I replied. This man made me nervous.

He accepted the beer I offered, sitting at the kitchen table. He was wearing a denim jacket over the white T-shirt this time, and pulled vials, syringes, cigarettes and cotton swabs in a baggie out of various pockets.

I watched silently, then blurted, "Michael and I have some history, so I'd rather not have to call him to reach you."

Why did I feel like a twelve year old?

"That's fine. I'll give you a number where I can be reached."

I grabbed a piece of paper and took down the phone number, stuffing it in the pocket of my jeans as Joanne and Michael came into the room.

"What's going on?" Michael asked, looking at me with knotted eyebrows.

"Nothing yet," Daniel replied, giving me a half smile while he pulled the outer cap off a syringe.

I'd already brought down the distilled water and cotton balls, watching as Daniel mixed a hit for me and for Joanne.

"Michael can do me," Joanne said. "Come on to the bathroom."

"Go upstairs," I said. The last thing I wanted was to listen to them knocking around in the bathroom just ten feet from the kitchen.

With a wink over her shoulder and a returned roll of the eyes from me, they headed up the staircase.

"Are you ready?" Daniel asked, pulling the brown leather belt out of his pants.

I let out a deep breath and sat down in front of him.

"Shoot," I said, giggling at my own pun.

He looked at me without speaking. I stuck my arm out and watched as he placed the belt slightly above my elbow.

"Hold this," he said, giving me the end after he looped it through the catch while bypassing the prong.

"Make a fist." He rubbed the crook of my arm. "You've got lousy veins."

"Great," I replied, looking at the ceiling. I didn't want to see.

"Okay, I think I've found it," he said.

Unconsciously, I held my breath as I felt the prick of the needle.

"I've got a live one," he whispered. "Let up on the belt."

I loosened my grip on the belt end and opened my fist. Now I looked down and watched as the oily liquid went from the needle into my arm. With what seemed to be one motion, he pulled out the syringe and got the belt off.

"Put your finger here." He took my opposite hand and placed my own fingers over the small drop of blood at the injection site.

Like before, I was hit with a burst of heat exploding in my lungs and shooting out between my legs. I breathed out, expecting to see a flame.

"Oh my God. I'm going to pass out." My voice echoed and I put a hand on the table top for balance.

"You're fine," Daniel said, his voice even more soothing than usual. "Just put your head down for a minute if you need to. And don't forget to breathe."

I closed my eyes and as he spoke, my head began to clear. I was filled with such a sense of well-being that I felt I would float. My skin was electric, my hearing intensified, and as I opened my eyes, everything in the room seemed sharper, as if someone had fine-tuned the lenses on a set of binoculars.

"Wow," I said, again blowing out a full breath of air.

Daniel just chuckled.

"I need to urinate," he said, getting up from the table.

I sat with eyes half-closed until he came back, reveling in sensation. He sat down across from me, methodically gathering the works off the table.

"Oh, I forgot," I said, pulling a folded wad of cash from my pocket.

"Thank you," he said, putting it into his wallet without counting.

I didn't feel quite as tongue tied with a tenth of a gram of meth in my system as without. I started asking Daniel questions. What was it like in prison? Where did he grow up? How did you make speed?

He asked me stuff too. About Jamil, my favorite place to visit, whether I'd read certain books. Whether he was answering or asking, his speech was very precise, and it seemed like he thought about what he said instead of just talking off the top of his head like I usually did. I know that I was the only person in the room, but I felt like I was the only person in the universe and that he was supremely interested in everything I had to say.

I hadn't felt that way in a long time. I know Jamil loved me. It wasn't about doubting that. It wasn't even about thinking Daniel was gorgeous. It was his attention that simply enchanted me. I wanted to be absorbed into his presence. Later I would get annoyed with it, because whoever he was with at the time was the most important person in the universe, but tonight it was me and it was new and it felt good.

Michael and Joanne surfaced an hour later, shit-eating grins on both of their faces. Daniel didn't miss a beat.

"Annette and I were just talking about the Tarot. Are either of you familiar?"

"Don't be talking that mumbo-jumbo to me," Joanne said. "I'm a good Baptist girl."

"I can see that," Daniel said, granting Joanne the half smile.

"If you ask me, Baptists have their own mumbo-jumbo," I chimed in, trying to keep his attention.

"You could say that about all organized religion," he replied, turning towards me as we began a discussion of ritual.

Michael and Joanne quickly lost interest. They went into the living room with a deck of cards and bottles of beer.

We sat at the table for several hours and four more beers. At 9:00 in the morning, Daniel looked at the kitchen clock and declared, "I have to work today. I need to leave."

"You work?" I asked, surprised.

"Only when I have to," he chuckled. "Actually, it keeps my parole officer happy."

"Doing what?" I wondered. What did chemists do for a day job?

"I'm a prep cook at Bishop's House," he answered.

"Oh." Jamil and I had been there recently. It was a nice place. Had Daniel chopped the onions that ended up caramelized on my plate?

As he and Michael made their way to the door, I panicked.

"What am I supposed to do with this?" I asked, taking the packet of speed from my pocket.

"I'm sure you'll think of something," Daniel smiled.

"You can snort it, or drink it, you dork," Joanne whispered, as the men got into Michael's car and drove off.

"Oh." That didn't sound like nearly as much fun as having Daniel stick a needle in my arm.

I sent Joanne home with a portion of the speed, and attempted to ration myself over the next few days. I did try snorting some, but it hurt like hell. It felt sharper than cocaine, like tiny knives slicing my nostrils. I got high, but not with a rush like from the needle. The following day I liquefied the rest in water and drank it on an empty stomach. That actually did give me a hint of a rush, but it tasted awful, a metallic chemical burn. Later I learned that tin foil and lye were part of the ingredients.

By the third day I was out. By the fourth day I was climbing the walls. All I could think of was Daniel and speed and getting more of both.

Chapter Six

I T WAS NEARLY Christmas. Jamil would be home soon, in time for the Caribbean cruise we'd planned a year earlier to celebrate the New Year. I'd been looking forward to the getaway for months. No phone, no family—just the two of us.

But all that had changed in the last week. I thought about telling Jamil about the speed and not telling Jamil about the speed. I thought about how long he would be home this time and hoped, for the first time ever, that it would be a short stay. I contemplated the captive week at sea while pacing in my kitchen, a full committee waging battle in my head.

Call Daniel. It will be fine.

But Jamil will be home next week. I need to just cool it.

But I'll want some speed for the trip.

No you don't. You can't stay up all night on the ship cleaning the bathroom grout.

No, but I can stay up all night making love to Jamil. Maybe he'll try it too.

No. No. No.

And so I called Daniel. A woman answered.

"Could I speak to Daniel please?" I asked, trying my best to sound professional.

"Who's calling?"

"My name is Annette."

"And this is regarding?"

"I'm a friend of Michael's," I fibbed.

The phone was dropped with a clunk.

"Danny! Telephone!"

Danny? He sure didn't seem like a Danny to me.

"Hello?"

"Hi. It's Annette. From the other night," I stammered, suddenly afraid that he wouldn't remember me.

"Hello Annette. And how is your reality?" he asked.

"Fine, I think. I'm not sure what you mean. I'm all right," I stumbled. "I was just wondering if we might connect sometime soon."

I could hear him walking with the phone, shaking out the cord as he went.

"I could possibly get together in a few days," he said, his voice lowering a notch.

I let out a sigh.

"My boyfriend will be back in town next week. I was hoping to see you today. I was really hoping to see you today." *Please see me today. Please see me today.*

He paused.

"There is a possibility," he said slowly, as if thinking. "I need to catch the bus for work in a little while so it would have to be later."

"I could give you a ride," I volunteered. "No problem. Anywhere you need to go." No problem. For all I knew, he lived in Salem. But I'd drive to Seattle if it meant I could feel the way I'd felt on the meth.

"That would be cool," he answered. "I'll make a phone call before you arrive."

He gave me the address and directions. My stomach knotted. He'll make a call. It could be a dead end, but he'll make a call.

I dressed carefully, in jeans and a cable knit sweater, after trying on three different combinations. After stopping at a bank machine for cash I headed cautiously to southeast Portland, carefully following the map I'd sketched out. I found myself clenching and unclenching my fists as I drove, catching my breath against the anticipation of the rush.

I turned at the Kupie Cone on Holgate like Daniel had said, up a few blocks and onto a street of small bungalows with tidy yards. Another turn and I was in front of the gray house with white trim that he'd described, with another neat little lawn, though not quite as well kept as the neighbors on either side. A large orange tabby sprawled on the porch.

A woman came to the door when I knocked. She was pretty, a few years older than me, with blonde hair in a short pixie cut and probing brown eyes that looked me up and down from behind wire-rimmed glasses. She wore black slacks and a white blouse and as I later learned, was on her way to work at another downtown restaurant that I frequented with Jamil.

"Hi. I'm Annette," I said cheerfully, to mask my discomfort. "Is Daniel here?"

She let me in without a greeting, but once inside asked, "How do you know Danny?"

I hesitated.

"Through my friend Michael," I said, lying about the friend part, not sure if she'd know who Michael was.

She just stared, then turned and walked towards the back of the house and a small kitchen.

"Danny!" she yelled, turning to stand against the sink, eating from a bowl of cereal that had been on the pink-tiled counter. I followed and stood at the edge of the doorway, gazing at where the old linoleum floor met the hardwood of the living area.

Daniel sauntered into the kitchen from a second door to the hallway, combing his fingers through wet hair.

"Hello," he said, picking up his wallet from the kitchen table. "Annette is giving me a ride to work," he said, adding, "Annette, this is Diane."

"Nice to meet you," I said, doing my best to sound friendly instead of nervous.

"Have you eaten?" she asked, ignoring me completely.

"I'll eat at work later," he replied, turning towards me.

"Don't forget your key," she said, continuing to spoon cereal into her mouth.

He reached behind her to grab a single key from the windowsill and stashed it in his front pocket.

"Aren't you wearing a jacket?" she asked, as we moved towards the living room. "It's cold out."

"I'm okay," he said, indicating with his eyes that we should leave.

He didn't volunteer any information about this woman as we walked out, and I didn't ask. As we climbed into my Nova, he said, "I've talked to my friend, Robert. We can stop by his place for a package."

Portland is divided into distinct quadrants, east and west, north and south. We were headed to a restaurant in southwest via his friend's in northeast. Daniel attempted to give me directions, but northeast I knew. I had covered the ten-mile radius from the Coliseum to the Fremont cemetery since my cousins and I learned to ride bikes. Familiar with shortcuts from driving drunk on back streets, I wound my way through the stately homes of Alameda towards the more run down area near Irving Park. I got us there in ten flat.

"Remind me to call you when I need a getaway car," Daniel laughed, and then more seriously, "You'll need to wait out here. Do you have cash?"

I forked over a wad of bills and got comfortable, watching as the rain created miniature rivers on the windshield, rehearsing what I might say if anyone asked what I was doing sitting in my parked car in the middle of the day.

I was surprised when Daniel came back after just a few minutes.

"You can come in," he said through the rolled down window. "I told him there was an attractive woman in the car."

I blushed. I'd actually been fine in the car, but followed him up the driveway and into the back door of a huge barn of a house. We went straight down the stairs into the basement.

"Robert lives with his uncle, who knows nothing about this," Daniel said, leading me through a tidy laundry room and under the giant arms of an octopus furnace. Walking through a door with a hanging padlock, I was greeted by a scene from a sci-fi movie. Bubbling caldrons connected by glass vials and plastic tubes stood on a table, with electrical cords from hot plates at odd angles reaching for ceiling plugs. I wondered at how this was kept a secret. You could lock a door, but what about that chemical, almost sweet smell and the soft gurgling noise? I kept my mouth shut, but my face must've registered surprise.

As if he read my mind, Daniel said, "This is a lab. Robert is one of the best cooks in the city."

"And Daniel is the other one," said the short, wiry man who bounded out of an adjoining room.

"Actually, there are several," Daniel replied modestly. "Annette, I'd like you to meet Robert."

A shirtless Robert balanced a large beaker and a dishtowel as he reached to shake my hand. He was handsome in a hard-as-granite way, with shaggy brown hair and dark brown, almost black eyes.

"So where have you been hiding this lovely lady?" he asked Daniel, leading us through a door cut in a sheetrock wall to a small room crammed with a bed, an upholstered chair, a smaller chair next to a card table, and a video camera on a tripod.

"In Jantzen Beach," I answered, taking in the old Fillmore concert posters on the wall.

"Robert, are you making porn again?" Daniel asked with exaggerated disdain.

"Only for personal consumption, my friend," he answered. "Unless you'd like to see the latest?"

I sucked in an audible breath.

"No, thank you," Daniel replied. "I need to get to work. So, can you set her up?"

He could, and did, measuring out two grams of crystal. There was a bag of syringes on the bed.

Daniel eyed the needles, and asked, "Do you mind if we do this here?"

"Mi casa, su casa, brother," Robert answered, leaving us alone, but not before showing me the large vein on the back of his forearm that he used regularly. I was fascinated by the web of ropy veins sticking out on both of his arms, and on Daniel's as he took off his pressed shirt and hung it on the back of the straight chair.

I watched as Daniel quickly injected himself, closing his eyes for a moment as the rush worked its way through his system. I held my breath in anticipation.

When it was my turn, I tried my best to keep my eyes on his hands instead of his bare chest. Prison had been good to this man.

"You're tough," he said, stroking my inner arm in search of a vein. Keep looking, I willed.

He stopped, but kept his hand around my wrist, his knees straddling mine.

"If this is going to be your thing, you're going to have to learn how to do it yourself," he said, in his voice that felt like a caress.

I could feel myself blushing, again.

"Now?'

"No. I need to get to work. Next time."

He found a vein on the second try, and once more I was transported to the place where all was right with the world. The heat exploded through my body and I willed it to last. I sat with my eyes closed for several minutes, and when the dizziness passed, we gathered our things.

As we walked out towards the basement stairs, Robert was using an eyedropper to put a liquid into one of the vials on the table. He set it down.

"Good?" he asked.

"As always, my friend," Daniel answered.

I could only nod in agreement.

"Don't be such a stranger, Daniel," Robert said, shaking my hand and smiling. "You can bring her back any time." As we turned to leave, I noticed that he winked at Daniel. I made a point to remember where he lived.

"Are you okay to drive?" Daniel asked as we settled into the car.

"I'm fine," I replied, noticing how smoothly the car handled and how sharp my senses were.

Daniel directed me into downtown. Two turns off the Morrison Bridge and we pulled up in front of an ornate stucco building constructed in the late 1800's that had been converted to a restaurant. I slid into an empty spot right in front. Before getting out of the car, Daniel took paper and pencil from the glove compartment and wrote down a number.

"This is the phone in the kitchen, if you need to reach me," he said. "If you should ever have to come down here," he continued, "I would meet you at that door."

He pointed, indicating a narrow wooden door built into a fence that attached to the restaurant.

"Okay," I sighed. I held my breath a lot around him.

"This should last you, if you're careful. Will I hear from you before your man comes back?"

I was surprised that he remembered.

"He gets home on Sunday and then we leave for a week, so I'm not sure," I said, avoiding his eyes. Today was Monday.

"Well, be good. And Happy New Year," he said, pausing until I looked at him.

"Thanks. You too," I said in a small voice as he left the car and checking a watch that he pulled from his pocket, went through the small doorway.

I sat with my head resting against the seat back. I'd only had a few conversations with this man, but felt like I'd had sex every time I saw him.

For once the week flew by, between last minute Christmas shopping, speed-induced housecleaning and grocery shopping for Jamil's homecoming. Feeling stingy with the bag of dope, I intentionally avoided seeing Joanne, though we talked on the phone daily.

"I'm not so sure about this latest thing," she had said, talking in code about the speed. "It leaves me really cranky. I think I'm going to stick with Michael and the usual."

She could have the cocaine as far as I was concerned. With coke, all I wanted to do was chew on my tongue. With crystal I was productive, efficient, brilliant.

I picked Jamil up at the airport on Sunday evening, having slept most of Saturday night and into the day. I felt disconnected from the normalcy of parking lots and gate numbers until I saw Jamil, tall, dark and sleepy, walk through the door at the gate. God, it was good to see him.

"Habibi, my love!" I cried, enveloping him in my arms.

He hugged me back, dropping his suit bag to hold me, burying his face in my hair.

"I've missed you so much," he whispered.

It will be okay now. Everything will be okay. We love each other and that will be enough. Please let it be enough.

On Tuesday we had dinner with some business associates. Good food at a nice place with pleasant people, but my mind kept wandering to Daniel, and Robert, and the woman Daniel lived with. I had looked through a small window into another world, and I wanted more. This dinner conversation seemed so superficial. Had it always been this frivolous? What was Robert doing right now? Was he having sex in front of a video camera? What type of woman would do that? Was Daniel at work?

"Annette?" Jamil was looking me. "Elaine asked about our cruise."

"Oh, sorry. I must already be there," I said, smiling with my best imitation of sincerity.

I'd asked Joanne to grill Michael about this Diane woman, the roommate. Who was she exactly?

"According to Michael," Joanne had said conspiratorially, "she's his ex. They were together for years before Daniel went to prison, but now she wants him out."

"So they're not, like, together?" I asked, caring more than I wanted to.

"Not according to my source, baby cakes. Why?"

"Just curious," I lied. "She acted like his mother."

I played and replayed the scene in her kitchen through dessert, smiling and nodding as Jamil conversed with Elaine and Jim. I thought about my interaction with Daniel outside the restaurant. And about the baggie of speed that was hidden in my underwear drawer.

We wrapped up dinner at 9:00 and bid farewell to our companions on the street.

"Well, that was boring," Jamil said, smiling as we waved goodbye. "Should we go out for a nightcap?"

I paused as we turned toward the parking lot.

"Actually, I've got something at home for you to try," I said, measuring my words. "Remember how much we liked that pharmaceutical speed last year? I've got something better."

On the drive home I told him how Joanne had introduced me to this guy named Daniel who had this powdered speed.

"How did she meet him?" he wondered.

"Who knows," I said. "You know Joanne."

At home I brought out the stuff, and made us each a line on our coke mirror. I cut a plastic straw into thirds, putting two pieces back into our stash box. I could barely stand the thought of putting this in my nose instead of my arm, but first things first.

"This'll hurt," I said, wiping the tears from my eyes as I handed Jamil the straw. "And you don't need quite as much as with coke."

He took a breath and blew it out through his mouth, then drew the crystal into his right nostril.

"Shit!" he exclaimed. "That burns!"

Within minutes our conversation raced. We marveled at how great we felt. I told Jamil about Joanne's experience with sex, leaving out the "with-whom" part.

"Like we need help," he laughed, leading me to the bedroom.

Joanne had been right. I nearly lost my balance with the intensity of our first kiss as we stood in the doorway of our room. Jamil touched me with familiarity, but it was as if my skin had extra sensors. As he walked me backwards towards the bed, I hoped it would last forever.

He reached past a pile of pillows for a cigarette when it was finally over. "Damn," he said, running his free hand along my thigh.

"That's an understatement," I said, moving up onto my elbow.

For a few moments I caressed his chest and shoulders, mind racing.

"You know," I finally said, "you can inject this stuff instead of snort it."

"What?" he said, as he sat up and pulled the sheet over his lap. "How do you know? You've tried it?"

"Once," I lied. "With Joanne. It was really good. More intense than snorting."

I tried to keep my voice even, as if I were talking about the difference between regular and light beer.

"Are you crazy?" he asked, grabbing my arm. "Where? Show me."

Luckily, I hadn't bruised much this last time. I had to look for the slight greenish spot in the crook of my arm.

"It's not a huge deal," I said. "I think you'd like it."

I wanted him to like it. If he liked it, I could keep liking it.

"This is a big deal, Annette," he said as pulled on a pair of sweats and walked around the room. He listed all the reasons I'd given Joanne that first night.

"I know. I know. I thought the same things," I said, "but it's just different. Not better or worse. For God's sake, we've been snorting cocaine for nearly four years now. It's not like we don't use drugs."

"The needle is different," he replied. "The needle is hardcore. Don't forget about Abdullah."

Shit. I had forgotten about Abdullah, a cousin of Jamil's who lived in Florida. He was a really nice guy who'd gotten addicted to pain medicine and then heroin when the doctor stopped giving him prescriptions. He'd been fired from his job, and his Egyptian wife had moved back to Cairo. Jamil had been part of a family intervention that took place in Miami and was visibly crushed when he came home.

"Abdullah wants us to leave him alone," he'd said. "He loves us but says he isn't hurting anyone."

At the time I couldn't relate. I still couldn't. Jamil was the most important thing in my life. I'd do anything for him.

"Speed is different," I rationalized. "With speed you're efficient and feel great. It's not like a downer where you just zone out."

Jamil didn't look convinced. We let it drop, walking around each other gingerly. I threw on my sweats and went into the kitchen to clean what was already spotless. Jamil went into his office, coming down in an hour without speaking to me. He put in a videotape and settled in on the couch. Out of the corner of my eye I could see the back of his head, and beyond that, galloping horses from one of his Westerns.

We'll just be gone a week, I thought, as I wiped out a cabinet for the fourth time in two weeks. I can go without speed for a week. I can have a nice vacation with my true love. I can not be jealous and not start fights. I can stop thinking about Daniel. I can do anything for a week.

Christmas at Mom's house was strange. My cousin, Paul, who lived in Louisiana, had just gotten out of rehab for a cocaine habit. He'd always lived with his mother, so I didn't know him very well, but he used to be a lot of fun when he came up for the holidays to visit Mom's brother, Uncle Jack. While we were in high school, all the kids would sneak into the backyard for a joint, and then in recent years we had a couple of all-nighters with Paul, Marcie, Jeff and John. Cousin Richie had turned into a straight arrow, but the rest of us liked to party, especially at holidays. This year, Paul sat on the couch eating tortilla chips, trying a little too hard to convince the rest of us that life was great. Besides not sneaking upstairs to snort lines, he wasn't drinking either, so everybody else backed off. A show of support, I guess, but the party wasn't as fun as usual.

I'd snorted some speed before we got there, so was flying high even without booze. I could deal with less drinking as long as someone would listen to me. I made the rounds, avoiding Jamil, who didn't know I'd gotten loaded before we left. I finally cornered Marcie, going on and on about the upcoming cruise, as well as my plans for studying Arabic.

After about five minutes she eyed me suspiciously. "What are you on?" she asked, peering into my eyes. "Are you speeding?"

I lied and told her I'd gotten a few Desoxyn, a pharmaceutical amphetamine, from Joanne.

"You bitch," she said. "I'd kill for a week's supply of that stuff. I really need to lose ten pounds. Let me know if you can get more."

That worked. I went into the bathroom and looked at my eyes. My pupils were huge. If I stayed out of the bright light of the kitchen, and away from anyone in my age group, no one would catch on and I'd be fine. I felt fine. I felt fantastic.

Jamil was waiting outside the bathroom. He pushed me back inside, closing the door behind him.

"What's Marcie talking about?" he demanded.

"What?" I replied, avoiding his eyes.

"About wanting to get some of what you've got?" he said, reaching out to raise my chin so that I was forced to look at him. "What do you have that she wants?"

"Shit," he said, as soon as he saw my eyes. "You're high?"

"Oh don't over-react. I snorted it," I said, pissed off. "Last Christmas we were all fucked up on cocaine so please don't give me a lecture."

He laughed, though it sounded strained. "I'm just mad that you're holding out."

I'd gladly share my stash if he liked it and if it meant he'd let me like it. I took the tiny brown vial from my shoulder bag and pulled out a hit on my little fingernail.

"Here you go, baby," I said, scooping out another for myself, and then one more for him.

We both snorted a damp finger's worth of water from the tap to wash away the burn. John's little Lizzie knocked on the door.

"I gotta go!" she wailed.

"Just a minute, honey," I said, stifling a giggle.

Jamil grabbed me as I moved towards the door. Kissing me, he pushed me against the counter, running his right hand up from my waist to my breast.

"Let's go home soon," he whispered in my ear.

Two days after Christmas, we flew to Miami, stopping in Dallas just long enough to have a drink and get on another plane. It was good to be getting away from Portland, I told myself.

We arrived late in Miami, so stayed in the designated cruise hotel rather than troubling any of Jamil's family. Early the next morning we were at curbside with other cruisers, lined up to catch the shuttle that would take us to the docks and our ship. The van was full. I squished myself into a middle seat between Jamil and an older woman with overdone eye makeup and strong perfume. She tried to make conversation but I just smiled and turned away. This was my time with Jamil, I told myself.

Most of the cruise was a blur. Jamil and I drank a lot and napped a lot, and ate too much, and I longed to go home. I could not shake the image of Daniel walking through that little gate at work, or the touch of his fingers on my inner arm. I wanted him to shoot me up again, and talk to me in his deep, suggestive voice while I rode the wave of the rush.

It didn't help that the weather sucked. The sea swells felt like a roller coaster. People bounced from wall to wall of the narrow inner hallways like pin balls while on their way to one function or another. The moody December Caribbean slapped us around so brutally that Bahamian officials forbade our docking in Nassau.

But we went through the motions of having fun. Every night the disco was packed with newly moneyed Texas debutantes and their scotch-drinking oilmen's sons, New Jersey roofing salesmen and their wives, and the random Oregonian. Dancing was more about keeping balance than displaying any rhythm. I get queasy in the back seat of a car doing thirty, so I was wiped out the entire time. Between Dramamine, which I popped like breath mints, and Pepto-Bismol, which I drank like soda, I never quite threw up. I just felt like it the entire week.

We were assigned to a dining table with three other couples. Two of them had come together, nice enough people from Rhode Island. The third was from California. He was a little greasy, like you wanted to shower after spending time with him. His smile was too slick, his handshake too practiced, his "how are you, really?" a little too sincere. The girlfriend was blonde and bubbly, perfectly made up every time we saw her. I called them "Barbie and Ken."

We sat with them in the bar a couple of times, but only because they'd invited themselves to join us. Jamil was a friendly guy and enjoyed talking with people. He was comfortable making conversation with people he didn't know. Chitchat confounded me. So I smiled and nodded a lot while I tried to keep my lunch down and my mind on my boyfriend.

Finally, finally it was over. Miami was too muggy and too full of Jamil's extended family for me to enjoy, but I was grateful when we docked at last. I couldn't wait to go home, but Jamil had to go to New York for a meeting with Nadim, Khalid, and some banker, and I couldn't justify heading home on my own. Jamil would guess my intentions, so I continued to smile, and nod, and try like hell to keep my mind on my boyfriend.

New York frightened me. It was huge and noisy and I worried about getting mugged. I expected to get lost or have some cabbie yell out, "Hey! You don't belong here!" So I stayed in with the television on, riding the elevator to the hotel café for lunch when housekeeping knocked to make up the room.

I had phoned Joanne as soon as we reached the hotel and Jamil had gone up to his brother's suite. "Joanne! Sweet Jesus, it is good to be back on terra firma. Talk to me."

"Happy New Year, baby. Did you have fun?" she asked.

I wanted to lie. I wanted to say "Oh yeah, everything was great," but I couldn't. I started to cry as I told her about Barbie and Ken and the lousy weather and my constant stomachache and wanting to be home.

"Oh well. Live and learn. Sounds like cruising isn't your game," she replied.

I was comforted by Joanne's nonchalance. I wished I shared her attitude. There was very little that threw her. She did, however, have definite opinions on my dealings with Jamil.

"You need to pull yourself together," she went on to tell me after I whined a little more. "No man likes a moping-around woman. You're in New York City. Most girls I know would kill to be at the Plaza ordering room service, so you just quit your sniveling about wanting to come back to rainy, gloomy old Portland and enjoy yourself. At least make Jamil think you're enjoying yourself or pretty soon he'll find someone who will."

Easy for her to say. She wasn't the one sitting in the hotel room for hours while he attended business meetings, or at those long dinners where the other men brought mistresses and I wasn't supposed to tell the wives.

"Does Siham know that Khalid cheats?" I asked after a late dinner the next night, drunk and pissed off and feeling insecure.

"It's not your place to judge, Annette," Jamil had said. We'd been back in the room for an hour and he'd been on the phone to Saudi Arabia for most of that time.

But I did judge. And it scared me that Jamil just went along with it. It happened all the time when we traveled on business, whether it was the lawyer or the accountant or the cousin or the brother. They were rich and good looking, and full of themselves and Johnnie Walker. How could I know for sure that it wasn't Jamil with a blonde on his arm when I wasn't there?

"We've talked about this a hundred times," he said, dragging hard on a cigarette. "*I* don't cheat."

I slunk off to bed, burying my head in two of the fluffy hotel pillows to block out his phone conversation in the next room.

"Allo! Cav halek? How are you?" he yelled. Was everyone in Jeddah hard of hearing? I rolled over and hugged the pillows tighter around my ears as I fell asleep thinking of home, of Daniel, of speed.

I woke up in what felt like the middle of the night to the sounds of Arabic music and men's laughter. I grabbed a robe and stood in the door of the bedroom watching as Jamil and Khalid danced while Nadim sat on the couch with his hands folded over his belly.

"Hello Annette. These crazy brothers of mine are enjoying themselves. Come and join us," Nadim said, in an invitation that wasn't really an invitation. "You know that our father loved to dance?"

I shook my head and crawled back into bed with the realization that his family had solid hold on Jamil's allegiance. I wasn't sure if I'd ever even been in the running.

We flew to Portland the next morning. We'd been away twelve days that felt like a month. I wanted Jamil to meet Daniel. He'd see how the needle was okay. And maybe if I brought them together, I'd somehow shake this infatuation.

"Are you sure about this?" Joanne had asked. I could hear her smoking on the other end of the phone.

"Yeah. Jamil's uncomfortable that I'm dealing with someone he doesn't know. If he meets the guy and if he sees you doing it too, everything will be okay."

He hadn't actually said those words, but I know he'd feel better about the whole thing once he met Daniel and once he saw that Joanne hadn't turned into a raving addict.

"Well, I'd planned to give this shit up and go back to the land of snow, if you catch my drift, but just for you and just this one more time," Joanne had replied to my pleading. I knew I could count on her.

"Are you sure about this?" Daniel had asked when I called him the next day at the restaurant. Hearing his voice after so long made me catch my breath. I could hear him dragging on a cigarette, the clacking of dishes and chopping knives in the background.

"Yes. I've got it all worked out with Joanne on how we'll handle it. It will be fine." Please, oh please.

I could almost hear him thinking as he exhaled.

"Annette, I'm very protective of my identity and who I associate with. You know that I've been away and I'm not inclined to go back."

"No, no," I replied. "Jamil is cool. Trust me. Please." I loved hearing him say my name.

He took another drag and exhaled. "Okay, this once. But I reserve the right to exit at any time."

"Of course," I said, fighting the urge to jump up and down. As I hung up, I told myself it was the speed that I wanted.

I was wiping the kitchen counter when Jamil came in from his office the following evening.

"Hello my love!" he said cheerfully, taking off his tie and hanging his jacket on a kitchen chair. Rolling up the sleeves of his shirt, he grabbed a beer from the fridge and kissed the back of my neck. His moustache tickled. Daniel didn't have a moustache.

"Hey sweetie."

I reached back to stroke his head, my stomach churning.

"I called Joanne to get some stuff."

"Coke?" Jamil asked, straightening up.

"Speed, I think. Her coke connection isn't holding." We never said Michael's name.

"Hmm," he replied, walking to the living room. He turned on the evening news and stretched out on the couch. I stayed in the kitchen.

"She'll be here at around 7:00," I said. "We'll eat first." I'd picked up a pizza earlier in the day. Leftovers would be good to have on hand when we came down.

The comforting smell of hot crust, onions and bell peppers mingled with Jamil's cigarette smoke as I set a plate piled with slices on the coffee table, then sat at the far end of the couch and stared intently at the TV screen.

After the silent meal, Jamil changed into jeans and a T-shirt from New Orleans and grabbed another beer. We hadn't talked about the speed at all on the cruise or since we'd been home. He hoped it would go away, while I hoped he'd come around.

The doorbell rang at 7:10. I was in the bathroom and heard Jamil go to the door.

"Hello darling! Welcome home!" I heard Joanne exclaim. I knew she was giving him a hug. She really liked Jamil. Everybody did.

"Jamil, this is Daniel," she said as I walked down the stairs. They shook hands.

"Oh, hi," I said on cue, feigning surprise.

"I decided to bring the source with me," Joanne went on. "Where's the beer?"

"Oh, sorry," I said, "Come on in."

Daniel followed me to the kitchen, as did Jamil and Joanne.

"May I sit?" Daniel asked.

"Of course," Jamil and I said at the same time. I held my tongue and reminded myself to let him be the host.

"Let's get down to business," Joanne said, pulling up a chair. "And then you can tell me about your trip."

As if she hadn't heard all about it from me already. God bless her. Keep talking, sister. Just keep it normal.

Daniel brought out a small baggie.

"Try before you buy?" he asked.

"We're good," Jamil said, pulling out his wallet.

"Sure," I jumped in.

Daniel turned towards me. "How do you want it?"

I hesitated, but Joanne spoke up

"Fire us up," she said with attitude.

"You too?" Daniel asked casually, looking at Jamil.

"No thank you," Jamil answered, stubbing out his cigarette and lighting another.

"Are you sure you don't want to try it?" I asked, looking back and forth between the two men.

Jamil looked at me long and hard. "No."

"Well, get the mirror then, so you can snort some," I replied, pumped full of the adrenaline of anticipation, riding a line between pissed off and scared.

By the time Jamil came back with the mirror, Daniel was ready to go. He injected Joanne first, while I watched Jamil watch her. Daniel rubbed her inner arm and easily found a vein. She breathed out through her mouth and exclaimed "oh my" as he pulled out the empty syringe.

I was next. Please find a vein. Please find a vein. I closed my eyes, not wanting to see Jamil's expression. The shot hit me like a two by four. I hadn't been this dizzy before and took deep breaths as I fought the urge to fall over. I closed my eyes and lowered my head to the table.

"Is she okay?" I heard Jamil's voice through a tunnel.

"She's fine, man," Daniel replied, though he reached over and put his hand momentarily on my forearm. "Keep breathing," he said, "You're okay."

When I thought that my neck would hold up my head, I sat up and opened my eyes. "Whew! That was something else."

Daniel and Joanne chuckled. Jamil was tight lipped as he chopped out a line on the mirror. He winced as he snorted.

"You can drink it if that's not working for you," Daniel said. "Not the same punch, but it'll get you there."

Jamil hadn't said much to Daniel and didn't start now.

"Where's the deck of cards?" Joanne piped in. "Jamil, come play me a game of Concentration. It's a riot on this stuff."

The two of them moved the ten feet to the living room couch, leaving me in the kitchen as I attempted to get my bearings.

"I'll clean up," I said, still dizzy, knowing full well I should be in the living room with the man I loved but held like a magnet to Daniel.

We were quiet as he gathered up the works. I wiped down the already spotless table with a napkin from where I sat.

I looked up. Daniel was staring at me.

"How was your travel?" he asked.

"It was alright," I said softly. "Well, actually, a lot of it really sucked."

"Annette! Will you bring us a beer?" Joanne called from the living room, keeping me honest.

"You know you can call me," Daniel said quietly as I moved from the fridge towards the living room. "It doesn't just have to be for product."

My stomach jumped into my throat. I offered a weak smile as I passed him. Fuck yeah, I could "just call him." For what? For I'm not doing it, that's for what.

Joanne and Daniel stayed another half an hour, time for two more games of Concentration and a half-hearted attempt at small talk about our cruise. When they were gone, Jamil took my hands and looked me in the eye, dilated pupils to dilated pupils.

"I thought you were going to pass out. That was scary," he said.

I attempted a chuckle. "Yeah, that was intense."

"Is this guy okay?" he asked.

"He seems to be. I don't know him all that well."

"Joanne comes with some winners." He paused as he turned back to the couch. "He's a good-looking guy."

"He's alright," I said through clenched teeth. "I think he might be gay." Shut up, Annette. Don't dig it any deeper.

"Really?" Jamil asked. "I guess you never know."

Jamil left Portland a few weeks later. We drove up to Seattle for a long weekend, staying at the Four Seasons before he caught the polar route to London and then on to Saudi Arabia. He expected to be gone for at least two months after being home for less than two. We hadn't had any knockdown drag-outs, but there was a new uneasiness about us that didn't feel right. I'd always trusted Jamil implicitly, but something had shifted. I couldn't put my finger on it, but it had started to feel like we'd both decided to give up on us, though neither of us spoke it. We had each held on to our personal, private dream for a long time. Mine had to do with a 9 to 5 man and a casserole in the oven. His was about a woman who sat daintily at home until he returned. We were both off the mark.

On the morning that Jamil left the country, I sat on the closed toilet wrapped in the hotel's oversized terry cloth robe, running my fingers over the crook of my arm. All I really needed to do was leave this stuff alone. I told myself that it was Jamil that I wanted, our life together, and that the speed was coming between us. I said those words to myself while my body ached to experience the rush, the heat, the intensity of the meth. Standing to wipe the steam from the mirror, I looked at myself. *Leave it alone. Leave it alone. God, what am I doing?* I thought about my conversion and wondered if God even listened to me anymore.

Speed had exploded my mind. And along with cravings so intense that I barely recognized myself in their grip was a whole new set of questions about my life with Jamil. There was a certain independence that I associated with methamphetamine. It was my thing, my new friends, my secret. *Tell him. Tell Jamil that this isn't working. I can't keep saying "good bye."*

"Annette? We must leave now," Jamil said from behind the closed door. What was he thinking? Was he as confused as I was?

I cried as I put him on the plane at Sea-Tac.

"Hey, hey. This isn't forever," he said as he held me to his chest. "I'll be back before you know it. Or maybe I'll bring you to Japan on my way home."

"Okay," I said in a small voice, feeling like it was forever, knowing he wouldn't bring me to Japan. "You know I love you."

"I love you too," he said, one hand stoking my hair. "I'll call you from London."

Wearing his traveling cords and favorite blue pullover, he looked hung over around the eyes and already far away as he turned for a final wave at the jet way door. It felt like he wasn't ever going to come back.

Suddenly exhausted, I made my way through the airport in a daze, ignoring the happy families and tearful lovers that usually held my interest. I found the car where we'd left it in short-term parking and navigated my way onto the Interstate. It rained the entire way home: pouring, then drizzle, then steady, then mist, followed by an all-out downpour—all the northwest weather incarnations.

I drove non-stop, and when I pulled into my parking space at the condo three hours later, realized I'd been gripping the steering wheel the entire way. I didn't even get my bag out of the trunk but opened the door to the scolding cat, fed her, drank a glass of milk on the verge of going bad, and laid on the couch in the dark. I stared at the blank television screen for hours. A weak winter sun lit the horizon as I surprised the newspaper delivery guy while getting my suitcase from the car. I went upstairs to bed without unpacking. With any luck I'd sleep most of the day away.

Chapter Seven

"**H**EY. IT'S ANNETTE. How are you?"

"Good. Always good. It's nice to hear your voice."

I'd waited three days after Jamil left before I called Daniel. Even as I picked up the phone, I said out loud, "Don't do this. Don't do this," but it was if I had started a downhill roll on a skateboard and nothing short of a broken leg would stop the descent. And even that would just be a delay.

"I'd be interested in what you have," I said, trying to sound like I was talking about eggplant or bark dust or anything other than illicit drugs.

"That could be a problem," Daniel replied. "All of my people seem to be on vacation. I was contemplating getting back to work myself, but I'm short on supplies."

Vacation? Was there a meth cooks union? I later learned that Daniel and his cohorts made speed throughout the city, and stopped making speed throughout the city in unison, in an effort to confuse any law enforcement surveillance. If crystal from five secret labs was on the streets, the theory was that it would be harder to trace back to any one person.

"What kind of supplies?" I asked.

He replied vaguely. I later learned that, for Daniel, as a parolee, even having this conversation could be viewed as "intent," and could send him back to prison. "So where do you get this stuff and what does it cost?" I asked. Maybe I could help. Time and money I had plenty of.

He rattled off a store location. I was surprised. Who buys this stuff besides drug dealers? But hell, I could spring forty dollars for a beaker if that's all it would take to get me high. I arranged to meet him at the restaurant to drop off some cash the next afternoon, a Friday.

When I pulled up, he was standing outside the little door, smoking a cigarette, a food stained, used-to-be-white kitchen jacket over his shoulder.

He opened the passenger door just as I turned off the car.

"Hello," he said, smiling. "Let's go."

"Go? Where?"

"Shopping," he said. "I developed a sudden stomach ache and have the rest of the evening off."

I turned the ignition and pulled onto Third. "Where to?"

Daniel directed me out Front Avenue towards the store that sold glassware.

"You can just go buy this stuff?" I asked incredulously.

"It's for science class," he replied mischievously as we merged onto Macadam.

My foray into the manufacture of a controlled substance started out simply enough: twenty dollars here, forty dollars there; trips to the scientific supply store, or to the grocery store for lye or denatured alcohol. I knew I was getting sucked in and did my best to ignore a very tiny voice inside said that I was being taken advantage of. But I know Daniel liked me as a person. He always seemed glad to see me. This wasn't just about the money. And I liked him too as a person, an interesting guy. And I wanted what would come out of all those beakers and vials he was collecting.

It was over the span of a few weeks that the first batch came together.

"Aren't any of your friends back from vacation?" I asked, a week into the process.

"I want the next crystal you have to come from me," Daniel had replied, not giving me a choice.

It turned out to be more complicated than just going to the store. First was the gathering of the glassware, some new, and discards from guys like Robert and another fellow named Herb. Whatever had gotten dispersed when Daniel went to prison was called back in. There was a clandestine trip to Seattle to buy something called a precursor, and consultations with a guy named Hugh. I called Daniel once or twice and gave him several rides from his place to Robert's but could just listen and nod as he tried to explain the process. I couldn't quite make the connection between all this crap in a milk crate in my trunk and the stuff that nearly gave me an orgasm when he stuck it in my arm.

In the meantime, I continued the motions of my life. I talked to Jamil on the phone. I went to lunch with Joanne, for the first time not talking about what I was doing when I wasn't at lunch with her. I was constructing a secret world. I had dinner with my folks and celebrated Mom's February birthday, one eye always on the clock. The daffodils I'd planted the previous autumn by the back door came up, but I found myself walking past them without much notice. Everything I did, every conversation, felt like a placeholder for the speed. One ear was always listening for the phone, and I found myself wanting to stay home so I wouldn't miss Daniel's calls.

He'd started phoning every couple of days. At first the calls were brief and fairly businesslike. I was the primary investor. But soon we were talking about other stuff—Joanne and Michael, what I liked about London, what it was like for him in prison. With a drink or two under my belt, I was more comfortable with him and could tease when he spoke so formally.

One evening he excused himself from the phone so he could urinate. When he came back, I laughed, "So Daniel, you don't pee, you urinate. Tell me, do you fuck or do you fornicate?'

He laughed low and deep. "It's all semantics," he said. "Maybe we can talk more about it when I see you."

Finally, I got the call I'd been waiting for. Daniel's ex-girlfriend, roommate, whatever she was, was in Minnesota visiting family and he'd set up shop in her basement a few days earlier.

"Annette? It's Daniel."

As if I wouldn't recognize his voice.

"Hi," I said, afraid to say more and betray my anticipation.

"Ready when you are," was all he said.

"I'll be there in less than an hour."

It was 4:00, Friday again. Just as I hung up, the phone rang. It was Jamil.

"Hey, baby. What time is it with you? What are you up to?"

"I think Joanne and I are going to dinner and a late movie," I said, glancing at the kitchen clock.

We talked a little longer, about the weather in Kuala Lumpur, where he'd just arrived from Jeddah, his frustration with the company men there, our usual "I'm away and wish I wasn't," chatter.

"I'd better go," I said. "I need to pick up Joanne from work. I don't know when I'll get home, so I'll talk to you tomorrow."

"Okay, my love. I'll wake you up tomorrow."

He believed me. He so wanted me to be honest that he actually thought I was. I used to be. At least I used to want to be. Now I wasn't sure what I wanted.

I dialed the phone.

"Joanne? It's me. Listen, I'm with you tonight if anything comes up. We're going to eat and go to a movie."

"Well, well, well. What are we seeing?" she asked.

"Shit, I don't know. Pick something. I'm sure you won't be asked, but just in case."

"No problem-o, my friend," she replied. "You cover me, I cover you. That's what makes ours such a beautiful relationship. What are you up to anyway?"

She was used to me getting swept up by drunken strangers, not a premeditated lie.

"Nothing. Not really. I'm going over to Daniel's."

Joanne replied with a slow, nasty chuckle. "You don't say? When did all this start?"

"Nothing has started. Really. I'm just going over there to hang out."

"Hmm. Whatever you say, darling," she said. "But you'd better bring me some of that 'nothing' when you come home."

I laughed, somewhat feebly. "I thought you'd quit."

"Well, quitting is a good theory when you have something else to back it up, and right now I don't have anything else to back it up."

"All right," I said, and started to hang up.

"Annette," Joanne said, her voice moving from co-conspirator to parental, "you be careful. You don't know what you're getting in to here. Michael tells me that Daniel and his crew are big time. You could get into some real trouble."

"I'll be fine, really," I said, this time hanging up the phone for certain.

Really, I said to myself, I'll be fine.

I parked in front of Diane's tiny one-story house and walked up the cement path to the door. There was no answer. Tap. Tap. Tap. I tried again.

I stood on the little concrete porch for another minute, then opened the screen and tried the knob. It was unlocked. I cautiously opened the door and stepped into the living room. Lou Reed was playing softly from the back of the house.

"Daniel?" I said, "Daniel," a little louder this time.

"In the basement," I heard him yell. "Lock the door and come on down."

I found the door in the kitchen and walked down the steep, narrow staircase, becoming aware of a faint gurgling sound. As I ducked my head to avoid the overhang, I was surprised by the same heavy, sickly sweet smell that had permeated Robert's basement.

What greeted me was similar to what I'd seen at Robert's a few months earlier: cauldrons and vials and tubes with flowing liquid, and extension cords connecting hot plates to overhead plugs. I'd taken the one required science class in high school, but this looked more like a scene from an old horror film. In front of the various contraptions stood Daniel, leaning up against the basement's center beam. He was wearing worn jeans that rested on his hipbones and nothing else as far as I could tell. His jailhouse tan was faded; the veins on his biceps stood out like a topographical map. He appeared to have an erection, though I didn't allow my eyes to linger. He held a cigarette between his thumb and forefinger, and as he exhaled, said, "I just did the first hit off the first batch. It's good."

"Oh," I said, a potent mix of sex lust and drug lust coursing through my system. I'll be fine, I told myself.

He chuckled, with that voice that sounded vaguely erotic whether he talked about the weather or a recent film he'd seen.

"May I do the honors?" he asked.

"Please," was all I could muster, moving to sit on a tall stool.

I was completely seduced by the ritual. The measuring of the dope with the scale, the pulling the syringe out of its case, the adding of the water and the rolling of the cotton ball followed by the drawing of the meth into the rig and the tap, tap to make sure the air bubbles were out. It was beautiful and precise and methodic. Then came Daniel's touch, first to tie the rubber tubing and then to stroke my inner arm as he searched for a vein. And then the prick of the needle as it pierced my skin, the drawing back of the blood that meant he'd found a vein, the pushing in of the plunger and watching the speed enter my system.

Whooo. I breathed out through my mouth as he withdrew the empty syringe. Once again I was nearly at the point of orgasm, alone with this man not six inches from me with no shirt and nothing on under his jeans. If our eyes had met, I would've gone over the edge. Instead I closed my eyes and took a few deep breaths.

"Shit," was all I said.

He laughed slightly. When I opened my eyes, he was smiling. I held his gaze for three seconds and then looked away, lost in the clarity and sensation and awareness that was the rush.

"So, this is your lab?" I said a few minutes later as my head cleared.

"My lab for today," he answered. "They're usually fairly mobile operations, out of necessity."

"Of course," I replied, not wanting to betray my ignorance.

He described the process as he moved along the table, outlining extractions and additions and timing. I was only half-listening and barely understanding, content to simply be with him. After a few minutes he was silent, his muscled back to me. I watched as he checked temperatures and peered into vials. Time didn't exist, just the gurgle of the fluid moving through tubes. My legs got sore from sitting, and I had to pee, but I didn't want to leave the basement. If he forgot I was there, maybe I could stay.

Something was happening with the procedure, and his actions picked up a tempo from one end of the table to the other. I didn't move, watching as he pushed an errant curl out of his eyes, squinting as he held a lit cigarette between his lips. Just when I was certain that he had totally forgotten, me he said, "Come look at this."

He had a Pyrex dish on a hotplate and was stirring what looked like a thin layer of water with a glass stir-stick.

"Just watch. It's beautiful," he said softly.

As he stirred in a figure-eight the liquid thickened, swirling into patterns that followed his motions.

It started to dry along the edges as he took a hot pad and removed the plate from the heat. He continued a few gentle stirring movements as what was liquid just a few minutes ago turned to a layer of white.

"Oh my God!" I exclaimed. "Is that the speed?"

"Indeed, mademoiselle. See how clean it is. Some people prefer to leave some impurities in for a different type of rush, but I insist on a clean product."

He spoke with authority, looking at the dish like a proud parent. After it had cooled, he took a single-edged razor and began scraping the powder. I looked at the plate with longing while a series of light bulbs clicked in my head. Why couldn't I finance the operation and have a steady supply of this stuff? How expensive could it be, especially if he sold some?

I made the suggestion, and he smiled. Not a full smile, but one tinged with something I couldn't identify.

"Be careful what you offer," he said, and we let it drop.

We let it drop that night anyway. There was some conversation, but not much as he was entirely engrossed in his work. I drove home in the middle of the night to an empty condo that didn't need cleaning, wandering from room to room, images of the lab turning over and over in my mind. My initial investment didn't have to be a one-time thing, I thought. We could essentially be partners. It could work.

He didn't bring it up again, but over the next month or so Daniel asked, and I provided thirty dollars here, fifty dollars there, for various bits of equipment. We made several more trips to the chemical store for beakers and graduates and tiny glass filters, and plastic tubing by the yard. I developed a new vocabulary of chemical reactions, synthesis and pH levels. We never did talk about a return on my investment or the terms of this partnership.

After Diane came back from Minneapolis, Daniel set up shop in the kitchen of the one-bedroom house of a woman named Brandy. Brandy had two scary Dobermans, augmented breasts and frizzy blonde hair. She was missing an eyetooth and had been around the block several times by my estimation. She was pleasant but reserved the first few times we met. Were she and Daniel sleeping together? I didn't think so, because I'd been introduced to a guy named Brian who wandered in and out of her room in his boxers. I felt out of place with her and the dogs and the dirty dishes piled in the sink. I lived with a wealthy man and it showed.

My wealthy man came home during that first set-up phase for a couple of weeks. I didn't shoot up while Jamil was in Portland, but I did have a small reserve of speed to snort or liquefy and drink when he was at an evening meeting or business lunch. I had already passed the point of choice. If I had it, I used it.

Joanne and Anthony came over one night and we cooked a big Middle Eastern feast—leg of lamb, hummus, tabooli, stuffed grape leaves. It felt like our early, carefree days as Jamil and I rolled grape leaves side by side, working as a team before our guests arrived. As the lamb cooked, Joanne and I sang along to oldies as we chopped tomatoes and parsley for the tabooli while Jamil and Anthony played a few hands of poker.

We had our good moments, like that evening with Joanne and Anthony, but there was an almost imperceptible shift in how Jamil and I interacted. We didn't talk about speed at all. The conversation was conspicuous in its absence, but I didn't have to deny what he wasn't asking about. Twice I walked into the room when he was on the phone with one of his brothers and he switched from English to Arabic. It wasn't unusual for his conversations with family to slip in and out of Arabic, but this was different, intentional. He also seemed to make it a point to come into the bathroom while I was in the shower. Not unusual either, but I noticed him looking at my arms a lot. I tended to bruise yellow so there wasn't much to see that I couldn't explain away as old scars, but he never asked, just looked.

It felt funny, this talking about everything but the speed, but I played along. I called Daniel a few times at the restaurant when Jamil was out of the house, but that felt funny too. I was in limbo, like I was swinging on the monkey bars as a kid and had let go of one rung but hadn't quite grabbed the next.

Jamil took a cab to the airport when he left town. I'd always, always, gotten up for his early flights and had planned my morning around his departure.

"Don't worry about it," he said the night before as he placed another necktie in his suitcase. "I've already arranged a car."

I could feel my lower lip quiver.

"Jamil, this doesn't feel good. I always drive you," I said. "What's going on?"

"Oh habibi," he said with a deep sigh, drawing me to him. "It's fine. I'll just sneak out early and be back before you know it."

That wasn't true. He would be gone for at least a couple of months, if not more. We went to bed that night and made love in the dark. I was glad that he couldn't see the tears in my eyes. In the morning, with hair damp from the shower, he leaned over to kiss me good-bye.

"Don't get up. I'll call you when I get there." The cabbie knocked on the door and he was gone.

I felt Jamil slipping away and it made my gut ache, but at the same time I was being sucked into the vortex that was Daniel.

Chapter Eight

ANIEL. SPEED. SPEED. Daniel. The two were linked in my psyche in such a way that I still can't pull them apart. I called him later that day.

"I'm glad you called," Daniel greeted me, his deep voice more serious than usual. "There's been a disruption at Brandy's and I've had to shut down."

"What happened?" I asked. I'd been counting on scoring as soon as I was alone.

"I'd rather talk in person," he said. "Can I come over?"

I inhaled and squeezed my eyes shut. I usually went to him. Neutral territory. Public places, rarely alone together, and not at my place.

"Okay," I answered. "When?"

"I'll need to make a couple of stops so that I don't come empty-handed. Later this evening."

"Okay."

It was nearly 5:00. Later this evening; later this evening. What the hell did that mean? Why didn't I ask what time he meant? Shit.

The house was clean, but I vacuumed anyway. I threw out the dead bouquet from the dining room table. I'd bought it for Jamil's homecoming, but now the dried and browned blossoms looked like our relationship felt. Don't think about it. Just don't think about it. What would I do if Jamil and I split up? Don't think about it. We'll be fine. He loves you and you love him. This will all play itself out and we'll be fine. He'll stop minding about the speed, and he'll see that I've kept my promise to be faithful. He'll work less and be home more. It will work out. And in the meantime, Daniel was coming over.

I took a shower and put on make up that didn't look like I'd put on make up. I put on lace panties, took them off and grabbed a cotton pair, then went back to the lace. The jeans I put on had been a little snug after our cruise, but now buttoned easily. After three changes, I settled on a blue V-neck sweater, without a shirt underneath.

I spent a long time on my hair. Ponytail? No, it made me look like a pinhead. Maybe braids? No, I looked fourteen. How about pulling the front back into a barrette? Hippie throwback. Stop. Stop. Stop. It's just hair. It doesn't matter. I threw the barrette into a drawer. Leave the bathroom now.

I didn't want to sleep but went to my room and tried to read. There was a time when I read a couple of books a week, mostly bestsellers, but I hadn't finished a book in months. It was hard to pay attention to the pages when so much was going on in my head.

I reached for the television remote and wandered aimlessly through the channels, looking without watching, listening for a car. How would he get here? Should I have offered to pick him up?

It was after 10:00. I hated the waiting and wondering and anticipating. My stomach churned as I went to the bathroom and gathered my part of the works: cotton ball, alcohol, distilled water, cotton swab. I hesitated, contemplating leaving the accessories in my bathroom. No. Take them downstairs to the kitchen table.

I opened the front door, just in case. Mike, the neighbor who owned a sandwich shop nearby, was just pulling up. It was after 11:00. "Hi Mike." "Bye Mike." I stood with my back to the front door, then turned around and looked out the peephole. A car went by without stopping. Then one came the other way. Where was he?

I went back upstairs and lay on the bed. It was 11:47.

Was that someone knocking? I jumped up and ran towards the stairs, slowing to take a quick look in the bathroom mirror as I went by. I hesitated on the bottom step. Yes, it was a knock.

I looked out the peephole again to see the back of Daniel's head and an old beater pulling noisily away. I unlocked and opened the door.

"Hi," I said, moving aside so he could come in.

"Hello," he replied. "May I come in?"

"Please." As if we were at a fucking country club. Yes, come in, please. Let me take your wrap.

He stood just inside the door, hands in the front pockets of his jeans. He wore a blue-pin stripped cotton shirt underneath his denim jacket, a pack of cigarettes in the left pocket, who knows what else in the right.

"Would you like a beer or a drink?" I asked.

"A cold beer would be good."

I motioned for him to sit on the couch. We usually sat at the kitchen table. I grabbed two beers and perched gingerly at the opposite end.

"Here you go," I said. "Cheers."

"Yes, 'cheers,'" he replied, taking a long draw.

He set the bottle on a coaster and looked at me.

"Brandy is a lunatic," he said.

I'd considered that but was interested in why he thought so.

"I don't believe you met her neighbor, Debbie, a woman we call 'Rinse-bag.' She was picked up on a warrant two nights ago while she was working 82nd Avenue. Brandy heard this from another woman named Ruby and decided to dismantle the set up while I was at the restaurant because she is beyond paranoid and thought the cops might come to her place and think it was Debbie's and find the stuff and we'd all go to jail."

"Okay," I said with some hesitation. "So what was this Debbie doing on 82nd, and what on earth is a 'rinse-bag'? And why would the police come to Brandy's house because of it?"

"In the first place, the police wouldn't come to Brandy's house. That's the insanity, and why I'm so perturbed. Debbie is a somewhat pitiful whore who gives five-dollar blowjobs behind a convenience store on 82nd in order to support her habit. She scrounges empty bags of speed in order to rinse them out and glean the last molecule of dope, hence the 'Rinse-bag,'" he said, shaking his head.

Jesus. Five-dollar blowjobs? No wonder I felt out of place at Brandy's.

"So what does all this mean?"

"It means," Daniel continued, "that I am temporarily out of business and in search of a location. In the meantime, Robert was producing, so I stopped and got you this."

He pulled a dime bag out of his right breast pocket.

This was good. Let's do some now and talk about being out of business later.

I retrieved the cotton and other props from the kitchen, placing them on the coffee table between the two beers. Daniel pulled a syringe out of the pack of cigarettes and moved closer to me on the couch.

"I've only got one," he said. "I'll get you first, with the fresh tip, and I'll go after that."

After mixing up mine, he tied off my arm and began the stroking that I craved.

"You know," he said, continuing to rub my inner arm, "you are going to have to learn to do this yourself."

I'd been lulled by his touch but came to attention. He'd said this before, but I'd hoped he'd forgotten.

"Okay," I said. "Why, and when, and could it be later?"

He looked up at me with his hand still on my inner arm. "Why, because you need to take responsibility for this if you're going to continue. You've got lousy veins and it's better you than me poking around. When is 'soon' and 'no,' it doesn't have to be now."

I was relieved in the moment but worried. I didn't trust myself with free access to my veins. Plus I liked the connection to Daniel. Why would he want to spend time with me if all it amounted to was a drop-off? I really liked him touching my arm and breathing with me and being so close. Okay. Here we are. He's touching me now. He's found a vein and is pushing in the plunger on the syringe.

I wanted to cry with relief. The heat spread through my body and out the top of my head and between my legs and all was right with the world. I unconsciously let out a small moan.

"Well, well," Daniel said.

I blushed as I opened my eyes and looked away, closing them again to relax into the rush. I was acutely aware of the heat that coursed through my body and bounced off Daniel as he sat next to me.

He prepared his own hit and proceeded, after taking off his jacket and rolling up his shirtsleeve. I stared as the veins in the crook of his arm stood out. Unlike mine, he had no problem hitting the mother lode on the first try. I was envious. The stream of blood entering the syringe chamber was beautiful. When he hit the plunger, it was almost like he'd done me again. He closed his eyes as he pulled the needle out and placed a finger over the drop of blood that appeared.

"That Robert is a good man," he said, leaning back into the couch.

As we sat there quietly, I got something like a shiver, though I wasn't cold. Daniel reached over and touched my shoulder.

"Are you alright?" he asked.

"Yeah, I'm fine," I answered, jumping up from the couch. "Another beer?"

"I haven't finished this one," he said, looking at our half-full bottles.

"Oh. Right."

I sat back down.

And then, as if possessed, I said, "So what does a girl have to do to get your attention, Daniel?"

He cocked his head and smiled at me. "You've had my attention for some time now."

Again I had the feeling of being propelled along a path. My mind clicked over my options in a split second. I could laugh and go for the fresh beer. I could offer to take him where he needed to be next. I could think about my love for Jamil and all the promises I'd made to him.

Instead, I slid closer to Daniel on the couch.

"Well then," I said.

We held each other's gaze for just a second before I closed my eyes and moved in to kiss him. Oh Lord. I was lost, tumbling and twirling and falling. In love? In something. In deep.

I stood and kissed him again, pulling him towards the stairs.

"Annette?" he said from behind me, not moving.

I turned. "Yes?"

He paused, his hand on my waist. "Are you sure?"

I was never more sure of anything. Sure that it was wrong. Sure that my life was changing. Sure that there was no turning back. Sure.

"Yes," I smiled.

When we got to the bedroom, I hesitated.

"We need to go to the guest room. Is that alright with you?"

"It's your house," he answered, following me across the hall.

I led him into the darkened room and we kissed again. I unbuttoned his shirt and pulled it out of his jeans and off. As I took off my own sweater, Daniel said, "wait," and reached to turn on the bedside lamp. I crawled out of my jeans, and stood in my lace panties and bra as he sat down.

"You're so pretty," he said, his already deep voice soft with desire. I reached back over and turned off the lamp.

He stood to take off his jeans, then sat on the edge of the bed.

"Move up," I whispered and climbed on top of him.

To say that sex on methadrine is intense is a little like saying that chopping off your left arm with a dull kitchen knife hurts. Every nerve ending, every pore, every hair follicle, every square inch of skin is sensitized beyond description. I could almost hear the electrical currents crackling and arcing off the bed.

Finally being with Daniel after this prolonged build-up was a carnival ride—exhilarating and death-defying and dizzying and wait-I'm-going-to-fall-off-the-bed good. And I knew it must never happen again. But then it did, and I knew that it would again and again.

We didn't actually sleep with all that methamphetamine on board, but after being quiet for a while, Daniel asked for a glass of water. The sun was just starting to rise. I looked in the bathroom mirror at pupils as big as saucers, skin pale from lack of sleep and chemicals. Running my fingers through matted hair, I grabbed a T-shirt off the doorknob, wanting to cover what I had so freely uncovered a few hours earlier.

When I got back to the bedroom with the water, Daniel was sitting up, and in his jeans.

"Hey," he said, "I've got to get moving. If you get me up to the store, I can catch a bus."

"I can drive you," I said automatically.

"Great," he answered, buttoning his shirt. "May I use your bathroom?"

"Of course."

He went into the bathroom and I heard water running as I put back on the lace underwear and jeans, and pulled my sweater on over the T-shirt. Where did he need to go at 6:00 in the morning?

As we walked outside, Mike, the neighbor was just pulling out. Shit. I busied myself in my purse so as to avoid any eye contact. In the car I sat for a moment, waiting for him to drive away.

"Is everything alright?" Daniel asked, watching me watch Mike.

I exhaled. "It's not so good that the neighbor saw us coming out together."

"You don't get visitors?" he asked.

"Not men, and not leaving at the crack of dawn," I said. "I'm not sure how to explain this."

"I can't imagine that you'd have to," Daniel replied.

Maybe, I thought, but I'll check the driveway before we leave next time, assuming that there is a next time.

I drove Daniel to Brandy's and waited while he went inside to gather his things. He came back with a cardboard box, taped shut, and asked if it could stay in my trunk while he was at work. He then asked that I drive him to Diane's.

"So are you and Diane still a couple?" I asked, keeping my eyes on the road. "Michael says that you used to be but that you're just roommates now."

He chuckled. "Well, I don't sleep on the couch if that's what you're asking."

Joanne used to say, "Don't ask the question unless you're prepared to hear the answer." I always forgot that until after I'd opened my mouth.

"Diane and I were together for ten years before I went to prison. While I was away, she cleaned up and decided that she wanted to live a different life. She's being kind until I find another place to live. We have history, and a great deal of affection for each other."

Not sure if I fit in to this equation or even wanted to, I concentrated on going the speed limit. At Diane's I watched him retrieve a key from under a window box. He said, from the porch, that he'd call me later.

I got home and took a shower, then paced until after 8:00.

"Joanne? I've got to see you. Can you meet for lunch?"

"Sure darling. Pick me up out front at 12:01."

I arrived ten minutes early, tapping the steering wheel as I waited.

"What's up, sweetie?" Joanne asked as she settled herself in the car.

I headed towards a bar a few blocks away.

"I need to talk."

"I'm all ears," she answered, readying a cigarette and her lighter for the moment she got out of the car.

"Let's get inside first."

We sat in a corner booth, in the back. Joanne ordered lunch. I ordered beer.

"Okay, sugar, what's all the mystery?" she asked, lighting a second cigarette.

I took a deep breath. "I slept with Daniel last night. Well, we didn't sleep. At all. And, oh shit, what am I going to do?"

"Well it's about time you got some of that fine stuff," Joanne laughed.

"Damn it. I'm serious. This wasn't just a roll in the hay," I answered, my voice raising an octave. I took another breath and almost whispered, "This guy is something else."

"I'll bet he is," she chuckled.

This wasn't going the way I expected. I wanted sympathy. Direction. Guidance.

"Joanne, I'm really serious. This is a big deal. I've been thinking about him for weeks, okay, months. And Jamil isn't calling me like he usually does. And I can't even tell you how good it was with Daniel. I'm so confused."

Joanne exhaled smoke through a sigh.

"Annette. Annette. For one thing, you were high. Probably still are from the looks of you. Sex on speed is amazing. You told me the same thing about Jamil when he was home for Christmas. Second of all, Jamil is your man. You're going through a rough patch, but you'll work it out. You just need to get Daniel out of your system, knock off the speed before Jamil gets back, and go back to being the perfect little couple."

She looked at me as if I were nine years old and had forgotten how to tie my shoes.

"But I'll tell you what. I'd be taking my own sweet time getting him out of my system. That Daniel is one fine man."

I realized that she didn't get it. She really didn't get it. Jamil and I weren't the perfect little couple that she imagined. Maybe we had been once, but we'd been struggling for a while now. We were becoming strangers. I used to tell him everything and now I talked to him like I was an employee. This was more than a rough patch. And this was me taking a lover, not a one-night stand from some dance club. It certainly wasn't like when I left Eddie for Jamil. That was going from a bad situation to something good. This was going from a good situation to jumping into an abyss. I finished my glass and refilled from the pitcher.

"I don't know, Joanne. I just don't know."

She delicately placed a pickle slice on her tuna sandwich and looked at me.

"The thing is that you don't have to know," she said. "You just ride the wave until you tumble on the beach."

She laughed at her own joke while I concentrated on not making a head on the beer.

"Lighten up, girl," she said. "Enjoy yourself. It ain't nothin' but a thang."

I sat in silence as she finished her sandwich, tucking the little bag of chips into her purse.

"Now I know you're going to give me a taste before I go back to the office," she said, batting her eyes.

I reached into my purse to pull out the tiny plastic bag of speed and passed it to her under my hand.

"Go to the bathroom and do a line," I said. "And don't take all of it. It has to last."

"Please," she said, heading towards the ladies room.

I propped my elbows on the table and cupped my chin in my hands. What on earth was I going to do?

For now, I'd take Joanne back to work and go home. Maybe Daniel would call. Maybe Jamil would call. Maybe I'd learn to shoot myself up. Not yet. For one thing, I didn't have any syringes. For another, I didn't want to kill myself by injecting an air bubble or worse. And for another, I hoped to see Daniel again soon.

In the coming week Jamil did call, and then he didn't, and then he did again. There were moments when it felt normal. We missed each other. I could sense the ache in his voice to be done with the Japanese company men and his uncle and room service and just come home to me. But then he'd ask, —"So what are you doing today?" and I'd lie.

The truth was, I wasn't doing anything much other than waiting for the phone to ring. My already small world had shrunk even further. I did miss Jamil. It seemed like all I'd been doing for the last couple of years was miss him. And then, in wanders Daniel. Daniel, who looked me in the eye when he talked to me; Daniel, who never once took a phone call when I was with him. Daniel, who listened to every word I said and made me feel like I was the most important person in the world; Daniel, an ex-con, minimum-wage, part-time prep cook and drug dealer who was sleeping with his ex. Daniel, who supplied this new drug and shot me up; Daniel, who I couldn't seem to get enough of.

And so I waited, like I'd always waited. For Dad to come in off the road, for Eddie to come home from a card game, for Jamil to return to

Portland, for Joanne to tell me what to do. And now for Daniel to bring me methamphetamine along with his attention.

A few days later Daniel called to let me know that his problem had been solved. Diane had to leave for an extended stay to care for her sick father. He would re-set up the lab in her basement. I could expect product by the weekend, since everything else was in place. That was all he had to tell me, though I wanted more.

I was fairly judicious with my stash. I could make a quarter bag last six or seven days if necessary by just snorting a little when I got up, or skipping a day. But the skipping–a–day nearly killed me right from the start. The bag would talk to me just as surely as if it had a voice.

"Annette? Oh Annette? You know you want me. Come on. You can get more later."

I'd pace, trying to take my mind off of it, but the bag kept talking until I had it in my hand. "Just a little. It'll be okay. Yeah, that's it."

Daniel called back on Friday and asked that I pick him up from the restaurant. He was nearly ready for me, if I wanted to come over to Diane's and hang out. That was the most endearing thing he'd said all week. I was there at the appointed hour.

"Let's swing by the store so you can buy some syringes," he said, after "Hello" and "How are you?"

"Me?" I squawked. "I've never bought syringes before!"

He laughed. "Well, it's about time you started."

"What will they think? I don't look like someone who buys syringes."

"Precisely," he said. "In Oregon they can't legally turn you down, but the pharmacist over there gave me the evil eye the last time I was in. They can't turn you down, but they can give you crap. You are well-dressed and respectable. You'll have no problem."

No problem other than being scared. In the parking lot, I quickly jotted out a grocery list that included "insulin syringes for Aunt Betty." Attacking the list with purpose, I gathered milk and bread before wandering nonchalantly to the pharmacy with a knot in my stomach the size of Texas.

"What size, honey?" the clerk asked.

"Uh," I referred to the piece of paper, "100cc—is that right?"

"Yep. Here you are. Do you want to pay for your groceries too?"

I found Daniel in the music section.

"That was easier than I thought," I gushed. "So who buys these things?"

"Well, obviously, diabetics, and addicts," he answered. "There's a big heroin problem in this town you know."

"Really?" I was shocked. "Heroin?"

Until I met Daniel I hadn't known anyone who used the needle, much less heroin.

"Yeah, look around you," Daniel said, surveying the entrance area of the working class grocery store. "Who do you think all these people are? We're right up the I-5 corridor from Mexico. It's a veritable pipeline."

I looked at the people coming and going. Many were just normal folk, picking up groceries after work, maybe dragging a kid or two. But there were more than a few tough-looking characters, cheeks drawn, hair unkempt, eyes downcast.

"I just thought they were poor people," I said from my protected little world.

Daniel shook his head as he rolled his eyes. "Let's get out of here."

We made our way to Diane's, a bag of needles and a jug of milk in the trunk. When we got out of the car, Daniel said, "I worked all night, so we're almost ready to go. Robert has been here keeping things moving."

I put the milk in the fridge while Daniel headed downstairs.

"Excellent," I heard him say. My heart raced in anticipation as I followed him to the basement.

"Beautiful lady," Robert said, bowing to kiss the back of my hand. "Allow me to present our latest."

A plate full of the stuff sat on a table next to a large scale and a packet of bags.

"I have to take off, man," Robert said, dropping my hand and turning to Daniel. "I measured out my cut and put the rest back in the dish for you to divide up. If you're selling, I've got more buyers than I can handle."

"Let's talk later," Daniel answered. "Some of this is already spoken for."

I hoped he meant me.

"As for now," he continued, "Annette is going to have an injection lesson."

Oh shit. I knew this was coming. I smiled weakly.

"Good girl," Robert said, giving me a wink. "You'll be fine."

I followed the two of them upstairs and went to the bathroom while they walked to Robert's car. Splashing cold water on my face, I took deep breaths while wiping my sweaty palms on my jeans.

Daniel was at the kitchen table when I came out, setting up a hit. He looked up as I walked in the room.

"Sit down. We need to talk," he said, his mouth set in a thin line.

"Okay," I said cautiously.

"I need to tell you about methamphetamine," Daniel said, fingering the curl that fell over his forehead.

"Okay," I said again. What about it? I liked the way it made me feel. I liked him. What more was there?

"I don't know where you're going to go with this stuff and right now everything is cool, but I need you to understand that there could be a time when that changes. Over time, strange things can happen with speed if you're not careful. You could start to see things that aren't there and hear people that aren't talking to you. Always remember that if someone wants your attention, you'll know it. If you have to wonder, it's probably in your head."

"So you're saying I'll go crazy?" I asked.

"Not really," he answered, smiling now. "Well, maybe a little. A lot of it has to do with lack of sleep. You can't sleep on it now, but as your body acclimates you'll be able to rest and to eat. You need to do both. Speed has a lot of great qualities, but you need to take care of yourself with it."

I'd only done hallucinogens a couple of times because I was afraid of getting lost in my own brain. I didn't like the sound of all this. I certainly wasn't going to turn into one of those toothless wonders we'd seen at the store.

"Any questions?" he asked, looking me in the eye. I looked away.

I had lots of questions. Could I do speed every day? How could I insure a steady supply? Did he like me? Would he go to bed with me again? Now?

"I don't think so, "I answered.

"Fine. Now for your lesson."

"Do you think I'm ready?" I asked, hoping he'd say no.

"Of course."

Daniel handed me an empty syringe to get familiar with how it felt to maneuver. He showed me how to tap out air bubbles from the chamber, letting just a drop of liquid come out of the tip. He then showed me how to tie off my arm with a belt or surgical tubing, using one hand and my teeth to make the knot.

"Tight enough to pop your veins, but not so tight that it cuts off your circulation. Make the knot loose enough that you can undo it once you've got a vein."

I took a deep breath, focusing on the sequence. Mix the hit. Get rid of the air. Tie off. Stab. He helped me find what appeared to be a vein, and watched as I stuck myself with the needle. It wasn't as bad as I thought, but it wasn't a vein either. We looked some more, prodding and rubbing my inner arm until something felt right.

Before I tried to hit again, he said, "You have lousy veins, Annette. That's part of why I want to turn this part over to you. I don't like the poking and prodding. People shoot up all sorts of places. When you're done, I'll tell you more about that."

I stuck the needle in what I hoped was a profitable vein.

"Okay, now pull the plunger out just a little bit," Daniel whispered. "Good, you're in."

I watched as the thin stream of blood, my blood, entered the chamber. I glanced up at Daniel. Now what?

He reached over to help me loosen the tie.

"Don't move or you could lose it. Now slowly push the plunger all the way down."

"Slowly?" I asked. I'd seen him do it quickly.

"You can get fancy later. Just go nice and easy, and when it's empty, pull it out quick and straight."

I followed the instructions, covering the small drop of blood at the puncture site with two fingers. I closed my eyes and felt the exquisite rush flow through my body, picking up speed as it hit my lungs. I breathed out.

"Good." Daniel said. "You'll do fine."

He got up and left the room, I assumed to let me settle in to my high. I continued to breathe deeply, following the sensation as it reached my toes.

When he came back, Daniel sat down and told me more about veins—what to use and what not to use. Arteries, never. The back of the hand was fine, inside of wrist, not; ankles and feet, not a great idea, but available; the neck only as a last resort. He told me about a woman who used the veins in her breasts, a guy who'd shot up in the vein in his penis, and ex-cons who went between the toes so the tracks wouldn't show when they saw their parole officers. I glanced at the raised blue veins on the backs of my hands as I turned my arms over and then back again. None of this related to me. I didn't plan on living on the dark side. I was just a tourist, a visitor. I smiled at him without speaking.

I followed Daniel downstairs as he cleaned up in the lab. I sat on the stool I'd claimed as my own and watched as he weighed and measured small and larger amounts of the powder into dime and quarter bags. He was more talkative now that the main work was done. He told me about his ex-wife, Pam, who had gotten pregnant in high school. She was now a manager at a local grocery store. Their twenty year-old son was in school back east. Daniel was an only child and his parents divorced when he was four. A deaf cousin cared for him while his Mom was at work.

"That's why I'm so comfortable with silence," he offered, like it was something he'd said by way of explanation a hundred times before. I didn't mind his quiet periods. I wasn't much of a talker myself.

"Let's go upstairs," he said after an hour. "I'm expecting a friend."

He walked behind me up the stairs and turned out the basement lights. Will I spend the night here? Will Jamil have called while I was out?

I settled in the kitchen while he put on a Marvin Gaye album. Sweet, sweet Marvin. Oh Daniel, please tell me that you want me to stay.

We talked while sitting at the little kitchen table, about being married to our high school sweethearts, how that went bad for both of us, about the traveling I'd done and that he hoped to do someday, the house he wanted to build with his bedroom in the space that most people used for the living room. We drank cold beer and listened to more music and talked and listened and talked some more in that timeless space that is methamphetamine.

Tap. Tap. Tap.

"Ah, Lorie is here."

He got up.

Lorie? I wasn't expecting a female friend.

She preceded him back into the kitchen.

106

"Annette, Lorie. Lorie, Annette," he said from behind her.

"Hi," she said enthusiastically. "Daniel has told me about you."

I tilted my head slightly and forced a smile.

She was tiny, thin in a way I'd never be, with curly dark red hair just barely to her shoulders and a wide, toothy smile. She looked a little younger than me, maybe twenty-four or twenty-five, and wore black slacks and a white men's style shirt open at the collar.

"I've got to get off my feet. The restaurant was really busy tonight," she said, sitting in the chair that Daniel had just vacated.

Daniel handed her a beer and offered a hit of speed.

"Umm. Not now. I'd rather get some sleep. I'll save it for the morning," she said, yawning as she poured her beer into a glass.

She went to the bathroom before even taking a sip, asking Daniel if she could take a bath.

"Be my guest," he said, and I heard her turn on the water in the tub.

I had a queasy feeling in my stomach. It felt like time to go home.

"Annette," Daniel said, reaching across the table to put his hand over mine. "Lorie and I work together. We've been hanging out for a few weeks."

"Okay," I said in my best "it doesn't matter" voice.

"Are you?" he asked.

"Yeah, sure. I mean, I live with someone, right? No claims."

"You're great." He smiled and squeezed my hand.

"I think I'll head out," I said, putting my hands in the pockets of my jeans as I stood so that he couldn't see them shaking.

"Alright. I'll call you."

I gathered up a handful of the syringes that I'd bought.

"Do I owe you anything?" I asked, picking up the bag of speed.

"No," he said. "This one's on the house."

On the house, my ass, I thought, marching to my car. I paid for most of this shit. And what am I saying about *my* ass? What about her skinny little ass?

I drove home on mostly deserted streets. At this hour of the night, the city was quiet. I was supremely alert, driving past the reservoir at Mt. Tabor, through neighborhoods rich and poor. Passing the statue of George Washington on 57th, I felt very competent behind the wheel. Driving home drunk with one eye closed used to make me nervous, but this stuff improved my perceptions. Beats liquor, I told myself as I tried to keep the image of Daniel and that little waitress out of my brain while winding my way back out to the island on as many back streets as I could manage before hitting the four-lane highway that would take me to the condo.

When I got home, I lay in bed until well after the sun came up, eyes wide open. I needed a hobby. I needed something. I decided to visit Mom.

"Knock, knock," I sang out in my best imitation of fresh-and-cheerful. I unlocked the back door and walked into the kitchen. "Anybody home?"

"You're bright and early," my mother answered from the kitchen table where mornings always found her with the crossword puzzle and a cup of coffee.

I sat down, looking past her through to the dining room shelf crammed full of knick-knacks. A lot of them were from my trips with Jamil: the Delft pitcher from Amsterdam, the miniature Eiffel Tower from Paris, a doll from Singapore. What kind of souvenir would I bring her from deep in southeast Portland? A spent syringe?

"Yeah. I have some errands to do so I'm getting an early start on the day."

In the last few years I'd been stopping at the house only briefly to say "hi" and keep moving. I didn't know how to talk about my life. Jamil loved me but he was rarely with me. When he was, we treated day like night, then stayed awake until the sun came up. And now Daniel and the speed. It was easier to be vague, though a part of me ached to tell my mother how confused I was, seeking solace from someone who wasn't likely to give it. Instead I sat at the kitchen table in twenty-minute increments and told my mother and myself that I was fine.

"When will Jamil be home?" she asked.

"I'm not sure. I think he's still in Malaysia," I replied. I didn't have to pretend ignorance at this point.

Thirty minutes later I was pacing in the condo from the living room to the kitchen and back. I had syringes and speed in my purse and they were talking to me. Loud.

Was it too soon to do more? What if I passed out and died and no one found me for weeks? What if someone knocked on the door or the phone rings? Fuck it. Where was the scale?

I found the little green plastic scale that we used for measuring cocaine. It was a discreet little foldaway that we'd purchased mainly for its cool appeal. It's not like Jamil and I had anything to measure. You didn't have to weigh out lines, and cocaine went pretty fast around our house—we had it, we did it. But it would certainly come in handy now.

I balanced the little cup in the prongs of the counter-weight, setting it to zero. I'm sure it wasn't accurate but close enough for what I wanted to do. Retrieving the bag of crystal from my purse, I measured out just under a dime.

Next came the syringe. I was very methodical, imitating what I'd now watched Daniel do a dozen times or more, adding distilled water and drawing the liquid up through a tightly balled piece of cotton.

Moving down that path again, I was an observer and a participant, watching my life change while not believing that it ever would. I had developed the habit of not thinking too much about the future. I could usually keep my brain occupied during the day, with wondering about Jamil, and now, Daniel, thinking about Cyprus, the family, groceries, anything other than the what-are-you-doing-with-your-life question. The hardest time of all was in those few minutes before falling asleep at night when there was no one in my head except me and God. I did whatever I could to avoid even those few minutes of quiet with a pretty effective combination of vodka and television. Enough of a stiff drink and I'd simply pass out with Johnny Carson. It was a little more difficult with the speed, but if I stayed up past exhaustion, I was out like a light when I did hit the bed. Don't think. Don't think. Just keep moving.

And now here I was moving ahead, moving ahead, slowly now. Me and the needle and a cloth belt around my arm, alone in the condo. Me, focused solely on the needle in my hand. Me and methamphetamine. Here we go. I held my breath.

I didn't hit a vein with the first jab, or the second. I looked at the back of my hand, tightening the fingers of my left around the wrist of my right. A number of veins stood up, begging for attention. I had a momentary flashback to an assembly in high school when a guest speaker talked to us about drugs. He had a petrified hand from hitting a nerve instead of a vein. I pictured the guy's darkened and useless appendage nearly every time I shot up in the hand from there on out, but it didn't stop me.

I got it the third time, feeling a little smug as I leaned back on the couch to enjoy the rush. I could do this. I'd be fine.

Daniel continued to come over, and I continued to have sex with him. He continued to leave when we were done, and I assumed, continued to spend time with Lorie. We didn't talk about either his relationship with me, or with her, or anyone else who might have been in his picture. He certainly didn't volunteer and I didn't ask, but I kept hoping that I'd win what I saw as a contest for his time and attention.

As confused as I was about Jamil, my relationship with him felt like my breath or my heartbeat—something that just *was,* not something that I thought about in relation to Daniel. In my mind, we were close to separated, though neither of us had said the words. I had slipped into confusion about what was real and what was a fantasy, whether fueled by the methamphetamine, or my own fears about speaking the truth. Jamil was real. I lived in his home; his shirts were in the closet, his picture on the wall. I used his last name when paying our bills and spoke to his mother several times a month. But I was sleeping with Daniel and was in that dangerous place of mistaking good sex for love; and I wanted a declaration from him, an intent, something to hang on to.

"So I'm really having strong feelings for you, Daniel," I finally said one evening in my kitchen, in Jamil's kitchen. "As in, I could almost say 'I love you.'"

He was silent a little too long.

"Annette," he finally said, in his deep and distinctive voice, "I do care for you but I'm very careful with my words. Once something is said, it is in the universe and takes on a life of its own."

I must've looked puzzled because he walked over to where I stood at the sink and put his arms on my shoulders.

"I promise you one thing," he said. "I may not tell you that I love you, but I promise to tell you when I stop."

That wasn't exactly what I wanted to hear, but it made sense in an odd sort of way. A lot of what Daniel said made sense, in an odd way, like his explanation of sleeping with both Lorie and me.

"Love isn't a commodity," he explained that evening. "Affection and pleasure aren't exclusive to one person. My having a connection with someone else has no bearing on my connection with you."

I had a hard time with that one, but really, really wanted to be a free spirit, the kind of woman Daniel would want to be with. But his philosophy made no sense in my world. I hadn't been faithful to either Eddie or Jamil, but I had intended to be. In my little and warped vision of life, fidelity mattered.

But, with Daniel I aimed for cool and groovy. Cool and groovy. I did everything I could to seem cool and groovy. Until the phone rang a week later.

"Hello Annette. It's Daniel. I need to ask something of you."

I'd been loading the dishwasher, which took weeks to fill these days.

I sat down.

"I need you to get tested for syphilis," Daniel said.

"You what?" I said, standing back up.

"Well," he continued, "Lorie thinks that she has it, so had to tell her partners, which means that I have to tell mine."

I was dumbfounded. I certainly wasn't going to go to my family doctor. What in the hell did he expect me to do? Go to the public health clinic, apparently, which is where he was headed the next morning.

I was downtown at 10:30 and watched Daniel walk towards me from down the block, hands in the front pockets of his jeans, eyes downcast. He smiled when he looked up and saw me. I was glad to see him, even if it was concerning a sexually transmitted disease that he might have passed on to me from his other lover.

"Let's walk," he said, steering me away from the County Health Department offices.

We traveled the few blocks to the waterfront without saying a word, settling on a bench near the seawall. He turned towards me with a chagrined smile.

"There is no syphilis," he said, explaining that Lorie had wanted to know if he was sleeping with me, so concocted a story about giving a guy a blow job and getting a sore throat and being tested in order to ferret out the truth.

"She'd told me she wasn't sleeping with anyone else," he said, shaking his head, "but somehow figured that oral didn't count."

"You expect her to be faithful?" I asked, surprised.

"Of course not," he said defensively, "but I do expect honesty. She said she wasn't being sexual with anyone else. Now I'm not sure."

It seemed out of character that he was so concerned with sex that she'd made up. Maybe cool and groovy was an act for him too.

"She could've just asked if you were sleeping with me," I said, thinking of my conversations with Jamil over the past few years.

"She wonders why you need two boyfriends when all she wants is one," he replied, looking across the Willamette River towards the freeway on the other side.

I sighed. I didn't subscribe to his "love is not a commodity" philosophy, but it wasn't a question that I had an easy answer for. Hadn't he told her the same thing he'd told me about having two girlfriends? I just looked at him and shook my head. He cupped my face in his hands and kissed me gently.

"Walk me to work?" he asked, and we said nothing more about it.

Chapter Nine

J AMIL CAME HOME unexpectedly. He hadn't called for several days, which was becoming more normal than not. I'd been in Diane's basement with Daniel and Robert all night watching them cook and came home via the grocery store at 8:00 in the morning. There was Jamil, sitting in the living room with a beer, his suitcase at the bottom of the stairs.

"Surprise!" he said, in a voice that sounded road-weary and more like an accusation than a greeting.

"Jamil! My God! You're home!" I exclaimed. Thank God I was alone. Thank God I didn't smell like sex with another man. Thank God that all my works were hidden away upstairs and thank God I had a bag of groceries in my arms.

I went to the couch and snuggled into his lap, avoiding his direct gaze. My pupils, undoubtedly, were huge.

"I've missed you," I whispered into his neck, inhaling a mixture of cologne, travel sweat and beer. That much was true, mostly.

"So, is there anything I need to know?" he asked, immediately going into his "what-have-you-done-wrong-since-I've-been-gone?" routine. Normally we had a day or two of reunion before the interrogation started, but then, not much had been normal the last few months.

He was a little drunker than the beer in his hand would indicate. In theory he could be asking if there were any bills he needed to know about, or any phone calls he'd missed while in transit, or any news of my family. But we both knew what he was asking.

"Nope. Borings-ville around here," I answered, covering all contingencies.

He grabbed my wrist. "Really?" he asked.

"Oh sweetie, yes 'really.' You seem tired. Why don't you go up and have a shower and a nap."

I was surprised at how easy it was to lie to him. Of course, in the past, we'd be tanked up on cocaine and cheap wine when we had this conversation, a truth serum if there ever was one. In the past when I'd confessed to an indiscretion that I completely regretted, it was because I completely regretted it and wanted Jamil to know how much I missed him and how lonely I got. If he could only understand that, he wouldn't travel so much. But that was the past. There was absolutely nothing to be gained from admitting that Daniel and I were lovers. Nothing. I would finally take Joanne's admonishments to heart. This was a story that did not need to be told.

"I don't trust you, Annette," Jamil said, with an undercurrent of anger that I hadn't seen in him before.

"Is something wrong?" I asked, with a knot in my stomach.

"You tell me," he said, his accent thickening through the jet lag. "I call here all times of the night and day and no one answers. When you do answer, it sounds like you'd rather be someplace else. You've cheated on me twice that I know of. Why am I supposed to think that anything has changed?"

"Wow," I said, oddly calmed by his accusations. "You ask me to change my ways and I do that and now you're angry? If I don't answer the phone at night, it's because I'm asleep. If it was during the day, I was out. And you never told me that you couldn't reach me." I hoped he was bluffing.

He went on to tell me, yet again, how upset he was by the Michael incident. How hurt he was. He'd always told me that he'd accept the truth from me, so he had to carry on, but inside it was killing him to think that another man had been in his bed. The sadness I could empathize with. I wished that the episode with Michael had never happened. But then he got angry again.

"You came to me by being unfaithful to your husband. Why should I think you'd be any other way with me?"

"I don't know what it is you want from me, Jamil," I answered. "Why don't you get some rest and we'll talk about it later?"

There's nothing worse than telling a drunk that he should go to sleep.

114

"I'll rest when I'm ready to rest. What I want from you is to stop thinking with your pussy. You tell me that men think with their dicks. You're no better."

I slapped him, hard, scared as soon as my hand left his face. He grabbed my wrist and twisted my arm away from him.

"Don't you *ever* do that again," he growled, dropping my hand with a vengeance.

"Don't you ever speak to me like that again," I hissed, walking backwards from the couch as I grabbed my purse.

I slammed the front door and got into my car. Where in God's name had that come from? Why was he dragging up something we'd dealt with? There had been no indication on the phone these last few weeks that he was so upset. We'd fought before, but never like this. I'd never hit him before. I'd never hit anybody before.

My hands shook as I turned on the ignition and pulled out of the driveway towards the Interstate. There wasn't anywhere to go on the Island, unless I wanted to drive in a circle around the mall. I merged on to the freeway, heading south. Joanne would be at work. I didn't want to face my mother. Daniel and Robert had still been up when I left.

I headed back the way I'd come just an hour before, heart beating hard and fast in my chest, nearly holding my breath. I was angry and scared and confused and hurt, and unwilling to turn around and deal with the man that I lived with. How dare he sneak home like that? He was just trying to catch me at something. I was lucky he hadn't.

Robert was climbing into his beater as I pulled up.

"That was quick," he said as he powered up the noisy rig, gunning it as I walked up the path to the house.

"Be good," he shouted as he drove away trailed by a cloud of exhaust.

The door was unlocked.

"Daniel?"

He came into the living room naked, rubbing his wet hair with a towel. I tried not to stare at his flat belly and the ridge of muscle where his torso and pelvic bones met.

"Annette?" he said. "What's wrong?"

I started to cry, telling him as best as I could between sobs about Jamil coming home and the ugly argument we'd just had.

"Hey, hey," Daniel said, wrapping the towel around his waist as he walked me back to the bedroom. I sat on the edge of Diane's double bed, attempting to muffle my sobs with the back of my hand.

"Listen," he continued, "Lorie will be here in a little bit to take me to work, but maybe you can call me at the restaurant later."

I knew that he didn't have to be at work for at least a couple of hours. I hated the thought of Lorie coming over to Daniel and that little green towel. Wiping my nose, I pulled him towards me and nuzzled my face in his belly.

"Annette, Annette," he said, putting his hands on my head as I undid the towel. I'd take care of things so there wouldn't be anything left for her. Sex was easy, sex was power; my way of distracting myself or the person I was with. It was easier than saying, "I hurt. I'm scared. I don't know what to do."

"I rarely orgasm from oral sex," he said as I kissed his stomach.

"I like a challenge," I replied and continued.

Show him, I did, and in short order. He chuckled as he wiped himself with the towel when it was over.

"You are an amazing woman."

"Don't ever forget it," I answered, grabbing the other end of the towel to wipe my mouth.

"So it might be awhile before I can see you again," I said, "or even call. I have no idea what's going on."

He agreed to give me an extra bag of crystal, just in case. I'd pay him later and call when I could.

It wasn't that I specifically wanted Lorie to find me there, but I was just a little glad that her car rounded the corner as I was pulling away. Syphilis, my ass, I thought, as I waved and smiled.

The condo was silent when I returned. The living room blinds were up, morning sun lighting dust particles in the air. Tiptoeing quietly upstairs, I found Jamil asleep on top of the bed, curtains drawn. Pulling off his shoes, I tried to undress him, but he was dead weight. I covered him with a blanket from the hall closet, shutting the door as I left.

Going back downstairs, I emptied the dirty clothes from his suitcase, and started a load of laundry. Back in the living room I picked up his briefcase and set it on the coffee table. He frequently sent me to retrieve one thing or another from it, so I didn't feel particularly guilty about opening it now.

Cigarettes, his lighter, pens, random papers, nothing out of the ordinary. I picked up a matchbook from a restaurant in Sydney. I hadn't realized that he'd been in Australia. He had told me he'd be coming home from Kuala Lumpur. There was a phone number written inside the cover in what appeared to be a feminine hand. "How original," I said out loud as my stomach flipped.

Maybe I was naïve, but I believed Jamil when he said he was faithful. I'd never had any reason to doubt him, even with my acting out. He was an honorable man. Maybe the gap between what I said and what I did had gotten too big to navigate. Despite our recent estrangement, it hadn't occurred to me that he might actually be on the verge of leaving.

Later that afternoon, after staring out the window at the river for an hour, I picked up pizza, Jamil's favorite hangover food. His sleep would be screwed up for a week, but I could give him dinner at a regular time in order to help him acclimate.

"Jamil?" I said quietly, setting a tray with pizza and a cold beer on the bedside table. I opened the curtains slightly so that the late afternoon light leaked in.

He was groggy, though roused by the smell of food. He sat up and took a sip of the beer, then asked for water instead.

He ate silently, and then pushed aside the plate.

"Hey," he said.

"Hey to you," I said back.

He looked at me with tears in his eyes, and drew me close.

"I love you so much. I'll always love you," he said.

"Baby, what's wrong?" I asked, not wanting to know.

"We'll talk later," he said, kissing me.

We made love in the exquisitely painful way that signals the end, where you try to pour every ounce of love and history into your caresses, and fear and sadness and desire all bump up against each other. We came together and I started to cry, crossing the line from pleasure to pain somewhere in the middle of the orgasm.

Jamil held me tight as I tried to quiet my sobbing.

"What happened to us?" I asked, as my breathing slowed.

He didn't answer, but I felt his tears on my neck.

"You'll always be my best friend," was all he said.

The next morning, Jamil and I slid around each other in the condo, very polite, very tender. Finally he said, "We need to talk."

I sat at the kitchen table across from him as he told me he was moving to Detroit to be with his family. They needed him right now. It was his duty. I stopped listening after the "I'm leaving."

"I've asked Tim Collins to start looking for a house or a condo for you because my intention is to sell this place as soon as possible," he said.

I could only stare at the surface of the table.

"I don't know what to say," I finally said, as I turned towards him. "This seems so sudden."

He sighed, looking at me for the first time.

"Does it really, Annette?" he asked.

Maybe not. But we loved each other. How can you say "good-bye" to someone that you love?

"Will you come back? Will I still be your girlfriend?" I asked stupidly. "What about loving me forever like you said?"

My lip trembled like an eight year old.

"I have to go out," was all he said, putting his hand on my shoulder for just a moment before he turned and left.

One hand flew to cover my mouth and the other held my stomach as the door closed. I continued to stare at the tabletop, unable to form a coherent thought, unable to move. This wasn't unexpected. Of course it wasn't. But even though the tiny voice inside had been whispering for a while now that Jamil and I were headed for an ending, it was still a shock. I had hoped to delay the inevitable, as if ignoring the problem would make it go away. The phone rang somewhere around noon. I didn't answer. For much of the day I sat on the couch staring at the river, swallowed by grief, trying not to think about the logistics of splitting up. I was in bed before Jamil came home. He crawled in quietly and fell asleep with his back to me.

Chapter Ten

HE NEXT FEW months moved ahead on steroids. Time sprinted on, despite my attempts to ignore it. Jamil had stayed in town only a few days after his disclosure, very polite, very kind, very loving, but not saying a word about his plans. I knew there was more to the story than what he'd told me, but I wasn't getting it from him. I called Joanne several times a day.

"Joanne, I think he's getting married. I think his mother finally must've fixed him up," I cried into the phone.

"And?" she'd replied, "you expected something different from all this? He's an Arab, dear. How many of his cronies do you know that are actually married to their American girlfriends? The question isn't whether or not he's getting married; the question is what are you going to do when he does?"

She was right, but I didn't want to admit it. It was going to be different with me. He always told me that since he was raised in the States, he could do what he wanted. I couldn't acknowledge that this might be what he wanted.

I twisted a strand of hair around my finger. "What do you mean, what am I going to do? I can't do anything about it from here, and I certainly can't just fly to Detroit."

"I mean," she replied, "what are you going to do, as in you'd better take him up on that offer to get you settled someplace before he changes his mind."

And so that's how I found myself barely two months later, sitting in the empty living room of a cute little place five minutes from the house I grew up in, crying my eyes out because I couldn't decide which carpet to have installed. If I didn't decide, then it wouldn't get done and if it didn't get done, I couldn't move in and if I couldn't move in, Jamil would come back and everything would be alright.

I locked myself in various bathrooms, at the condo, or the new house, or my mother's, injecting as much speed as I could at a time. I'd quickly stopped even trying for the veins in my arm and now regularly shot up in the backs of my hands. It was quick and it was easy and for those few moments of the rush, I forgot that my life was falling apart.

I saw Daniel regularly. I had become the full-time girlfriend with Lorie somewhere in the background. I was completely absorbed with Jamil leaving, doubled-over with grief. Daniel sat with me as I cried and told me stories about his own painful breakups. And he kept me supplied with crystal meth.

"But you don't understand," I wailed. "He loves me. He can't do this to me," simmering in a stew of anger and self-pity. I saw a lawyer, only to learn that Oregon didn't recognize common law marriages.

"Let me get this straight," the legal aid lawyer had said, pushing blonde bangs out of her eyes as she straightened her glasses. "He is co-signing your mortgage, is providing a monthly allowance and is leaving you with several thousand dollars worth of jewelry and a nice wardrobe? My advice is to be very thankful and leave it alone."

I don't know what I expected, or even what I wanted. Jamil was being kind, more than kind. I loved him. I hated him. And he wasn't returning my calls. It's hard to navigate a break-up when the person leaving simply disappears.

I met with Tim Collins at the office, who handed me the keys to my new home. It had a breakfast nook that opened onto the backyard, a half-bath on the main floor, two bedrooms and a full bath upstairs, and a little workshop under the basement stairs with a door that locked.

Daniel liked that little workshop.

"You realize that this is perfect, don't you?" he said as my tour of the place took him under the stairs.

"Perfect?" Nothing was perfect as far as I was concerned.

"If you ever wanted me to set up my operation," he continued, not quite asking.

I thought about it, for about fifteen seconds.

"Great. Let's go for it."

So, I moved into this newly carpeted house that contained some new furniture, whatever hadn't been nailed down at the condo, and the makings of a meth lab under the basement stairs.

Little by little, Daniel moved in too, though we never called it that. First came the glassware and tubing and odd bits of lumber that he hauled into the basement under cover of darkness. Then the toothbrush, followed a week later by a laundry basked full of clothes and a box of cassettes. He placed them methodically in the extra bedroom, taking care to hang the shirts and fold the four or five pairs of pants. I sat on the floor and watched.

"What's in the bag?" I asked, looking at a brown lunch sack at the bottom of the laundry basket.

"My good shoes," he answered, removing a worn but polished pair of black wing tips.

"If you take good care of things, they will last forever," he said, placing the shoes on the floor of the small closet, on top of the sack.

All I'd ever seen him in was jeans and tennis shoes or slippers. We sometimes went to a nearby tavern for burgers, or to Starry Night, a converted downtown church, to hear a band, but I wondered about that part of his life that included dress shoes and the gray slacks he now hung carefully. The ex-wife, the son back east, the deaf babysitter, two years of college and his own home, the yearbook photo he'd shown me of the smiling young fellow with the 1960s pompadour. He'd graduated high school nearly ten years before me. How did that guy in the picture become this curly haired meth cook who often seemed to be performing for an audience, even when we were alone?

I'd probably never know. Daniel talked for hours about philosophy, whether Nietzsche's or Lou Reed's. He espoused Lao Tsu's premise of non-doing, and thought Charlie Watts was the best drummer of all time, but he rarely talked about his own life or plans, other than the immediate of driving to Brandy's or Robert's for a sale or a buy. It was a very present-oriented existence and it frustrated the hell out of me, me who liked at least the illusion of planning out my days and weeks. With Jamil I'd always kept a date book full of flight information, lunch dates, appointments, calls to make. With Daniel, if I could even think in terms "with Daniel," there was nothing. My calendar was blank, empty-page after page of clean white sheets.

I'd slipped into that emptiness without even being aware of it. A year earlier I'd been with Jamil in New York, riding in the back of a limo on the way to dinner at an ambassador's apartment. Yesterday, I drove with Daniel to some speed cook's ratty apartment in Hillsboro and split a bottle of cheap wine with the guy and his stripper girlfriend. It felt like a dream, like I was in a fog and unable to see more than two feet ahead. I was just vaguely aware that the structured life I'd always wanted of casseroles and predictability was farther away than ever, and that it mattered less and less as the days became months. The life of an addict, though I wouldn't have used that word at the time, is very focused on the end result, which is making sure you have what you need. It was like moving through time with blinders on; weather, seasons, none of that mattered, or was noticed. Summer was hot, and then it wasn't. I took out the fans, then put them back in the closet. I did laundry, and sometimes turned on the new music video channel, but all activities revolved around the time I spent in my bathroom with a belt tied around my arm.

I was sleeping some. Daniel had been right about that part. After a few months on a regular dose of speed, I'd developed the ability to rest for at least a few hours. I'd taken the mini-refrigerator from the condo and used it as a bedside table. Stocked with beer, I put a syringe full of speed on the little shelf inside the door before going to sleep.

When Daniel did crawl into bed, usually as the sun was rising, he would reach to hold me, often falling asleep with legs twitching before we fully embraced. Quietly, I would slip off to the bathroom for my first hit of the day, preparing to outrun the demons that sleep had held at bay.

Daniel had quit the dishwashing job and was working full time in my basement, which could mean that he'd be up for three days in a row running a reaction, or that he would disappear for a couple of days to deliver product. Through it all, I was shooting speed, several times a day.

I played games with myself when Daniel was gone, watching the street from behind the curtain in the front upstairs bedroom, telling myself that the next car would be him, or the next, or the fifth one coming from the north. It wasn't a busy street.

When I wasn't actively waiting for Daniel, I wrote long letters to Jamil, begging him to come home, to talk to me, to help me make sense of what was happening. I wrote to Kate, in London, saying how much that I missed him and could she please convince him to call. I phoned his mother's house every day for two weeks.

"Oomi? Hi. It's Annette again. I'm just wondering if Jamil is there?" It felt a little funny to still call her "Mother."

There was silence on the other end, the kind of long silence where your stomach goes in a knot and you know you shouldn't have dialed the phone but you did it anyway.

"Annette. You know that it is midnight?" she answered, her accented English heavy with sleep.

"Oh my gosh, no. I'm sorry. I wasn't thinking about the time difference. I'm so sorry. Can you give Jamil a message?"

I could almost hear her lips tighten like they did when Jamil used to talk about quitting the family business. I could picture her in the hallway outside her room, various photos of Jamil and his brothers and their children on the wall, in a long flannel nightgown, eyes dark with kohl even at bedtime.

"Annette, you must stop this calling," she said. "You must leave him alone."

I bit my lip to keep from crying. A tiny "okay" was all I could muster before hanging up. He wouldn't answer my letters or calls, and now his mother had shut the door on me. I imagined her telling the aunties and brother's wives about my calls, clicking her tongue as they all shook their heads. I wanted to disappear from the earth, but more than that, I desperately wanted to talk to Jamil, to see him, to remind him of how much he loved me, to beg him to let me down easy.

My own mother, I avoided. I didn't want to answer her incessant questions about what had gone wrong, when would I start looking for work, how come I looked so tired?

Joanne had quit even snorting speed but came by after work once or twice a week for a beer. We'd sit in the backyard or on the porch, sometimes with Daniel or Robert, sometimes just the two of us. She'd dropped Michael, saying he'd gotten too possessive.

"I don't let my husband tell me what to do and I damn sure won't let somebody else's man tell me what to do," she'd said, leaving it at that. I didn't ask any questions. I had no need for Michael.

On a breezy June evening, she sat on my front steps while I pulled weeds from the small flowerbed off the porch.

"Have you heard from Jamil?" she asked, looking away when I sat back on my heels.

"Don't you think I would've told you if I'd heard from Jamil?" I said, brushing a stray hair from my eyes. "I haven't talked to him for at least three months, since that time he called from London to talk to me about Tim Collins and the money."

Joanne sat silently for a minute, examining the label on her bottle of beer.

"What is it? What do you know?" I demanded, as I stood and dropped my garden gloves to the ground.

She looked at the sky, back at her beer, and then at me.

"Sit down. Here, beside me." She patted the step.

"I'm not sitting anywhere. What is it?" I said, my voice rising with each word.

Joanne looked from me to the beer and back again.

"Oh, honey," she said, "He got married."

The neighbor's lawnmower that had been whirring went silent. The wind stopped. Joanne on the porch looked far away, like I was seeing her through the wrong end of a telescope.

Just as quickly, it all came back—the mower, the shouting kids in the street, the breeze rustling the branches of the tall pine next door, and I felt like I'd been hit in the stomach. I grabbed my gut and closed my eyes.

"Annette?"

"I don't understand," I finally said. "When? How do you know? Why didn't he tell me?"

She lit a cigarette and reached to pet the cat that rubbed against her brown legs.

"Well, he called Anthony a couple of nights ago, from Paris. It happened about a month ago. They're on their honeymoon."

"You've known for two days and you didn't tell me?" My voice cracked. I needed to sit down.

"Hold on. Hold on," she said, raising one hand. "I shouldn't have had to tell you. That low-life should've been a man and told you himself."

I sat down beside her and leaned in, my shoulders starting to shake as I tried to hold back the tears.

"Just let it out," she said, moving to wrap her arms around me.

My head on her breast, I sobbed for this loss, this final blow, this ending.

Finally, in what could've been ten minutes or thirty, I uncurled myself from Joanne's embrace and saw that she was crying too.

"I've ruined your shirt," I said, noticing the mascara streaked on her chest.

She flicked at the yellow blouse.

"It's alright. It's just a shirt."

We sat, saying nothing, staring at the street. The kids kept playing. The sun was still shining, the cat rolled on her back in the lawn.

"I just kept thinking he'd be back," I finally said. "He's always traveled so much that I was trying to pretend he was just on one of his trips."

"I know you'll need to deal with this in your own way and in your own time," Joanne said, by now peeling the label off the beer, "but you do need to figure out what you're going to do. I'm worried about you, Annette."

"I don't know. I don't know" was all I could say.

A couple of times, Joanne opened her mouth as if she wanted to say more, but didn't. She was my best friend, my sister, my heart, but I didn't want to hear what was under her words of concern: quit using drugs, get a job, take care of yourself.

When Joanne drove away an hour later I was as alone as I'd ever been in my life. Daniel had left with Robert the previous day, and for once I was glad he was gone.

I drove to the still partially furnished condo. Sometimes I went out there to check the mail but mainly just to have something to do. The Island had been home for six years. It was where I still went for groceries and gas, craving familiarity and routine. I'd fill up the tank, then pull up to the condo where I wandered through the rooms and stared at the river.

I drove straight there, the car on auto-pilot. The longest day of the year was approaching, so the sky was still light at 9:00. The sun had gone down behind the west hills but still cast a glow.

I pulled into the parking spot, my parking spot, walking to the door I'd been in and out of hundreds of times. The potted arborvitae on the step drooped pitifully.

I put the key in the door, but it stuck. I pulled it out and tried again. Nothing. I knew that was the key but tried everything on my ring—my house key, my mother's, the padlock on the basement room, the car key, the condo.

Mike, the sandwich guy, pulled up as I continued to fumble.

"Hi Annette. Everything okay?" he asked, getting out of his car with a bag of groceries.

"Hi Mike." I tried to sound chipper. "My key won't work."

"Do you need to use the phone?"

"Sure," I answered, not sure who to call.

We'd been neighbors for years, but I'd never been in Mike's place. The condos were nice that way. People said "hello," and might visit in the parking area, but privacy was revered. Once your door shut, you were in your own world.

Mike's place was the direct opposite of ours. It was disorienting, with the kitchen to the left instead of the right, the stairs to the right instead of the left. His TV was in a different place, as was the couch. I stood in the entry.

"The phone is in here," he said, motioning me to follow him to the kitchen.

I rummaged in my bag for my address book in order to call Tim Collins. I'd called him so many times over the past few months, you think I'd have his home number memorized. But, I had to look it up each time I called about the mortgage documents, or with a question about the monthly deposit, or to ask if he'd talked to Jamil.

"Tim? Hi. It's Annette. Sorry to call so late, but I stopped out at the condo to water the plants and my key doesn't work."

There were no plants, but he didn't know that.

He was silent on the other end, this guy in a suit who'd become the go-between for me and the man that I loved.

"I'm sorry, Annette. The lock was changed. I thought you knew that."

"Oh. Well. Okay. No, I didn't. Thank you."

I hung up. I'd be damned if I showed him any emotion. Pleasant and business-like was what Mr. Collins got from me.

"Is everything alright?"

I'd forgotten about Mike but now turned to face him. He'd poured a drink and now stood with his back to the kitchen sink.

"Yes. It's fine. A misunderstanding," I answered.

"Can I make you a drink?" he asked, holding up his glass in a partial toast.

I hesitated. He was a nice enough guy, a boater, permanently ruddy faced from a combination of bourbon and sun, with a receding hairline that made you wonder if he was an old thirty-five or a young forty-five. I'd been in the sandwich shop a few times with Jamil, on the slough side of the Island. He always had a wink and an exaggerated flirt, safe because I was Jamil's woman, part of his M.O. as the proprietor.

"Sure," I said. "Do you have vodka?"

"Anything for the little lady," he replied, pulling a bottle of Stoli from the freezer with a flourish.

"Ah, the good stuff," I replied. Keep it light, keep it chatter.

"How's this?" He held up the highball glass, showing two fingers of liquor.

"A splash more," I answered. I didn't like the taste, but strong would be good.

"A girl after my own heart," he answered, adding ice and 7-Up.

His hand brushed mine, though it didn't need to, when he handed me the drink. I could see where this was headed, and I didn't care.

"I'm sorry about you and Jamil," he said, like he didn't want to say it but thought he should. Nice day out. Did you see that story in the paper? Sorry your life is over.

I smiled, saying nothing.

"Did you hear that they've raised the homeowner dues?" he asked, taking my cue.

"No, I hadn't heard."

We moved to the living room where we sat in side-by-side overstuffed chairs. I knew he'd been married once, but other than the two chairs, there was no evidence that anyone other than this single man spent any time here. I had a flash of Saturday night pick-ups at the local pub. How many women made it as far as this domestic viewpoint?

The sky was nearly dark and we commented on meals being served on various boat decks in the moorage below. It was peaceful. For just this moment I was in another world, a world of mixed drinks and ice cubes, of deck shoes and grilled burgers. Jamil, in Detroit or Paris or wherever he was with his beautiful wife, didn't exist. Daniel, his shoes in a brown paper bag, didn't exist. It was just me in a chair with a stiff drink, staring at the river.

127

I felt the vodka burning my throat, spreading warmth as it entered my system. That was something I'd picked up since I'd starting shooting speed, this minute attention to sensation and effect.

Mike has said something.

"I'm sorry," I said, turning toward him. "I was in my own world."

"I said, I've always thought you were pretty."

Here we go I thought, my mind just cloudy enough with drink and grief and this afternoon's speed to want to lose myself in his clumsy grip.

"You're a nice man, Mike," I said, bracing myself as he tried to squeeze himself onto the chair beside me.

"Let's move to the couch," I said, ignoring that he wasn't Jamil, ignoring that he wasn't Daniel, ignoring that he was Mike, the sandwich guy.

He lunged as soon as we sat down, a wet kiss taking in all of my mouth and grazing a nostril. I wanted to be into it, I really did, but as his fat tongue with his foreign breath and taste of Jim Beam pushed its way into my mouth and his hand grabbed my breast as if it were a softball, I pushed against his chest.

"Mike. Stop. I'm sorry. I can't do this."

He moved back and I felt him deflate against me.

"I'm sorry," I repeated. "I shouldn't have. I have to go."

He sat up and wiped his mouth with the back of his hand, looking at me with bleary eyes. "It's fine. Really."

I picked up my purse and keys from the kitchen table, continuing to apologize as I turned towards the door. My last glimpse was of him moving back to his chair as he picked up his drink.

I sat in my car, catching my breath. This was all wrong. I needed to go home. But where was that? The condo felt like home, but I was locked out. Numb, I drove back to my little house, over streets that were deeply familiar. I told myself that this was home as I took the long way and drove up Fremont, past the grade school where we'd smoked cigarettes on the roof, and the insurance agent's office that used to be the dime store. This was home, I told myself, pulling into the driveway of this house I now slept in. That was my big black cat on the front steps. My mailbox.

It looked like Daniel had been there and gone as evidenced by a pair of jeans crumpled on the bathroom floor and a still damp towel hanging on the rack.

The phone rang twice before the sound registered. Who would be calling so late? The lines crackled as I put the receiver to my ear: international.

"Jamil? Is that you?"

"Yes. Yes, it's me. How are you? It's good to hear your voice."

My voice caught. "How do you think I am? Is it true? Joanne says that you got married."

In the silence that followed, I willed him to say "No," "No, of course not," "No, what a silly idea," but instead he said, "Yes. Yes, it's true. I'm sorry."

"Where are you?" I asked.

"In Paris."

He avoided all reference to his new wife, but said he'd be in Portland the following week. He'd call me.

"Can I pick you up? Which day?" I pressed for details.

"I'm not sure," he said, "I'll call."

When he hung up, I went to the dresser and pulled my stash box out from beneath my underwear. I removed a syringe, the little green scale, the dope, and a cotton swab. Getting a capful of water from the bathroom, I sat on the small, gray upholstered chair near my bedroom window. I mixed a hit, not out of any desire to get high, but to get different. I searched the back of my hand and forearm for a vein, momentarily focused. I tied off and shot up, closing my eyes as I laid the empty syringe on the TV tray that doubled as an end table. For a few minutes I was nowhere. For a few minutes I was nothing, just heat and breath and heart beat. But then it came back, hard. Jamil was married. Married, and not to me.

I sat in that chair all night. My back got stiff and my right leg bounced with restlessness, but I didn't move from that place. I stared out the window looking at nothing as the dark moved to light, vague shapes turning into houses and trees. I didn't actually think about killing myself, but for the first time in my life I wondered what the point was of going on? I knew way deep in my heart that Jamil and I couldn't have made it together, that I'd been hanging on to a fantasy for a long time, but his marriage felt like a betrayal. I wasn't ready to let go. I wasn't ready to face what letting go meant.

At the same time, I was aware that I was standing on a precipice. I thought about my time with Eddie, and Jamil, and now Daniel. Where was

I in all of this? None of it—the married life, the jet set, this subterranean existence with meth—felt like me. But what did? The enormity of "who am I?" rocked me into a fetal position. Maybe I should do another hit. It would be easier than asking myself how long I was going to wait for something or someone to live my life for me.

Some time that morning, before the sun was fully up, I heard a car pull into the driveway and a single door open and close. The vehicle pulled away and I heard Daniel's key in the back door. I listened as he placed a paper bag on the counter and walked down the basement stairs. After just a few minutes he came back through the kitchen and upstairs to my room.

I turned my head as he walked in.

"Hey," he said quietly. "I'm surprised to see you up." He sat on the edge of the bed to untie his shoes.

"Jamil got married," I said flatly, turning back towards the window.

"Wow," Daniel replied as he placed his shoes neatly at the foot of the bed and unbuttoned his shirt. "Are you alright?"

I was disintegrating from the inside out. I was a hollow shell, a black hole.

"Yeah, I'm fine."

He took off his jeans and stood unselfconsciously naked, looking at me for a moment before turning down the sheets. As he climbed into bed, I stepped out of my shorts and crawled in beside him, still in my mascara-streaked t-shirt.

"Hold me, okay?" I asked.

Spooning me from behind, he was asleep within seconds, legs twitching to an internal rhythm. I listened to his breathing and started to cry, holding my body still so he wouldn't know.

Chapter Eleven

IN THE FOLLOWING days I trembled through the motions of my life, though at this point there weren't too many motions to go through. I did call Marcie and let her know about Jamil but asked her not to tell anyone else.

"Not yet, Marce. I'll tell Mom after he's been here. I just can't deal with all the questions and the sympathy."

Marcie knew I was using speed but didn't know about the needle, or the lab in the basement. She'd been over just once since I'd moved in.

"So what's going on with you?" she had asked after the grand tour that skipped the basement.

"What do you mean? Nothing. Jamil and I split up and he helped me get this place. End of story," I'd replied, avoiding her eyes.

"Bullshit, Cuz," she answered. "At Christmas you looked high. Now you look strung out."

It can be hard to lie to someone you've known since you were born. Marcie and I smoked our first cigarette together, stole penny candy from the dime store, shared our first joint. She'd gotten pregnant in tenth grade and now had a couple of kids and a really nice husband so we didn't see each other so much, but she knew me even better than Joanne. And bullshitting her was hard.

"Okay, I'm using the speed pretty regular. It's been tough with Jamil being gone. I just need to stay busy and not think about stuff."

That much was true, although "busy" was a relative term.

"Well, you don't look good," she said as I walked her to her car. "I could just kill Jamil. You be careful."

"I will. I'll be fine," I said, waving as she drove away.

It had been a long time since I'd had a drink with Mom and Aunty Ruth and Marcie, or stopped at Joe and Mamma Lea's for a beer. It had been a long time since I'd called Joanne for a lunch date, or gone with her to the clubs. It was a long time since I'd spent time with anyone other than Daniel and his cronies. I was so tired. My body felt heavy, and it had become an effort to interact with anyone, much less family. I hadn't even protested when Daniel said he was going to a wedding with Lorie.

"Have a good time," I said, almost on afterthought adding, "Jamil will be here next week. We need to clean things up, and I don't think it's a good idea that he knows you're staying here."

Daniel looked at me with a raised eyebrow.

"He's married, right?"

I shook my head. "Yeah. But for now, anyway, he's paying my bills and I don't imagine he'd be real thrilled with thinking he was supporting you too."

"Don't worry about that," Daniel replied icily. "I can take care of myself. I'll come back tonight and take my things to Lorie's."

"Daniel, Daniel, wait. That isn't what I meant," I said. "I don't feel that way at all. I just don't want to give Jamil anything to be angry about."

"Yeah, I get it," he said, walking out the door as Lorie pulled up.

Now it was her turn to smirk. I plastered on a smile and waved as she drove away with Daniel sitting beside her. Bitch. I felt sick inside, thinking of Daniel being at her place for a week, or maybe more. What if he didn't come back?

He had to come back. The lab was here, and she lived in an apartment. He'd be back. I'd be fine.

I was ready for him every day, but Jamil still hadn't called a week later. I'd looked at the lab after Daniel left with the intention of cleaning it up, but there was too much I could mess up. I locked the door and figured I'd keep Jamil out of the basement. The rest of the house was spotless.

I called Daniel at Lorie's mid-week. I was nearly out of speed. He was still holding from the last batch and said that I could come over.

Lorie was at work when I got there. She lived in a cute little apartment off a busy shopping street. I heard Daniel say "Come in" as I walked up the steps.

"Hi," I said. "Thanks for letting me come by."

"No problem," he said from the couch, rolling a joint. "Do you want to sit?"

I sat next to him, careful not to be too close or too far away.

"I'm sorry about the other day. I didn't mean to upset you, but I need to think of my bills and the money."

Daniel looked at me as he licked the rolling paper and twisted the joint closed.

"I understand, Annette," he said. "I was projecting some old shit onto you, so no problem. When can I get back to work?"

I smiled, and once again thought that he was just about the coolest guy I'd ever met, and how he loved me as much as I was beginning to love him. As he put the baggie of pot back into the cigar box he used for his stash, I moved towards him, running my hand up his chest.

"I've missed you," I said, kissing him, first pecks and then long and deep.

"I guess you have," he chuckled, kissing me back as he placed the stash box on the floor.

I climbed on top of him on the small couch and began to move, pleased at his erection.

"This isn't working," he said, with one leg on the floor.

I got up and looked towards Lorie's room.

"I don't know," he said, but I continued to kiss him, my hand now inside his jeans, the other unbuttoning my blouse. I wasn't wearing a bra.

He gave a little moan and said, "Screw it," and we moved to her bed, still kissing, pulling off our clothes.

Afterwards, we lay facing each other and he reached for a cigarette.

"You are a bad, bad woman," he said, laughing gently.

"I am," I answered, "and you'd better believe I'd kill you both if you ever brought her to my bed," a little surprised by the chill in my voice.

"You're going to need to look at these double standards of yours," he said, still lightly, but not laughing. "You're going to get yourself into a lot of trouble or get really hurt one of these days."

I brushed him off. I had a moment of vague unease that let me know he was right. But I was certainly not equipped to look at my inconsistencies. Not while I was lying, wet with sex, on another woman's bed with the boyfriend we shared.

Daniel came back to my place later that night. I showed him how I'd camouflaged his things in the spare room closet, just in case Jamil did some kind of inspection when he visited. The basement was another story. Daniel needed to get up and running, but we needed to be able to break it down quickly when Jamil showed up. We would lock the door, but I didn't want to be in the position of locking it with an active reaction in process. Sanity would have said to wait until Jamil had come and gone. A dwindling supply of dope said otherwise.

So, Daniel got back into the groove. This had been our first real argument, and we made up for it during breaks in the lab by having sex in the basement, on the carpeted stairs going up to my room, the couch, and up against the wall in the kitchen. We'd always been hot, but now we sizzled. Brandy came by and we rode with her to a guy's house in Estacada to pick up some glassware. On the way, Daniel sat with me in the back seat so that I could give him a blow job. Brandy cackled as she drove and said she wished it were her doing the honors.

Back at home later that evening, we'd ended up in bed for what seemed like hours.

"Gotta take a break, babe," Daniel laughed at one point, extracting himself to grab a beer from the little fridge.

"Give me that," I said, grabbing the cold bottle to hold against my sweating neck.

Propped up with pillows, Daniel said that he had something he'd like me to try. "Have you ever injected heroin?" he asked, tipping back the beer.

"Uh, I think you know that I never shot up until I met you," I replied.

"Heroin is my first love," he said, with obvious affection. "You might like it. It can really enhance sexual pleasure."

Now he had my interest, but still, heroin?

"Maybe" was as far as I would go.

As crazy physical as we were during that time, hopped up on methamphetamine and our own natural chemistry, the lab was sacred. Daniel never even kissed me in the lab. We barely talked while he was working. Sometimes I would sit on a stool and cut aluminum foil into strips, to be soaked in lye and mercuric chloride, and one time he let me adjust the nearly finished product by adding hydrochloric acid with an eyedropper until the Ph was compatible with human blood so that it wouldn't sting going in your arm. I was sent to the grocery store to buy lye, or rubbing alcohol, and sometimes I'd clean up and leave a little bouquet of flowers on a shelf. Mostly I sat quietly and waited. Waited, waited, waited for my chance to sample the product or to get Daniel upstairs and to bed. It sometimes took days.

The process in the lab had finally wrapped up at about 6:00 in the morning a few days later. By 9:00 Daniel and I were both flying off the new batch and he was packaging goods to go. Robert knocked on the back door an hour later.

"Hey pretty lady," he said, stepping into the kitchen. "Let me know if you ever get tired of this clown," his head motioning towards the basement, "even if it's just for a night."

I laughed, "Okey-dokey."

In one move, Robert was next to me at the sink, his hand rubbing the back of my neck.

"I'm serious, Annette. Daniel and I have often shared, just like you're sharing with Lorie. You just let me know."

His mouth was close to my ear, and he spoke softly, but without whispering. An electric current shot through my body.

"What have we here?" Daniel asked, walking up from the basement.

"You better keep an eye on this one, brother," Robert said, dropping his hand and turning towards Daniel. "I was just letting her know how it was in the old days when we were just one big happy family."

"Well that was then, my friend," Daniel answered.

They continued the banter about sharing girlfriends, which I'd been vaguely aware of from conversations with Daniel. I searched both their voices for clues. Was Daniel upset? Was it a joke? There was little doubt in my mind that Robert was serious, but how serious?

Daniel left us alone in the kitchen for just a moment while he grabbed his jacket. He must not be too worried. I wouldn't leave my girlfriend with someone like Robert if I were worried. I continued to wash dishes, but feeling Robert's gaze, turned to look at him. He was standing against the opposite counter, arms crossed, looking at me with a smile.

"I am serious," he said again, just as Daniel came in.

Daniel walked over and gave me a long, hard kiss. "So am I," he whispered.

Daniel never kissed me in front of his friends. I'd commented once on how he never acted like we were together when we were around people he knew, especially his women friends.

"Keeping my options open," he'd laughed, but I knew he meant it. So what was this bullshit with Robert? He chided me for having double standards, but this seemed pretty close to one of his own. I was glad that he didn't want me sleeping with his friend, but Robert's comment about Lorie stayed with me.

The next day I drove to my bank in the Hollywood District. Coming back, I thought I saw Jamil drive by in the opposite direction.

I had to get cash to Daniel so kept driving, but bolted into the house when I pulled up.

"Daniel! I think I saw Jamil. I'm going out to the condo," I yelled as I ran down the basement stairs.

"Are you sure that's a good idea?" he asked, looking up from the scales. "He'd probably call if he was ready to see you."

"You'd better clean up here before you and Robert leave, and lock the lab," I answered as I bounded back up the stairs and out the back door.

As if I'd just sit home. I was sure it had been Jamil. It wasn't his car, but there was no mistaking that profile. I'd know him anywhere. Jamil, my love. Why hadn't he called? How long had he been here?

My mind raced as I drove to Hayden Island. What would I say? Would he be happy to see me? As I rounded the Safeway and headed towards the condo, I panicked. What if that hadn't been him? I slowed down.

The same black car I'd seen was in Jamil's parking space. I parked, then ran to the door and knocked, holding my breath. I could tell that someone was looking through the peephole. I tried to smile.

Jamil opened the door.

"Oh, it is you," I said, out of breath and barely holding back my tears. "Why didn't you tell me you were here?"

"This isn't a good time, Annette," Jamil said, holding the door nearly closed.

Through the gap, I could see Tim Collins and another man sitting on the couch with an open briefcase. My lip trembled.

"When will it be a good time, Jamil?" I was whining but couldn't stop. "I miss you so much. I just want to talk and spend some time together."

His eyes softened.

"I'll come to your house later. In a few hours."

I was so happy. "I'll make you dinner," I said.

"We'll see," he replied. "I have to go."

The door shut, and there I was, alone on the step, the man I loved not three feet away. I turned around and stood against the wall for just a moment, my heartache overcome by a racing mind. So much to do.

I careened into the parking lot of the grocery store, stopping at the pay phone on my way in. I tried my house and then Robert's. No answer. Lorie? No, I didn't want her to know that Jamil was back. I dialed Brandy's number.

"Brandy? Thank God you answered," I said breathlessly. "Have Daniel and Robert been by yet?"

"No. I wasn't sure when they were coming over. Are they out and about?" she asked, voice raspy from years of cigarettes and yelling at her dogs.

"Yeah, they're on the move, or will be soon. Listen, this is important. I need you to let Daniel know that Jamil is here and will be at my place later. Can I use you for messages?"

"Yeah, sure," she said, "but you know Daniel—he doesn't stay in one place for very long."

I hesitated. "Well, just ask him to leave word with you where I can reach him. I don't know when I'll be able to call again."

I hung up and hurried into the store, picking up chicken, vegetables and a can of garbanzo beans for hummus. I picked out two bottles of white wine and some nice cheese and red wine for after dinner. The meal would be perfect, with everything that Jamil liked.

It was early. He had said a few hours, which would mean at least 6:00, more likely 7:00. After unloading the groceries, I opened all the windows in the house to fade any lingering smell from this last batch of dope. Going to the basement, I lit candles in glass jars, making a mental note to check on them in an hour. The smell of the lab was powerful at times. Someone who didn't know wouldn't know what it was, but it was definitely something that couldn't be overlooked. We'd had fans going all night, so it wasn't too noticeable, but I wasn't sure if that was just because I was accustomed to it. I sprayed air freshener just in case.

I decided to do a once-over house cleaning. Maybe I should do a hit of speed first, so I wouldn't run out of steam. Actually, I should wait until after Jamil came and went. He didn't need to see me with saucer eyes and fresh tracks.

But now the debate was on, and once I'd gotten to the point of wondering whether or not I should shoot up, the shooting up always won. I tried to talk myself out of it all the way up the stairs and into the bathroom, sitting on the closed toilet, opening up the bathroom drawer, pulling out the works. Don't do this. Just wait. You don't want Jamil to see you high. Fuck it.

It was getting harder and harder to find a vein. It sometimes took a good hour before I was successful, and I frequently wasted a hit before I found a vein I could use. Daniel had told me about saving my "blood hits," for cleaning later. It was pretty disgusting, and I hadn't admitted to him I was doing it, but I had a little jar of bloody dope in the freezer. Each time I added to it I told myself I should throw it away, but it was full of good speed. One of these days I'd wash it up like he'd told me about. It was my own blood, I reasoned.

I hadn't told Daniel that I'd tried shooting up in my breasts either, where the blue veins showed through like back roads on a map. I'd used the big veins on the sides of my torso too, and once in my thigh, though that had gotten nasty and looked like it would leave a scar. Brandy knew someone who worked for a vet and had passed on some antibiotics. She was turning out to be a friend.

I searched my arms and the backs of my hands. I hadn't been using very long, not much more than a year, but many of my veins had already retreated in self-defense. I decided to go between the breasts. It wouldn't be so obvious if Jamil were paying attention to my arms. I made the hit a little short since the rush from those veins was intense, as in knock-you-on-your-ass intense, as in direct-to-the-lungs intense. It was interesting how different veins had different feelings. With the veins in the sides of my stomach, and in the thigh, the lung rush was slightly delayed. I could actually feel the speed travel up through my body. In the chest, it was "blam!" right now.

With my hand over my left breast, I held the skin taut and stuck in the needle, drawing blood from the shallow pierce. Slowly I pushed in the plunger, watching the speed enter my bloodstream just inches from my heart. Immediately I breathed out a blast of hot air. Dizzy, I sat on the closed toilet, savoring the lightheaded euphoria. Dear God, make it last. My neck was rubber, too weak to hold my head. I let it drop to my chest, putting a hand out to touch the wall for balance. I took long, deep breaths with my eyes closed, opening them now as I raised my head. I chuckled. That was a good one.

As my sense of balance returned, I meticulously cleaned the counter and hid the works in one drawer and the stash in another. I had a small bag of syringes underneath my mattress. I took the few I'd kept out for immediate use and placed them inside tampon wrappers, inside the tampon box, another trick that Brandy had shown me. That worked really well for carrying an outfit in your purse or pocket.

The house was already clean. I was aware of not getting caught up in a tweak, like the time I'd cleaned every inch of grout in the bathroom with a toothbrush, but moved through the rooms with a vacuum, emptying ashtrays of Daniel's brand, throwing stray cotton swabs into a drawer. Scanning the living room, I picked out an old soul album to play when Jamil got there, something we'd listened to together a thousand times. I couldn't wait to see him.

I made hummus, grinding the garlic with lemon juice in the blender before adding tahini and garbanzo beans, just like Jamil had taught me. I kept a few beans out and added them to the finished dish with some parsley as a garnish, streaming a little olive oil over the top like he preferred. I squeezed more lemons for the chicken, mentally going over the spices I'd need. Jamil cooked from memory, only rarely calling his mother for directions, ingredients shifting depending on what we had in the cupboard, or how much he'd been drinking. I threw in a little of everything: cumin, red and black pepper, cardamom, turmeric, lots of garlic and chopped vegetables.

I glanced at the clock. After blowing out and hiding the candles in the basement, I put the barely marinated chicken parts and all the vegetables in a dish, covered it with foil and stuck it in the pre-heated oven.

I'd done well while caught up in the hustle of getting ready, but as I slowed down I could feel sorrow rise up from my gut. I stopped it at my throat by holding my breath. I did not want to start crying. Not now.

I showered after double-checking the oven. I didn't wear much make up these days, but for Jamil I'd at least use mascara and do my hair. I put on jeans and a loose fitting gauze shirt, lightweight so that the long sleeves wouldn't seem strange on a summer evening. It wasn't yet dark, but I lit a few low-watt lamps upstairs, moving to do the same on the main floor. Bright lights and I were a thing of the past. Dim was good.

The savory smell of roasting chicken permeated the house. I placed candles on the table and set out my good dishes. It was perfect.

As if on cue, the front doorbell rang. It could only be Jamil. Everyone else used the back door.

As I opened the door and saw him standing on the porch, so tall and handsome, his dark eyes conveying both longing and concern, I melted into the puddle I'd been trying to avoid. I collapsed into his arms before he even got off the porch.

"I've missed you so much," I cried, my face buried in his chest.

"Hey, hey," he said, trying to walk me backwards into the house. We ended up on the couch, my face still buried, though my tears were slowing. He held me, with one hand stroking my hair.

When I caught my breath, I sat back.

"Hi," I smiled shyly.

"Hi back," he said, smiling the smile that told me he still loved me. "Something smells good."

We effortlessly moved into all-is-well mode. We perched respectfully on the couch as he tossed back handfuls of smoked almonds while drinking scotch on the rocks.

"The place looks good," he said, eyeing the room. In contrast to the "I only live here part time" beige that he'd kept the condo, I'd painted the walls pale blue with navy trim around the fireplace. No river view, but it was peaceful, with a bushy palm in one corner, and a mirrored screen in the other to camouflage an empty wall.

"Thanks. It's home, I guess."

My lip trembled.

"Jamil, I miss you so much. I wish we could turn back the clock."

He took a long swallow of scotch, leaving nothing but ice, then reached and took my hand. "Let's just have a nice evening," he said.

All right. Nice evening. I would try.

He lit the candles on the dining table, and followed me to the kitchen to bring out dinner. It felt like it had felt hundreds of times before, except that now he was married to another woman and I was sleeping with my dealer.

Jamil exclaimed over the hummus, tender chicken, and the perfectly cooked rice. Warm pita, a salad and dish of Kalamata olives and feta rounded out the table.

"All that's missing are the grape leaves," he joked, referring to the time we'd stuffed one hundred grape leaves for a party.

We sat at the table talking about his brothers, the business, the weather, drinking faster than we ate. I tried diligently to stay in the mode of civilized ex-girlfriend, but I didn't feel like an ex-girlfriend. As far as I was concerned, Jamil was cheating on me with his wife. I was his woman and always would be.

We finished one bottle of wine with dinner and opened another before I cleared the table, piling dishes on the kitchen counter. Turning to take the empty plates Jamil handed me, I looked him in the eye.

"Jamil, please tell me one thing. Would this marriage have happened at some point anyway?"

He shook his head and was quiet a minute before answering. "I don't know, Annette. Maybe. Maybe not. She's a good woman. You'd probably like her."

"Oh, please don't. I can't even begin to have that conversation," I countered.

Jamil wasn't being a shit. He seemed genuinely thoughtful. But I wanted to pretend that the actual wife was some sort of cutout figure, a paper doll in a hijab, not a living, breathing and possibly nice woman wearing jeans and shopping at the mall.

"I said it before, Annette," Jamil said, his accent more pronounced now that he was living with family and slurring ever so slightly from the drink, "you'll always be my best friend. I'll always love you."

I moved into his arms, a feeling so comfortable and familiar that I couldn't imagine another woman in my place. We kissed, and I led him upstairs to my room, with the dim lamps now casting a soft glow. We undressed and I lay down, motioning for him to join me. He sat on the edge of the bed, leaning over to kiss me. As he sat back up, his eyes moved towards my chest.

"What's this?" he asked, his finger tracing the inside of my left breast.

"I don't know, a scratch from the cat I suppose," I said, moving to pull him towards me again.

"Wait a minute. What is that?"

Jamil stood up and turned on the bright overhead light as I reached to pull up the sheet.

"Is that a bruise?" he asked, uncovering me.

I didn't say anything. Fuck. Why hadn't I checked?

"Annette. Look at me," he said, desperate anger in his voice. "How did this happen? Did another man do that to you?"

"Jamil, I . . . I"

He grabbed one of my arms. There were several small bruises on the back of my forearm and down near my wrist.

"Do you think *this* is sexy?" he asked, yelling now.

"Jami, please. It's nothing."

"I don't believe you," he said, pulling on his pants, then shirt. His hands shook as he tied his shoes.

"I thought we could have a pleasant evening. I thought that you wanted to see me, and you come to me like this?"

I was crying, sheet pulled up over my knees. Tell him. Tell him the truth. Tell him it's the needle.

But I didn't. I let the man I cared so much about walk out of my house believing that the bruises on my body were from some man mistreating me. I was willing to protect my drug use at his expense. I couldn't admit to him that I was strung out, and strung out bad. Until that moment I'd been unable to fully admit it to myself.

I rocked on the bed as I heard his car door slam, hugging my knees. Without any real strategy, I pulled on the clothes I'd left in a pile by the bed and ran down the stairs. I grabbed my purse and keys and sat for a minute behind the wheel to catch my breath before pulling out of the driveway. With one eye on the road, and one on the rearview mirror, I drove towards the Island, grateful for the nearly deserted double lanes on the highway, hoping to catch him.

Jamil's car wasn't in its spot at the condo. Shit. I hadn't thought that he might not come here. I sat, fingers drumming the steering wheel, then drove back the way I came. At the now familiar pay phone in the grocery parking lot I dialed Joanne's number with a coin from the car ashtray.

"Joanne? It's me? Have you seen Jamil?"

"Girl, do you know what time it is?" Joanne asked. "Both of y'all are crazy. Yeah, he's here, downstairs talking to Anthony, about what I don't know and don't want to know. I do have to go to work tomorrow, in case everyone forgot."

I let her rant, breathing with relief.

"Don't let him leave. I'm coming over," I said, barely waiting for a reply.

"As if I could stop him," she answered, hanging up before I could say anything else.

Joanne and Anthony only lived a few miles away. I was there in ten minutes, mind racing the entire drive. I needed to tell him the truth. I could see Jamil and Anthony in the living room through the front window as I parked. Joanne was in the hall doorway in her long blue robe, arms folded across her chest.

I knocked, hearing her say, "It's Annette. Open the damn door."

Anthony opened the door, reaching to hold the screen. He shook his head as he let me in.

"Could we have a minute?" I asked, looking from Jamil to Joanne to Anthony.

"You can have the rest of the night, at home, as far as I'm concerned," Joanne said. "I'm going back to bed. Don't wake me when it's over."

Anthony looked to Jamil. "Are you alright, man?"

"Yeah. Yeah. I'm fine," Jamil answered, not yet looking at me.

I sat next to him on the couch after Anthony walked to the kitchen. I put my hand on his and took a deep breath.

"Jamil. Please listen to me. I'm so sorry I didn't tell you the truth. The bruise wasn't from a man. It's from the speed."

He looked at me and pulled away his hand.

"What are you talking about?" he asked, sounding drunker than when he'd left my house.

I let out a long breath, and raised my sleeve.

Here. See the bruise on my wrist? It's from the needle."

Jamil shook his head from side to side, touching where I'd pointed, pushing the sleeve up further.

"And on your chest?" he asked.

"Yeah. There too."

He closed his eyes and sat back on the couch, leaning his head against the cushions. He was quiet for what felt like forever. Finally, he reached to finger his mustache like he did when he was upset.

"Have you gone absolutely mad?" he asked, finally opening his eyes to look at me.

I didn't have an answer. How do you explain something that you don't understand yourself? What I did instead was defend. I talked calmly about our drinking and the cocaine and how this was just another venue. I talked about my pale skin that bruised easily, and how efficient I was around the house, searching for a logical explanation. He wasn't buying.

"Listen to yourself, Annette," he said, shaking his head. "This is bullshit. You are addicted and your life is a mess and that's all there is to it."

"Addicted is a pretty strong word," I said. "I think I have a handle on it. You'll see. I'll be fine."

He paused. "Well, you'd better be. I can't go on supporting this. I care about you, and I'd never see you suffer, but this can't continue. Not on my bank account."

"Oh Jamil," I said, trying hard not to cry. "I will be fine. You'll see. I so appreciate all the help you've given me, but just a little while longer and I'll be able to be on my own."

Doing what, I had no idea. Hell, I sometimes had a hard time getting out of the house. What was I going to do for work?

I hadn't realized that Anthony was standing in the kitchen doorway until he spoke. "You know, Annette, my new pastor had a pretty tough past. He'd be a good guy to talk to if you wanted some help with this thing."

"Thanks, Anthony, but I'm doing okay," I said, with less conviction than weariness.

"Jamil?" I said, turning to him. "Can I follow you home?"

He looked from me to Anthony and back again. I noticed a bottle of scotch and an empty glass on the end table.

"Okay."

He weaved as he stood up.

"Are you okay to drive, buddy?" Anthony asked.

Jamil waved him off and walked out the door.

"I'll call you tomorrow," he said over his shoulder from the porch.

As I left, Anthony shook his head at me, like he'd done when I came in "You need to get yourself together, Annette," he said quietly as I walked out. "For his sake if not your own."

"Good night, Anthony. Sorry to keep you up."

Jamil's sake? What about my fucking sake? Nobody was thinking about me when he went off and got married. Did anyone stop to think that maybe I wouldn't be in this situation if Jamil had stayed in Portland and married me?

For the time being I would go home with Jamil and he would remember that he loved me and everything would be fine. I would think about getting a job, and I would lighten up a little on the speed and it would all get figured out.

I followed Jamil out to Hayden Island, glad that the streets were quiet as I watched his rental car wander from the left lane into the right and then back again. I stayed far enough behind to keep an eye on him without getting in the way. As we exited on to the Island he slowed, fairly creeping the final bit to the condo. We parked side by side and he nearly fell up the parking lot curb, slumping against the doorjamb while he fumbled with his keys.

"Come on, sweetie. Let's get you upstairs," I said, pushing him from behind in an attempt to keep him upright.

He was wasted. I led him to the bedroom where he half-sat, half-fell on to the bed. I got his jacket and shoes off and maneuvered him onto his side, shoving a pillow under his head. Grabbing a light blanket from the hall closet, I covered him, kneeling by the side of the bed with one arm around his chest.

I wasn't tired. At all. I decided to run by Lorie's, and then maybe home. Jamil would be out for hours. I'd be back.

I wound my way to Lorie's apartment over side streets. The lights were on in the living room when I pulled up. Strolling up to the porch as if it were the middle of the day, I lightly tapped on the screen door.

Lorie answered, in her waitress clothes.

"Hello, Annette," she said, very politely. I didn't ever think she was glad to see me, but she always acted like she was.

"Hi. Sorry to bother you, but is Daniel here?"

Daniel walked up behind her and out on to the porch.

"We'll just be a few minutes," he said.

Lorie hesitated. "Look, it's late," she said. "Come on inside."

I tried to be as nice as her. I really did. But I always felt a little sick to the stomach when the three of us were in the same room, like I'd just gotten kicked and was about to be kicked again.

"Cool," Daniel replied, stepping aside so that I could enter.

It was a sweet 1950's apartment, with a decent-sized living room that opened directly into the kitchen. I sat at one end of the couch as Lorie walked towards her room.

"I'm going to take a bath," she said with a slight glance at Daniel.

He sat on the one easy chair, and then moved to the couch beside me as the bathroom door closed behind her.

"You got my message?" I asked, after I heard the water running.

"Yes. We got to Brandy's shortly after you called. How was your visit?"

Daniel had a way of talking out of the side of his mouth when he asked a question. I waited until he looked at me before I answered.

"It was okay. He figured out that I've been shooting tons of dope and that didn't go over so well."

"What did you expect?" he asked, this time looking me in the eye as he spoke.

I disintegrated when he looked at me like that. He could be arrogant, and I didn't trust him any further than I could throw him with his one extra girlfriend and who knows how many others, but I was still drawn to him, even when I was watching my life fall apart. Especially when I was watching my life fall apart.

I moved closer on the couch and put my hand on Daniel's chest. I don't know what I'd expected from Jamil. That he'd welcome me with open arms. That he'd tell me his marriage was a sham. That he'd say it had all been a mistake and that I should move back to the condo the next day. My drug use hadn't figured into my fantasy at all.

"Annette." Daniel took my hand and placed it in my lap. "Not here. Not now."

God, he could be a bastard. I was sure he'd rather be in the tub with his Lorie, but I wasn't going to give up so easily.

"I miss you." I whispered, knowing it wasn't exactly true.

He let out a short burst of quiet laughter as Lorie turned off the water.

"You miss me when I'm not there but don't like me much when I am."

"Oh God, you know that's not true," I whimpered. "I've just had a lot on my mind lately. You know how much I care for you."

He reached up and cupped my face in both hands.

"I'm not sure whether that's the truth, or if you just don't want to be alone."

"But I'm alone all the time," I protested. "Jamil was always gone, and so are you."

He smiled and shook his head. "That's not what I mean."

I knew what he meant, and he was right, though I could only partially acknowledge it to myself. I just never had been by myself; it wasn't that I couldn't be. From my parent's home, to Eddie, to Jamil and now Daniel, there had always been an anchor, a steadying force. I was aware that Daniel was more of a sail than an anchor, but he was the person who let me say that I wasn't alone.

We both looked up as the water in the tub started to drain.

"You'd better go now," he said, standing up. "You should have enough speed to last you a few days."

I did. I had more than enough, plus a vial full of used cottons.

Daniel walked me to the door and out onto the porch. I put my arms around the small of his back and drew him into me, kissing him long and hard.

"Annette, Annette," he said, gently pushing me backwards down the steps.

"Can I call you here?" I asked.

"Yes. After 12:00 is best," he answered, turning to go back into the apartment, to Lorie fresh from her bath, wrapped in a towel.

Noon was when she went to work.

"Bye," I said, smiling sadly over my shoulder.

I drove home, leaving the car in front rather than pulling into the driveway. I sat after turning off the engine, making sure that lights were out in the neighboring houses. I didn't know the people on either side, other than to wave as we went in or out. That was fine with me. I walked quickly up the driveway and through the side door. Without turning on a light, I tiptoed through the dark kitchen and up the stairs.

Just a small hit of speed, to get me through to morning, just a little one. To hold me over. I weighed out less than a dime with the little green scale. I went through the ritual of mixing it with water, rolling the cotton ball, drawing it up. No matter what I told myself, this was really more about the kick than the energy, so I skimped on the water in order to get more of a jolt. The process hadn't yet ceased to fascinate me. I looked for a vein, finding a potential on the back of my forearm.

I got it on the first try. That was unusual, but I certainly wouldn't fight it. Push it in fast so I can feel it. Exhale. Yes, that's it.

I stole into the guest bedroom in the dark and opened the closet. Daniel's wing tips were still there, in their paper bag. I smiled, confident in his return.

Going back to the bathroom, I puttered in the drawers for half an hour. I was just about to start cleaning under the sink when I realized that it was dawn. I had to get back to the condo, pronto. I fed the cat and shut the door, grabbing the paper off the front porch as I went to the car.

Nothing interfered with my drive. I pulled into my parking spot, like I always had, and reached for the key that I'd taken off Jamil's ring. Closing the front door ever so softly, I took off my shoes and tiptoed up the carpeted stairs into the bathroom. I scooted out of my pants and top, leaving a small pile next to the tub.

Mimicking a yawn just in case he was awake, I stole into the bedroom, but Jamil was in the same position as he'd been when I left. I went quietly to the other side of the bed and gently let myself down. I stayed there quietly for a few moments before working my way under his blanket.

He stirred as I put an arm over his chest.

"Where have you been?" he mumbled, pulling me closer.

"Way over here on the other side of this king sized bed," I lied, "waiting for you to wake up."

"Give me a minute," he said, rolling on to the floor. "Shit. I am so hung over."

"I've got just the cure," I answered.

"What, a drink?" he asked, stumbling towards the bathroom.

I heard the toilet flush, and water running in the sink. He came back naked, with damp hair and smelling of toothpaste.

"Come here," he said, getting back into bed.

It was so good to make love with Jamil. We knew each other so well, anticipating and responding to the other comfortably. I looked him in the eyes as we kissed, then closed them against the vision of the wife and his new life without me. For just those few moments I wanted to believe that our love was as strong as ever. Afterwards, we lay side by side, holding hands. He turned towards me, reaching up to brush away the tears that streamed down the side of my face.

"Hey, none of that," he whispered.

I smiled, but kept my eyes closed. He leaned over and kissed me on the forehead, then rolled over.

"I have to meet with Tim and another guy a little later about that project in Reno," he said. "I'm going to sleep a little more. Tim will be picking me up here."

"I'll be gone before you're awake," I said, running my hand along his torso and down his thigh, memorizing the feel of him. "Do you need anything before I go?"

But he was already asleep or pretending to be. I left a glass of water and a note on the bedside table, telling him how much I loved him and hoped I could see him again before he left. I wrote down my phone number and signed it with the funny little face that I'd always used on our notes and letters. As I closed the condo door behind me and pulled out of the driveway, I thought about doing more speed, a decent-sized hit this time. I might wait another hour or so, but maybe not.

Chapter Twelve

I WAITED THREE days before phoning Joanne at work.

"Hi. Sorry about the other night," I said.

"Ya'll are crazy is all I've got to say," she snapped back, the click of typing in the background. "So what *are* you going to do?"

"I didn't know that I had to do anything," I replied.

Joanne was usually behind me all the way, no matter how crazy or timid or half-assed my decisions. I wasn't used to her questioning me, though it had been happening more and more.

She sighed on the other end of the phone. She'd been a little distant since she and Michael broke it off, but I had just chalked it up to me spending most of my time with Daniel and not calling her as often as I used to.

"You're going to think I'm the crazy one," she finally said.

"What do you mean?"

"I've been going to church with Anthony," she said sheepishly. "I'm not sure about all the whooping and hollering, but I'm kind of thinking that I want my marriage to work."

"Wow," I said. "This is new."

"Yeah, well, there's something else. I'm pregnant."

"Oh my God. Pregnant? Are you sure it's not Michael's?"

She laughed. "Yeah, I'm sure. That's all I'd need is to pop out a little white baby, probably smoking a joint."

I laughed with her and offered my congratulations, though it felt odd. She'd always said that she didn't want kids to tie her down until she got older, and certainly not religion. Would Joanne as a church-going, pregnant, truly married woman still be my confidante and the ringleader

150

of our two-woman circus? Could she still be my friend? The part of me that was shooting dope on a regular basis was just a little relieved that she was occupied with something other than my habits.

I didn't see Jamil again before he left later that week, though he called from the airport. There was heaviness in his voice that reminded me he wasn't just going back to a lovely wife, but to the pressures of his uncle and the rest of the family. I felt angry and responsible at the same time.

I called Daniel as soon as I hung up the phone, double-checking the time. It was 12:05. I arranged to pick him up in two hours, giving him time to gather his things and break down the beginnings of a lab he'd started in Lorie's bathroom.

When I got there, I let myself in after a quick knock. Daniel was at the kitchen table with a man I didn't recognize. They barely looked up

"We'll be done in a minute," Daniel said.

It was odd; he always made a production of introducing me to his friends. My breath caught as I noticed a pistol on the counter. The man, who looked Native American or Latino, with a black ponytail and copper skin, gave me a slight nod as he left, putting on sunglasses before walking out the door. I looked back and saw that the gun had left with him.

"What was that all about?" I asked.

Daniel didn't respond immediately, still working on whatever was on the table, his back to me.

"That was a new connection," he finally answered, turning in his seat. "I bought some chiva for you to try."

I must've looked puzzled.

"Heroin," he said, "Black tar, Mexican. I thought it would make a nice homecoming."

I nodded, though my stomach did a flip. Since he'd first mentioned the desire that I try it, I'd learned from him and through bits of conversations with Brandy and Robert that Daniel had been strung out for several years before he went to jail. That was part of what got him arrested, getting sloppy while using the heroin, and was the real reason that Diane had broken it off with him. She'd been strung out too at one point but got clean and didn't want any part of him loaded on smack.

I didn't understand heroin. Brandy said that she didn't get it either, but both Robert and Daniel talked of it in alternating loving and disgusted tones. It was soothing, it was a killer; it was satisfying, it would

151

steal your life away if you let it. I wasn't sure I wanted to try it, but I was curious. What I didn't know at that point was that Daniel and Lorie had been using regularly for a few weeks.

He was agitated on the way to my house, pointing out where I could cut in front of other cars or where I might turn to avoid a light. As soon as we got inside and took the glassware downstairs and some clothing upstairs, he asked if I was ready.

"Ready for what?" I asked, standing at the kitchen sink.

"To try this," he answered.

It was the middle of the day.

"I'm nervous," I said, walking to join him at the table.

He looked at me from beneath the errant curl that never strayed far from the center of his forehead and said, "It will be fine. I'll make sure that you're safe."

It was that simple. He would keep me safe. This ex-con meth cook who borrowed money and my car, who left for days at a time, would keep me safe. What did that mean exactly? I'd felt safe with Jamil, though certainly not Eddie, and truthfully, I was on my own more than not with Jamil. Maybe I was the one keeping myself safe. In that case, I would trust that Daniel wouldn't let me overdose today. It was that simple if I didn't think too hard about it. I'd become very skilled at not thinking too hard about anything other than my next fix.

Daniel got out the usual works, along with a kitchen spoon that had seen better days, and a lighter, and proceeded to melt the heroin into a liquid while the heat cooked out any impurities. He measured a small amount out for me and wanted to watch while I shot up.

"I don't know," I said. "It sometimes takes me a while. I don't think I want you watching all my poking and prodding."

He took my wrist in his hand and turned my arm over and back again. Scabs and bruises dotted the backs of my hand and on up my arm.

"What a mess! Where have you been going?" he asked.

"My hands mostly," I said and hesitated, "and a few times between my breasts."

His expression saddened as he looked at me and shook his head from side to side.

"Annette, Annette. What have I done? Let me look."

I was still for a moment, taking in the bookshelf stacked with Middle-Eastern and Indian cookbooks that sat behind Daniel, and the calendar with photos of the Oregon Coast on the wall. I unbuttoned my shirt, showing him the small scar to the left of center between my breasts. He ran his finger over the spot.

"It's not like this is your fault," I said, buttoning back up the shirt. "I'm an adult. I know what I'm doing."

He chuckled. "Yeah, right."

Now it was his turn to be quiet. He looked at both my arms, and then took my face in his two hands as was his habit. He looked on the verge of tears.

"You need to be careful. Really careful. Not just with the veins in your chest, but with this whole deal."

I laughed. "Now you tell me."

We sat in silence for another few minutes. I'd like to say that I reflected on where I'd been and where I was going, but mostly I just sat.

"Hey," I finally said. "I'll be fine. I am fine. Are you going to let me try this stuff or what?"

Daniel cocked his head and gave me his half smile. "Yes, let's go ahead," he said, handing me a piece of rubber tubing. "I'll do you. Tie off your left arm."

This was sweet, and reminded me of those long months ago when we'd first met and I lived to feel the touch of his fingers on my inner arm. This time he stroked the forearm and the back of my hand, and then the back of my forearm.

"I think I can hit this," he said, tracing the vein that went from the outside of my wrist up towards my elbow.

I'd used it myself a few times. Positioning my arm for his access was a little awkward, but it worked.

I waited. The rush was different than with the speed. I felt dizzy and like I wanted to throw up.

"That's good," he said as I told him. "Having to vomit is good."

Good for who, I wondered, as I tried to relax into the sensation. After a few minutes, the nausea passed and I could feel myself drifting. I wasn't asleep, but I wasn't awake either. It was like I wasn't quite real in the world, like I didn't quite exist and it didn't matter.

Daniel smiled. "My turn," he said.

I sat there, thinking that maybe I should respond, but not having the energy or the interest to open my mouth.

I watched through my fog as his head dropped nearly to the table.

"Are you okay?" I asked.

"Shhhhh" was all he said.

We sat at the table like that for what seemed like an hour. At some point he suggested that we go up to bed. We each undressed slowly, very slowly, then lay down beside each other.

"What do you think?" he asked, facing me.

"I'm not sure," I answered.

We made a half-hearted attempt at having sex, but at some point must've passed out. When I woke up, it was dark, and he was still out cold. I tripped to the bathroom, pulling out my stash of speed. Fuck this, I need some zip.

I guess there are some people who prefer downers, but I was definitely not one of them. I can sleep on my own time, thank you. Daniel had given me some Quaaludes a month or so earlier, again on the premise of enhanced sex. I was out like a light. Ditto with codeine. I'd try just about anything but realized that I didn't like hallucinogens and I sure didn't like downers. Give me a solid upper any day.

Over the coming months, Daniel drifted more and more into the heroin. I'd find him nodded out over a plate of speed in the basement, the hot plate on. I sent away for a tiny ear alarm advertised for truckers to keep them from falling asleep on the road, but he wouldn't use it because he liked the nod. I was concerned about my house burning down.

I went to the basement less and less, telling myself it was too far to go just to see Daniel loaded. In truth, I was becoming more and more paranoid, and found myself worried about who I would find downstairs. It was getting easier to simply stay in my room. We rigged up a little dumbwaiter through the laundry chute. Daniel would bang on the furnace pipe, which meant I could pull up on the string of twine from the second floor to find a small bottle of crystal attached. I was becoming a self-contained unit.

Daniel started keeping even odder hours, and the people who came to my back door were stranger and stranger, with a hint of danger that I hadn't seen with the speed freaks. I posted a sign:

> No coming or going between 3:00-6:00am
> If you are here at 3:00, you will need to stay until 6:00.

That had its drawbacks too. Brandy and a couple of women came over one night at 2:00 and at 7:00 the next evening, were still there. I called Daniel upstairs to my bathroom.

"What the fuck is this, and when are they leaving?" I said, pointing into the bathroom.

He let out a slow whistle as he looked and saw blood in thin streams on the counter and the mirror.

"That Brandy is a messy one," he said. "I'll get her to clean up. They should be going soon."

I'd taken to sequestering myself in my room when he had people over. I was pissed off a lot of the time, at Daniel, at the heroin, at Joanne for abandoning me. Because I'd become vocal about disliking people at my house, Daniel stopped taking me with him to his friend's. That was fine with me.

The exception was Robert. We stopped there one night to borrow a piece of glassware and found him in the basement with a syringe taped to his left forearm.

"I got a good vein and don't want to lose the motherfucker," he laughed.

Robert had also started using lots of heroin. I liked him better on speed. On speed he was cocky, sexy, funny. On heroin, both he and Daniel were muted, slow to react. When they laughed, it was at some private joke.

I came down to the kitchen one morning after a few hours of sleep, waiting for my first hit of the day until I got something in my stomach. I was good about regularly drinking a protein shake and having a piece of whole-wheat toast. I took vitamins too, in an effort to stay healthy. Most days I convinced myself that it was working.

I gritted my teeth against the sound of the blender as I added a banana and three scoops of protein powder to a cup of milk. I blended in some honey and poured the mixture into a tall glass, then walked over to toast some bread.

I was brought up short. There was a gun on top of the toaster. A fucking pistol on my toaster.

I had always been adamantly anti-gun. Eddie's parents had a gun in the house, and once or twice it came out during a drunken argument. I knew that most people who were killed with guns were killed by people they knew, and I knew that me and mine drank too damn much to be trusted with loaded weapons in the house. I had very few bottom lines, but this was one of them. And here I was staring at it, bottom line, black and shiny, on my toaster.

I walked over to the top of the stairs and listened into the basement. I thought I could hear Daniel talking with someone, though sometimes I wasn't quite sure anymore. No, this was definitely a conversation, and they were moving closer to the stairs.

I stepped back towards the sink and took a long swallow of the shake to calm my empty and now jittery stomach. Daniel came up first, followed by the Native fellow who had been at Lorie's house. Again, there was no introduction, just a slight nod and an "I'll see you later man."

The guy started to open the back door, hesitated, then walked around to pick up the gun. He looked at me as he lifted his sweatshirt and stuck it into the waistband of his jeans. I didn't say a word, nor did he.

When he was gone, Daniel turned and smiled. "Good morning. I thought I heard you up here."

He was loaded on heroin. I could tell by the way he bent slightly at the waist as he talked to me, scratching the side of his face, his smile more vacant than focused.

My stomach flipped as I spoke. "I'm really not okay with guns in my house Daniel."

He made an attempt to stand up straight and brushed the curl from his eyes. His hand moved to the side of his mouth as he spoke. "Don't worry about it. It was one gun, for twenty minutes."

"That's not the point. I don't like the idea of people who have guns coming over," I countered, my voice rising with conviction.

"Jesus, you are so damned uptight," he said, turning around to make his way slowly back down the stairs.

He was fucked up. I could see that. I could also see that this might not be the best time to have this conversation. But over the next few days, we did have it, several times.

Me: "I don't want your friends at my house."

Him: "Fine."

156

And so, Daniel was there less and less. He rarely slept with me anymore but would come and go in the middle of the night straight to the basement. A few times I went down to visit with him, like I'd done when he first set up shop, but our conversations were strained, and he frequently took phone calls while I was there. One time as I was walking down the stairs, I heard him say, "I love you too" before hanging up.

"Who was that?" I demanded.

"Lorie. Why do you ask?" he said, his back to me.

'You just told her you loved her?"

He turned to look at me. "And?"

My lip quivered and I turned to go back up the stairs. I had realized that I didn't love this man, but I sure didn't want him loving someone else. Where did that leave me? What about all his concerns about not putting casual words into the universe? What about that?

He left soon afterwards.

I was alone, a lot. I sat in my room, or my bathroom, searching for veins, shooting speed. It was taking longer and longer, sometimes over an hour for one hit. And then I'd tweak in a closet or venture down to organize a kitchen cabinet or go through a drawer. Any trace of normal activities was dwindling fast. I rarely saw my parents for more than ten minutes at a time.

I tried heroin a few more times over the next months, thinking it might grow on me. One time Daniel fixed me up when I got cotton fever, an achy feeling that felt like cramps in my bones. It came from shooting up impurities, dirty speed, and the belief was that heroin was the cure. The fever passed, but whether or not it would've on its own, I had no idea. I simply spent the day half asleep in my bed, vaguely aware of summer sounds in the neighborhood—a screen door slamming, an ice-cream truck tinkling, the crack of a bat during a street game.

Mostly I didn't like what heroin was doing to Daniel. Despite our early, fascinating conversations there had always been a distance between us, but he was now drifting further away. I found myself yelling at him, telling him that he needed to stop the heroin. Just like I'd done all those years ago when Johnny had suggested that I cut back on my drinking, Daniel told me to mind my own business.

Once he did try to quit, sort of, but after two nights of wringing wet sheets and his moaning and screaming from my bed I said, "I've got cash. Make your fucking phone call." I drove him to an apartment in

Southeast with a bag between his legs in case he threw up, rocking in the seat against the cramping. As much as I'd come to hate the heroin, it was worse seeing him like this. No one should be in so much pain. I waited outside in the car for nearly an hour, slumped in the seat, nervously watching any cars that passed.

He finally came out, head down as a shield against the bright sunlight. He said nothing as he got in beside me. I pulled away, staring straight ahead.

"Move to the left," he said, an edge of desperation to his voice. "You're bumping too much in the curb lane."

I looked over to his lap. He held a lighter to the bottom of a spoon that contained a tiny bit of the black tar and water.

"Can't you wait until we get home?" I pleaded. There were cars all around us on the busy street.

"No."

I kept one eye on the road and the other on him as he tied off and injected the dope.

"Slow down," he mumbled. When I did, he opened the car door to vomit into the street.

He shut the door and sat back. Inhaling hard against my gag reflex, I watched the relief move through his body one muscle at a time. We said nothing the rest of the way home.

From then on, Daniel used the heroin full time. He was away more than he was at my house. I'd stopped loaning him my car and had stopped listening for the back door to open in the middle of the night.

One afternoon when he'd uncharacteristically been at my place for a few days, I came into the kitchen from upstairs and heard his moan from the basement. Running downstairs, I found him passed out behind the bar. That overdose was a turning point. I really didn't want him dying in my house. Within a week he moved out.

I called Joanne.

"He's gone," I said.

"Who?" she asked, as if there were hundreds of people with clothes in my spare bedroom closet. Church hadn't made her any less of a smart ass.

"I asked Daniel to leave," I replied, suddenly very tired.

"Well, as fine as he is, I could see that that man was no good from the beginning," she said.

Now she tells me.

"So, what are you going to do?" Joanne asked.

I hesitated. I knew that, just like when Jamil got married, she was hoping I'd get straightened out, and give up this mess. But to me, "what are you going to do" meant "where will I get my speed?"

"I don't know what I'm going to do," I answered and excused myself from the phone. The last time I'd called, she'd started up on the Jesus stuff. Not forceful at all, but telling me how much better she was feeling about herself and life now that she'd found the Lord. Part of me was glad she was taking care of herself for the baby, but it was like I didn't know her anymore. And I certainly didn't need any lectures.

What I needed was some dope. Daniel had left me with about a week's worth, if I stretched it. I was nearing the end of that, and had already beat the hell out of my cottons, cleaning the solution through glass filter paper that I'd grabbed from the lab works as Daniel was on the way out. I wasn't yet at a point of desperation, but my stash was dwindling. I called Daniel at Lorie's. We hadn't necessarily parted on angry terms. What he'd told me was that he couldn't live with rules, and while he respected my right to an opinion, it was merely that—my opinion. It seemed like a lot of bullshit to me, the heroin talking. But, I was getting annoyed with people at the house and him missing for three days with my car and the cigarette burns on my couch, so I let him go without an argument.

Lorie answered the phone. I checked my watch. She must be on a new schedule.

"Hi Annette," she said, recognizing my voice. "Daniel isn't here. He's been at Sandy's for a few days."

Sandy. Sandy. Why couldn't I place Sandy? Oh shit. Sandy was a woman who hung out with the heroin people. She was tall, with dirty blonde hair and faint acne scars on her cheeks.

"Is he working over there?" I asked. "Do you have a number?"

He was and she did. We kept our conversation short and to the point. I called Sandy's.

"Hi. I'm trying to get a hold of Daniel. Is he there?"

"Who's asking?" The voice on the other end was raspy and coarse.

"This is Annette. A friend."

I heard the phone being set, not so gently, on a table and someone walking away. A door opened and closed. I waited.

I was about ready to hang up when Daniel came to the phone.

"Annette. How are you?" he asked.

"I'm good, Daniel. It would be nice to see you."

He paused. "I'm pretty tied up for the next few days. I don't have anything you might want, if that's why you're calling."

"That's not the only reason," I said, "but any suggestions on where I should look?"

"Robert, or that friend of Brandy's would be the obvious choices," he said, his voice taking on a slightly tense tone.

"Good idea. I'll call Brandy." I didn't want to acknowledge to Daniel that I'd rather call Robert.

This time it was my turn to hesitate. Despite our differences, I still considered Daniel my boyfriend, and I wasn't yet ready to call myself single, though single is exactly what I was. Single with complications. Single with a habit.

"I would like to see you, Daniel," I said, my voice softening from business to girlfriend. I was sure that he missed me too.

"I'll call you in a few days," he said.

I heard the raspy voice calling his name.

'I have to go. I'll talk to you later," he said, hanging up before I could say goodbye.

I barely hesitated before calling Robert, arranging to go to his place later that evening since he said that he didn't want his uncle to be around when I came over. I'd never seen the uncle or any evidence that anyone actually did live upstairs, but I'd play along if it meant my connection.

I dawdled around inside the house for the rest of the day, dusting furniture, killing time. I couldn't spend too much time in the yard without feeling like an alien. I was sure that all the neighbors were looking at me through closed curtains, whispering that there was something wrong with me.

I wandered around the main floor, avoiding the basement. I didn't like going down there, especially now that I was alone. It gave me a creepy sensation. Like in the yard, it felt like someone was watching me. The kitchen was pretty safe. My bedroom and my bathroom were the safest, though sometimes getting from one to the other was risky. My world continued to shrink.

I dressed carefully to go to Robert's. I hadn't been alone with him since the time he'd come on to me in the kitchen. I knew I was walking a fine line by going to his house but I wanted what he had. Maybe I wanted more.

It was after 10:00 when I pulled up. I parked and walked up the driveway to the side entrance. Robert answered my quiet knock almost immediately, as if he'd been waiting right inside the door. His hair was wet, like he'd just showered, and the tendons on his neck stood out as if he'd been clenching his teeth for a year. It looked to be crystal methadrine, not heroin that was coursing through his veins.

I like guys with an edge and Robert was razor-sharp. Small and wiry, his weren't jailhouse muscles. He'd been in Viet Nam and prison twice, and had a tattoo of a woman on his upper forearm that moved when he flexed his muscles. Most of the speed cooks I'd met through Daniel had the drawn look of men who were tough and didn't eat much, and Robert was no exception, though the sparkle in his dark eyes offset his normally hard expression. I'd spent a lot of time secretly looking at him when he and Daniel worked together in my basement, or when I'd spent hours waiting in his.

And here I was, alone with him, pissed off at the fact that Daniel was at Lorie's, or Sandy's or wherever he was, curious to see if he was still interested.

"Pretty lady," Robert said, motioning for me to precede him down the basement stairs. I could feel his eyes as I walked in front of him. As we neared his area, he reached in front of me to open the door, brushing against my arm.

I moved towards the chair where I usually sat, but he directed me to a stool at the card table where he'd been measuring out the dope.

"You can sit here," he said, gesturing.

"Ah, the big people's table," I joked.

I was feeling a little cocky, a little reckless

"How much do you want?" he asked, putting his hand on my shoulder, running it slowly down my arm.

"As much as you want to give me," I countered, catching my breath.

It felt like someone else was talking or like I was an actor in a movie.

He tilted his head. "You know how much I want to give you," he said, his hand resting on mine.

"Let's finish the business part of this," I said, as I slid my hand from under his to reach for my wallet.

He counted out the bills as I tucked the quarter bag into my purse.

"Do you want to try some?" he asked.

Of course I wanted to try some, especially if it was some of his and not some of mine. He mixed up a strong hit from the pile in the dish.

"Will you help me?" I asked, remembering how good it had felt to have Daniel stroke my arm, and not wanting to fumble around with my lousy veins in front of him.

Robert looked at me. "Daniel told me you were using the veins in your breasts."

I took a deep breath before answering, "Yeah, but that's not what I had in mind."

Robert didn't take his eyes off mine but took both my hands in his. Finally, he looked down, moving each arm around and up and down, seeking a viable vein.

"You need to lift some weights," he said as he had me clench and un-clench my fist, finally having me reach up and grab the back of my neck, looking for the vein that went up the back of my upper arm. "This is one you can't really do yourself."

He wasn't as polished as Daniel, but he got a vein on my forearm after two tries. He slammed the plunger and I almost immediately felt the heat move through my body. I was dizzy, but not in a bad way.

I sat on the stool with my eyes closed, slightly wavering as the speed settled into my system. I felt Robert behind me, his hand on my shoulders.

He leaned over and spoke into my ear.

"Relax into it. Enjoy the ride."

I leaned back into his chest as his hands massaged my shoulders and moved forward down my chest. He spun me around on the stool so that I was facing him.

"Stand up," he said, his hands still on me.

I did, drawn into the sensation.

"Do you want me?" he asked, brushing my lips with his.

I nodded and opened my mouth to kiss him.

He was rough. His kisses were strong and hard as he gripped the back of my head and worked his tongue inside my mouth. I tried to relax into it, to enjoy the ride, but wished he'd slow down.

He backed me towards the bed and pulled my shirt over my head. I wasn't wearing a bra.

"Beautiful," he said, stroking my breasts. "Take off your pants."

I complied, and he held me as I went back onto the bed. He'd taken off his own pants and now climbed on top, entering me without any formalities. Suddenly I was scared, and wanted to be somewhere else.

He noticed that I was crying and slowed his motions.

"What's wrong?" he asked.

I sniffled. "This isn't right. I shouldn't be doing this."

"You're kidding," he said, resuming his thrusts.

I turned my face away and waited for it to be over. What in the hell was I doing here? It surprised me that he came fairly quickly, moving out of me and off the bed in the same motion.

I was still crying quietly as I sat up and reached for my clothes. I was stunned when he raised his hand, back-handing the side of my face.

"Don't you ever pull that, with me or anyone else," he said gruffly. "That 'I want it. No I don't' bullshit. Fucking take what you ask for, bitch."

The shock of getting hit had stopped my crying, but now my eyes welled up from the pain as I reached to feel my face. There wasn't any blood, but he'd hit me hard enough to have broken the skin on the inside of my mouth. I put on my jeans and shirt without looking at him and walked to the table to grab my purse, making sure to not turn my back.

"Oh get out of here," he said with a measure of disgust in his voice. "I'm not going to hurt you."

I walked quickly towards the door where Robert caught up with me, jeans on but no shirt. He put out his arm to block my way up the steps.

"If Daniel gets word of this, I'll come looking for you," he said, looking me in the eye.

"It's okay," I said. "No problem."

"We're cool?" he asked, dropping his arm to take my shoulder.

"Yeah, yeah, we're fine. I'm sorry for flaking on you," I said, keeping my voice calm.

I managed a weak smile but averted my eyes, walking up the stairs at a normal pace, no rush, no hurry.

Thank God I only lived a few miles away. My hands shook as I held the wheel, driving up the dark back streets to my house. I'd gotten myself into situations with men in the past where I wished I could turn the back the clock and put my clothes back on but never before had I felt in danger. It's okay. It's okay, I repeated to myself over and over, flinching at the shadows cast by trees and buildings as I drove home.

My hands were still shaking as I put my key in the side door. I let myself in and double-locked the screen and the door, going to the front to make sure the chain was on. I leaned back against the front door, sinking to my seat as I cried, sticky from sex, my face throbbing. The cat jumped off the couch and meandered over, rubbing against my knee. I picked her up and buried my face in her soft fur. "Oh kitty, what am I doing?" I cried.

I was scared and hurt and alone. I missed Jamil. I wanted him to wrap his arms around me and tell me that everything would be alright.

Edgy from the speed and Robert, I went into the kitchen and poured myself a stiff vodka, topping it off with some flat soda water from the back of the fridge. I held my breath against the taste. It burned going down. Why did everything that I liked burn? Maybe my choices were caustic. Maybe I wasn't doing myself any favors.

There was a rustling outside. I whirled around and saw what looked like Robert on the front porch. He'd moved away from the window as I'd turned. My heart pounded as I turned off the kitchen light and walked slowly towards the door. I glanced at the clock. It was only midnight.

I did my best to creep up to the window without making myself visible. I didn't see anyone, so more boldly looked out, right then left. Nothing, but I was sure it had been him. I re-checked the lock.

I circled the main floor in the dark, testing all the window locks and drawing the closed shades even tighter. I grabbed a couple of blankets from the hall closet, along with some tacks and made my way through the house. I secured blankets over the beautiful gray, retractable shades on the front and side windows. A prickly flowering quince outside the dining room window would keep anyone from peeking in, but I did cover the slider in the kitchen with a blanket, and the over-sink window with a large towel. I went back to the front door with another large towel and covered the small viewing window, but not before looking out. It was windy. Had I seen someone or not? I decided that I wasn't taking any chances, no sir-ee.

I grabbed another drink and went upstairs to my room. The shades were drawn there. I felt safer on the second floor, but only turned on a small, twenty-five watt lamp so I couldn't be seen from outside.

What was that? I held completely still and stopped my breath. There. It sounded like someone on the roof. Okay, that was probably a little crazy, but not entirely. If Robert was really angry with me, it made sense that he'd try to get into my house by whatever means he could.

I tiptoed to the bathroom and got out my works, coming back to the bedroom with a small cup of water. I positioned myself in the chair in the corner so that I could see everything around me, placing the drink and all my drug stuff within reach. I moved the phone closer too, though couldn't imagine who I'd call or what I'd say. The police? And tell them what? I turned the television on at low volume. After a few minutes, I turned the sound off so that it wouldn't distract me from any other noises.

It had only been about an hour since I'd shot up at Robert's, but I decided to go for it again. It was going to be a long night and I wanted to be alert. It took forever. Like over an hour forever. I couldn't get a vein and couldn't get a vein and couldn't get a vein until I wasted two hits. This sucked.

I finally found what seemed to be a vein on my thigh. By that point I was probably aiming at shadows. It stung a little going in, and there was hardly any rush, but I didn't care. It was done.

I sat still for a long time, maybe fifteen or twenty minutes. I knew I wasn't dying, but it felt like my life was passing before my eyes. I reached under the chair and pulled out the journal where I explored my situation without actually naming what was going on. The last page I'd written on was a week earlier. The script was barely recognizable as words, then scrawled off the page. I'd gone back the next day and added, "No, I don't have a problem."

I turned to a fresh page and thought about my life, and scarier, where I was headed. It was time to get honest. I wrote:

It just took over an hour to shoot up, in search of a high that became more elusive with each stab of the needle. I seem to have been on self-destruct mode since I was thirteen. What on earth could I have done before that age that was so terrible that. I have to punish myself for it on a daily basis? Where will this end?

I was completely and utterly at a loss as to what to say or what to do or what to think. I was fucked. That much I did know. Anything else, I couldn't even speculate. And so I sat, with my back to the wall, the phone within reach, a tall vodka in my hand while I waited for the sun to come up.

I did remember when Daniel sat me down and told me about the potential for hearing voices that weren't really there, but I hadn't told him that I'd been hearing them lately. They stopped right when I shot up, retreating in the heat of the rush, but they always came back. I'd ride the rush, then get into some tweak, whether rearranging the contents of the medicine chest or picking an imaginary pimple, and they'd start, just a whisper. "Annette. Annette." Or a low hum with what seemed to be bits of words that I almost understood. What in the hell were they saying?

The worst was in the grocery store, walking up and down the long echoing aisles with all those little cans looking out at me. I'd been so glad when Safeway went to twenty-four hours. There were fewer people to contend with at 3:00AM, and the folks you did see were usually just as weird (or wired) as me and tended to steer clear.

I heard them now. Was it Robert on the roof? Was Daniel in the basement with someone? Oh God, please let the day come.

The sun did come up, as it generally seemed to do, though no amount of coaxing from me could ever make daylight come or go any faster. That pissed me off, as did the need to sleep at all. There was so much to do. I was in the process of cleaning out all the kitchen cupboards and was lining them with contact paper. I'd chosen white, with a blue checked design. Getting the lines to match was no small task, but since I was alone most of the time, it didn't matter. The days all ran together. I rarely even knew what day it was anymore and had taken to looking out the blinds before answering the phone so I would know the weather. Seasons meant nothing. The passing of time meant nothing.

I made a daytime trip to the store a few days after the Robert incident. I needed milk (which had become my staple food) and candy bars and beer, and was nearly out of syringes. I'd stopped using the fake-note-from-my-aunt routine, but did put them on my grocery list, as if a box of insulin syringes merited the same attention as a jar of peanut butter or a roll of paper towels.

I made my way through the aisles, adding cat food and toilet paper to the cart. Steering towards the pharmacy, I took a deep breath and conjured a cheerful smile.

"Hi," I said to the tech, looking up from the grocery list in my hand. "I need a box of 27-gauge insulin syringes please."

She smiled back, her tight-lipped little grin looking as forced as mine felt. She said, "Just a minute," and made her way back to the pharmacist, a greasy-haired man with glasses propped on the end of his nose. He was there a lot.

I stood nonchalantly, taking a pencil from my purse to check off items on my list, all four of them. As I looked up, I saw the pharmacist peer through the little window at me, over his glasses. Without saying a word, he turned toward the tech and shook his head "no," resuming whatever it was he was doing. My stomach flipped. It wasn't illegal to buy syringes in Oregon, but the pharmacist had discretion. I was fucked.

The tech seemed embarrassed as she came back to me empty-handed.

"He said 'No'," she said, evading my gaze.

"But," I stammered, "what am I supposed to do now?"

Even I heard the desperation in my voice. She glanced back at the pharmacist, who was now out of sight. Reaching behind, she picked up a pack of ten syringes off the shelf and slid them across the counter.

"Here," she said, not meeting my look.

I paid, quickly and gratefully, slinking away to pay for my other things in the grocery line. My hands shook as I wrote out the check. Jamil was still giving me an allowance, which I knew was just one conversation with his brothers, or one intoxicated phone call away from being yanked. I was so fucked.

When I got home, Lorie's VW was parked in front. I pulled into the driveway and entered through the side door. I could hear someone in the basement.

"Daniel, is that you?" I yelled down the stairs.

"Yes. I'll be up in a few minutes," came the reply. By the sounds of it, he was in the lab. I couldn't tell whether or not he was alone.

I set the bag of groceries on the counter and took the syringes upstairs. I didn't want him to ask for any. They had to last.

When I came back down, I reached to move the sack to unpack it. I instinctively stepped back as I saw a gun on the counter. Again, a gun in my house.

I walked to the dinette table and sat down with a big sigh. Years later I would hear someone say that there came a point in his life when he couldn't lower his standards quickly enough to match his behavior. The gun wasn't mine, but the whole rest of the story was. How much longer could I explain it all away?

Daniel came into the kitchen as I pondered. He had a paper bag, filled with what I assumed was glassware.

"Hi," I said. I was surprised at how good it felt to see him, to see anyone actually.

"Hey," he answered back, softness in his eyes that I hadn't seen on the day that he'd left. He put his hand on my shoulder and held my look.

"Do you have any time for me?" I asked, reaching for his hand.

He chuckled but used his eyes to indicate the back door. I looked and noticed the same dark-skinned guy standing silently in the shadow at the top of the stairs. I could feel my lips disappear as they tightened.

"Maybe later," Daniel said, turning to walk out.

Before opening the door, the other fellow reached over and picked up the gun, again sticking it in the waistband of his jeans, under his baggy T-shirt. He looked at me without speaking, just the slight nod. I was beginning to think he was mute.

Daniel stepped back and kissed me on the forehead.

"I miss you," he whispered. "I'd like to come back."

"I'm not going anywhere," I said, closing and locking the door as he left.

Chapter Thirteen

I WAS ALONE in the basement after painting a second coat of yellow on the walls in the laundry room. I wasn't much on detail, sometimes painting over cobwebs onto the porous concrete rather than halting my progress to clean. But stepping back, I saw that it looked nice even with a few lumps, nicer than the dirty white it covered. I found myself staring, paintbrush in hand. Yes, it was time to sleep.

The phone startled me to attention. I didn't answer very often these days. But it was 3:00 AM. Only Jamil would call at this hour. I bolted up the basement steps, paintbrush in hand, lurching towards the wall phone that hung near the sliding door.

"Hello?" I gasped, expecting to hear the cracking of an international line.

"Annette? Honey, it's Mom. It's your father. There's been an accident. They think he had a heart attack at the wheel. John is on his way over to take me to St. Vincent's."

Heart attack? Accident? This didn't make any sense.

"Annette? Will you meet us there?"

"Of course. I'll be there by the time you are," I said, mind reeling. A heart attack. An accident. I'll be there.

I knew how to get to the hospital because Jamil had surgery on his sinuses there several years earlier. That had been crazy. He'd snorted coke the night before going in to have his nasal cavities cleared, and then a week later pulled out all the packing himself in order to do more lines. And he talked about my drug use? He and Joanne, and especially Anthony, all seemed to forget about our all-nighters, our snorting coke off the table tops at that restaurant downtown, our beer-for-breakfast days.

I pulled into the nearly empty parking lot and sat for a moment. Checking my reflection in the rearview mirror, I chastised myself for leaving the house without cleaning up. Running my fingers through my hair, I patted my cheeks to bring color to my face. I looked like I hadn't slept in several days. I hadn't.

Striding into the peaceful lobby, I made a beeline for the empty information desk.

"Hello? Hello?"

A stocky Latino man in a tan uniform vacuumed an area behind the desk. He looked up. "No one will be here until 6:00," he said. You should go to the Emergency Department."

Doing my best to remember his directions (left, then right, then a hard left or was it right?) I followed the long, silent hallways. Reaching the ER, I stood in line behind a woman with a wailing toddler. Hurry. Hurry.

I was given directions to the Intensive Care Unit. Oh my God. Intensive Care. I got there just as John and Mom showed up.

"How did you get up here?" I asked.

John looked me up and down. "How did you get here?" he said, then whispered "You look like shit. What in the hell are you up too?"

Mom looked like she was about to crumble to the floor. I ignored John and took her arm as we rang the buzzer to gain admittance through the locked doors.

Directed to Dad's bed, we stood silently staring at the tubes and wires attaching his body to an array of machines. He was pale, with wisps of salt and pepper hair pointing at odd angles.

"The dispatcher said that he must've already stopped the truck," Mom said quietly as she stroked his hand. "He said that the truck 'gently rolled' into a ditch. 'Gently rolled,' he said."

We stood in a semi-circle, watching the heart monitor beep, beep, beep in a steady rhythm. A bag of saline with potassium dripped through a large needle into a vein on the back of his hand. I glanced at my own flattened veins, clenching and unclenching my fist, stopping only when I noticed Johnny watching. I reached for Mom's hand.

One of the two nurses in attendance made her way to us from the next bed, a stern looking woman with what I hoped was more knowledge than bedside manner.

"Cardiac makes their rounds at 6:30," she stated, as if we should've already known. "You can't stay here that long. Wait in the lobby just outside the doors and we'll call you when Doctor has something to tell you."

Chagrined with our apparent naiveté, we silently made our way to the tastefully upholstered benches as directed.

Mom sat and closed her eyes. She folder her hands in her lap and moved her lips silently in what I assumed was a prayer. I looked away. John paced, finally announcing that he was going for coffee.

"Come with me, Annette." It was a statement, not a request.

Hands stuffed in his pockets, he strode two steps ahead of me back through the corridors towards the mostly dark cafeteria. The coffee station was open, and a lone attendant manned a register.

"There are machines in the hallway for snacks," the woman said in a heavy West African accent. "The lines open at 6:30."

"6:30 seems to be the magic number around here," I wisecracked, attempting to deflect John's apparent judgment of my appearance.

"Sis, you look like you've been through the wringer," he said, steering me towards one of the dozens of empty tables. "I used to hear gossip about your drinking. I don't hear anything anymore, and what I'm told is it's because you don't go anywhere."

"Jesus. I'm glad everyone is so interested in my social life," I snapped, adding four sugar packets and three tiny creams to my cup of coffee.

"Who is this Daniel character? Marcie thinks he's no good. I ran into Joanne at the gas station last week and she just said "humph" when I mentioned his name."

"I didn't know I needed your approval to go out with someone," I bristled. "It's none of your business."

"Oh come on, Annette." John rubbed his left hand against his barely-there whiskers, the same way that Dad did when he was annoyed.

"We need to get back to Mom," I said standing up.

Walking back to the ICU without speaking, John's vague accusations and my defiance created a palpable wall.

"Mom, I'm going home to get some sleep. I was up late talking to Jamil on the phone from Jeddah," I lied. "Call me when you talk to the doctor and I'll come back up."

Mom looked tiny and confused. I knew I should stay. But John's piercing look, and the knowledge that I was now seven hours from my last hit of speed allowed me to turn and retrace my steps back to the second level of the parking structure.

He didn't look so bad, I told myself on the drive home, and again as I climbed the stairs to my bathroom stash. He'll be fine. Mixing up a hit as I sat on the closed toilet, I looked in the mirror. Okay, maybe some sleep would be good. Carefully recapping the full syringe, I carried it tenderly to the fridge bedside table, cradling it safely in a napkin on the narrow door shelf. Stretching out on top of the covers, I was out within seconds.

I'd been vaguely aware of the phone ringing while I slept, though the ringer on the bedside phone had been turned off for months. But there it was again. Okay. Okay. I rolled over.

"Hello?"

"Where in the hell have you been?" It was John. "It's Wednesday afternoon, for God's sake. You went home at the crack of dawn on Tuesday."

"How's Dad?" I mumbled through my guilt.

"Going in to surgery. They're going to do a double-bypass in the morning. Marcie took Mom home a few hours ago to rest. You need to bring her back up here. Now."

"Okay. Okay. Get off of my back. I'll be there."

Damn him. Damn all of them. Why couldn't Marcie take Mom back and I'd go later? Damn it.

Reaching for the pre-mixed syringe, I made a fist over and over. Holding my right wrist tight with my left hand made several small veins stand up. I tied a fabric belt that I'd picked up in Mazatlan with Jamil right above my wrist bone. Breathing deeply, I flagged the vein below my index finger on the first try. Yes. Adjusting the position of my hand, I balanced the needle while untying the belt. Very carefully I held the needle with my left hand and injected the serum. That's it.

The rushes were changing; not as intense as when I'd first started shooting up. I'd been making my hits strong, with a lot of crystal and just a little water, filling the entire outfit with barely enough room for the tip of the plunger to stay in. It made hitting awkward, as I stretched my finger span to be able to push the needle in without yanking it out of my hand, or arm, or breast. But different was still good. While not exactly jolted awake, I came to attention, taking a quick shower before dressing and heading to Mom's.

She came out of the side door as I pulled into the driveway, looking even tinier than when I'd left the hospital.

"I was watching through the front window," she explained as she fastened the seat belt. "What took you so long?"

I knew this was more of an "I'm scared, let's hurry," statement than an actual request for information, so I remained silent. I'd gotten pretty good at knowing what people meant even if they didn't say anything. It was almost like I could hear their thoughts.

"Annette? I asked if you'd told Joanne?"

"Sorry. I was concentrating. No, I haven't talked to Joanne. I'll call her later."

Joanne, Joanne. I hadn't talked to her more than once or twice since she'd told me she was pregnant, and those very brief conversations had been stilted.

"What are you up to?" she'd ask.

"Nothing much," I'd reply and there'd be nothing else to say. Nothing else to say to the friend who used to know my every thought.

I was conscious of Mom speaking, but only random words made sense. Surgery. Long recuperation. Union steward. Insurance.

Dropping Mom at the entrance, I parked on the same second level, now full of vehicles and daytime traffic. Making my way down the stairs and into the lobby I followed Mom's scribbled directions to the Cardiac Unit to find her, John, Marcie, and Aunty Ruth huddled on plastic chairs around a small coffee table.

"They said I can spend the night," Mom beamed. "I want to be with him before he goes in to surgery."

John explained that Dad had been conscious earlier in the day. Said he wasn't scared, but looked it. Everyone else looked scared.

"Do you want to go in Annette?" Mom asked, taking my hand.

"Maybe he's asleep," I stammered, wanting to go anywhere but into his room.

Mom walked me down the hall and into his double room. There was no one in the second bed. His eyes were closed, and his hair had been slicked back.

"They took him off oxygen?" I asked.

Before Mom answered, he spoke. "Yeah. They said that's the one thing I'm doing okay at."

"Oh Daddy." I cried as I took his free hand.

"I'll be fine," he said as gruffly as a person could say from a hospital bed. "I want you kids to take care of your mother."

Dropping his hand, I stepped back. "Of course we will. Don't worry about anything. Mom, I'm going back to the lobby."

Making my escape, I was relieved to see that the others had left, presumably to the cafeteria. I sat, then paced, then sat again as Marcie appeared with a carrier full of coffee cups.

"Coffee? Tea? Hot chocolate?"

I laughed. "No thanks."

Marcie tilted her head as she looked at me. "You look pretty rough. This must be really hard on you. I can't imagine how I'd feel if something happened to Mom."

"Yeah, I could barely sleep last night," I lied. "So John said that you didn't have very nice things to say about Daniel," I prodded, prompted by her apparent belief that I was tired, not high.

She stammered. "Well, I didn't exactly say anything bad. You know I've only met him the once when I came over. But truthfully, Annette, he seems a little shady. Granted, he's a looker, but sort of scary. He just doesn't seem like the kind of people we usually hang out with. Joanne said he's a dishwasher or something? How does he afford that MG he was driving?"

"Here's your Mother," I said, turning to hug Aunty Ruth. After a few minutes of commiserating I excused myself.

"I'll be back tomorrow for the surgery," I said, already walking away. "Tell Mom I love her."

I heard John call my name, but I didn't turn around.

I was nearly out of dope and hadn't been able to reach Daniel since before Dad's accident. It would be easier to beat my cottons instead of trying to track down a supply at this point. Bringing all the works to the kitchen table, I poured the saturated end bits of cotton swabs from the miniature jam jar where I stored them into a small, clear ashtray. Dry now, but previously soaked with methamphetamine, they would yield at least two tenths of a gram, if not more. Adding distilled water from a syringe kept for just that purpose, I used the loose plunger from yet another needle to press the dope out of the cotton. When the liquid had

174

become suitably viscous I poured it through a small circular glass filter placed in a funnel in order to remove any stray cotton strands or other impurities. Then, as if it were a new batch, I poured the liquid into a glass dish and heated it on the stove, waiting to watch the magic as it thickened and began to dry.

The phone rang just as I took the plate off the burner. Tempted to ignore it, I glanced at the clock. 2:00PM. What day is it? I looked out the window to check the weather. Sunny. Check. I'm good. I'm okay.

"Hello?"

"Annette? Where are you?" Joanne shouted. "Your father just got out of surgery. You need to be here."

"Nice to talk to you too," I answered. "I figured there didn't need to be a bunch of us standing around, so I decided to wait." That's what I told myself anyway. I could make myself believe anything about my intentions if I said it firmly enough.

"You're full of shit is what you are," she replied, and I could almost hear her shaking her head. "Listen, I'm getting out of here myself so I won't see you. But it's Anthony's birthday this weekend. Come down to Slabtown on Saturday. Charles and some of the old crowd will be there. We haven't seen you in ages."

When did she start sounding like Momma Lea?

Without committing, I got off the phone and into the shower where I rubbed my arms and pumped my fists in an effort to raise a vein. Successful on the third try, I dressed carefully in long sleeves and now baggy jeans, trying to comb my bangs in a way that would camouflage my eyes. If it weren't for my pupils, you'd never know I used speed, I told myself, ignoring the tiny scabs on my chin where I'd spent too long picking at blackheads. I'm fine. I'll be okay. Keep moving.

Dad was in the hospital for over a week, and back at work within three months. Hard as nails, Aunt Ruth said over tinkling highballs a few weeks after that. Hard as nails.

I did go to Slabtown for Anthony's birthday, a feeble attempt at reclaiming my life, my old life. Entering the tiny club crouched nearly under the freeway, I felt like a shadow. These were not my people. This was not my scene. Not anymore. Watching Anthony with his hand on Joanne's protruding belly felt peculiar, unreal. But, she cleared a spot for me, just like always, and just like always, I played with the ice in my glass. People were looking at me. I needed to go.

A hand on my shoulder startled me so that I visibly jumped. "Whoa, Annette. Didn't mean to scare you. I'm not that bad, I hope."

It was Eddie. She hadn't told me he would be here. Was this some sort of a trap?

"Hi Eddie. How are you?" I said something else, but didn't complete my sentence. Daniel said that I did that a lot.

He looked at me quizzically, smiled, and turned to speak to Anthony. I whispered in Joanne's ear. "I'm meeting Daniel. I need to get out of here."

She seemed sad as she looked at me. "I'll walk you out," she said, getting up to follow me to the door.

Standing outside, she put a hand on my shoulder. "Annette, Annette. Where have you gone? I want my best friend back."

I opened my mouth, but nothing came out. "I'll call you," I said as I walked away, holding back my tears until I'd made it around the corner.

I was home within twenty minutes, locking the door and the double lock, making my rounds to make certain all was secure. The blankets were over the main floor windows permanently now. Peeking into the backyard, and towards the driveway, I chanted "I'm okay. I'm okay." "I'm okay" I repeated, breathless from the stair climb to my room. I settled on to my little gray chair with a comforter over my lap, scanning the room for intruders. What was that noise? It's the wind. I'm okay. I'm okay.

Chapter Fourteen

I DID SEE Daniel off and on over the coming weeks, but usually at Lorie's, or very briefly at my house. I didn't like all the comings and goings at my house, so it felt hypocritical to be hanging around with his friends. Plus I didn't like any of them all that much anyway. Mostly I just stayed at home. The weather had started to turn and the rain and the darkness intensified my feelings of desperation.

I felt backed into a corner with no way out. I wasn't sure that I truly wanted a way out, but I was aware that the walls of my house were closing in. Twice I phoned Johnny, hanging up when he answered. I briefly passed out in the kitchen after the second call. One minute I was standing with a blender full of protein shake in my hand, and then next I was on the floor, thick liquid spread around me. I dialed John again, but again hung up.

My birthday in October was marked with a small meal at my Mom's. Had it really been two years since the trip to Italy? I'd been so worried about missing the annual celebration if Jamil bought the place in Cyprus, and now it was as if my family members were strangers. My brother didn't even come over. Marcie stopped by for a beer on the way to her mom's place, looking uncomfortable as she asked how I was doing.

"I'm fine," I said, avoiding her eyes. I'd gotten really good at talking to people without looking at them. I could even put on a full face of make-up without looking myself in the eye.

"Annette," she started, then looked away.

I excused myself to the bathroom before she could change her mind about talking to me. Besides, it was time to go home. I'd shot up a few times before in my mother's bathroom but never with her there. I checked the medicine cabinet and stuck a couple of Dad's anti-depressants in my pocket, along with a couple of pain pills from when he'd hurt his back. I wasn't a pill taker, but it was good to have a stash to trade.

Days and nights were unending and unchanging. I finished painting the laundry room and did loads of wash and polished the woodwork and wrote letters to Jamil and stared out the window and shot up and then shot up some more. I hadn't seen Robert since that night in his basement and I mostly saw Daniel when I wanted some speed, or when he came over for sex under the guise of picking up something from the basement. I was alone and it suited me just fine.

The doorbell rang on a late October afternoon, a clear and cold sunny day. My stomach leapt into my throat as I moved aside the towel that covered the window and saw Jamil. I opened the door and fell into his arms.

"Oh God, it's so good to see you," I cried.

He held me against his chest for a few seconds before taking me by the shoulders and moving back a step.

"Marcie is with me" was his greeting.

Only then did I notice my cousin standing off to the side.

"Can we come in?" she asked.

"Well, sure, of course," I answered, perplexed at the formality.

We sat in the living room. I was surprised to see the two of them together. Surprised that Jamil was in town and hadn't let me know he was coming. Surprised at how good it felt to see them and how funny it felt to be interacting with people.

We engaged in a smattering of small talk. "How long will you be here?" "How is the family?" Jamil cleared his throat.

"Annette, I'm here because I'm concerned about you."

"We're both concerned," Marcie added, leaning forward with her elbows on her knees.

Here we go, I thought, smiling politely.

"Annette, we've arranged for you to get an evaluation. At a treatment program. We think you need help."

What were they saying? What did this mean?

"We have an appointment this afternoon for you to meet with a counselor," Marcie continued. "She'll make her recommendation after she talks to you."

Jamil pulled out his trump card before I could say a word. "Annette, I can't go on supporting you this way. You need to get help or find someplace else to live and a way to pay your own bills."

My eyes filled with tears. I had a hundred arguments why they were both wrong. Why I had this under control. Why he should still support me. And I used them all. For the next thirty minutes I pleaded and whined and cried and did my best to convince the two of them that my life really was all right. There was no lab in the basement. I rarely saw Daniel or his group. I was merely adjusting to life without Jamil and it was taking longer than I'd hoped.

But they held firm, though they each cried as they countered my arguments.

"You don't care about me," I finally cried out, collapsing onto Jamil's lap. He firmly pushed me aside and stood.

"Come on, Annette, it's time to go."

I was scared. I didn't want to move out of my house, and I was tired, incredibly tired. I let him lift me by the elbow and lead me to Marcie's car. I sent her back for my purse and keys.

"Jamil, how can you do this to me?" I asked when we were alone. "Why can't you just come home?"

He looked at me with sadness and pity. I turned away and closed my eyes, opening them only when we parked behind a brick building in northwest Portland. Walking through a tasteful lobby, they guided me into an elevator and then to a room where a woman in a business suit sat behind a desk. What could she possibly do for me?

I was reluctant to answer her questions about how much I used, how often and with whom. I knew that I couldn't pretend to not be using anything, but I cut the amounts in half.

"A gram lasts me about a week," I lied, trying to imagine what would be a reasonable amount of methamphetamine consumption.

"Can I see your arms?" the woman asked, what I took to be fake concern in her voice. I didn't trust her.

I lifted the sleeve of my left arm slightly to show minimal bruising. I rarely injected in my left arm.

"You know," this woman continued, dripping sympathy, "I am a former IV drug user myself. I understand."

Bullshit, I thought. You've never even seen a fucking syringe.

She continued, telling me that based on what I'd told her, I was chemically dependent and needed in-patient care in order to detoxify. They had a bed waiting. What had been pissing me off now set me into a panic. Stay here? Now? No. No. Not now. Not ever.

I argued. I had my cat to think of and bills to pay and hadn't packed anything and needed to talk to my mother. I couldn't possibly stay now. Again I pleaded and whined, this time laced with anger.

Finally, the woman looked at Jamil.

"Are you alright with this?" she asked him. "If she comes back tomorrow?"

"The day after tomorrow," I said. I had things to do.

"Annette, this is serious," Jamil said.

For the first time I really looked at him. He looked exhausted and his eyes were sort of puffy. He'd lost weight.

"I'll come back on Thursday. I promise."

Marcie opened her mouth as if to speak, then sighed and looked away. I was free, for another day at least.

None of us spoke on the way home until we turned on to my street.

"I'll set things up with my brother tomorrow," I said, looking out the window.

"If you don't, I will," Marcie fired from the back seat.

Jamil reached across me to open the door. "You don't have too many choices at this point."

"Jesus Christ. Don't threaten me," I said, getting out of the car.

"I'll be here on Thursday at noon to pick you up," Marcie said, moving to the front seat. "Let me know if you need me to do anything tomorrow."

"And you, Jamil? Will you be here?" I asked, speaking through his closed window.

He rolled it down an inch. "I'm not sure," he said, avoiding my gaze as he pulled away.

I had no doubt that Marcie would be back promptly at noon the day after tomorrow. I also had no doubt that Jamil meant what he'd said about my choices. I was pissed that he'd threatened me financially, but it had worked. I didn't want to be out on the streets or back at my mother's house.

I tried to reach Daniel first, leaving messages at several of his known haunts. Actually, the first thing I did was shoot up, trying not to imagine going without. Other than two days when Jamil had held me captive the previous summer, I hadn't gone a day without speed in close to two years. And those two days had been horrible. I literally could not lift my head off the pillow and when I finally did, I was ravenous and irritable beyond reason. What would it be like to go through that now, after all this time?

What did one pack for detox? Miss Priss had said to not bring much. I threw a couple of T-shirts, some pajamas, an extra pair of jeans, a toothbrush and a tube of hand lotion into my overnight bag. I didn't intend to stay long.

I went through the mail that had been sitting on my desk for two weeks, organizing piles of what needed to be paid and what could wait. Checking my bank balance, I saw that October's deposit had been made on schedule. Jamil hadn't cut me off, yet.

I phoned Joanne. "Hey stranger."

"Hey yourself. And how was your day?" She already knew.

"Well, how do you think it was?" I asked.

"So . . . great. You're going away?"

"Yeah, away to northwest Portland," I said. "It really makes me mad that Jamil is throwing his money around at me and making threats."

"Money or no money, you need to get your ass some help," she replied. "It's not the end of the world. You just go on and do it. Lord knows you've been through worse."

I couldn't think of anything worse but was unable to muster the energy to argue. I hung up after a curt "good bye" and tried Daniel again at Brandy's, Sandy's and Lorie's with no luck. I puttered around the house the rest of the night while waiting for the phone to ring, watering plants, packing and re-packing my bag, picking my face, hiding a stash.

The next morning I called my brother and told him I needed to come see him at work. He looked worried and a little nervous when he met me on the loading dock. A private guy, it probably bothered him that the other fellows saw us talking in the middle of his shift.

"What's up?" he said, looking past me to my car.

"I'm alone," I said. "Look, I need your help. I've developed a bit of a drug problem and Jamil is sending me to detox for a few days. I need you to feed the cat and check on the house."

"What are you talking about?" he asked, looking at me with a furrowed brow.

"Well, as you've suspected, I imagine, I've been using crystal meth for a little while now, and Jamil thinks it's gotten out of hand. I'm just going to take a little break."

He hesitated, peering at me. "Is that what was going on at the hospital? Is that why Marcie called me the other day? I didn't have time to call her back."

"Yep, I would imagine so."

I tried to play it off as no big deal, a minor annoyance. I didn't offer details. Communication was not my family's strong suit and I didn't intend to start now. On the other hand, I knew that I could count on John for anything. I handed him a key and told him I'd call in a few days.

As I turned to leave, he asked, "What about Mom?"

Shit. What about Mom? "I'll call her from there," I said, not intending to.

As I walked away, John came up behind me. He took my arm and turned me back towards him. "Are you sure you're okay?" he asked.

My eyes filled with tears. "Yeah, I'm okay, little brother. I'll be okay."

I left before he saw me cry.

I never did actually talk to Daniel, though I did tell Brandy where I was going and asked her to pass it on to him.

"Shit. Are you kidding?" she asked. "How long will you be gone? My cousin was away for six months and came back talking about Jesus."

"Whoa. Not six months. And no Jesus," I assured her. But truthfully, I had no idea what I was getting into. I was more concerned about the trouble I was trying to get out of.

Marcie showed up at 11:59. I'd just done a huge hit of speed, stashing the leftovers in a small container at the bottom of a cereal box in the kitchen. Just like Daniel had taught me, drugs and chemicals and needles and glassware are hidden in oatmeal boxes or syrup bottles or at the bottom of a laundry hamper. He'd always said that nothing was as it appears. He'd meant people, but it applied across the board.

I didn't wait for Marcie to get out of the car but grabbed my overnight bag and locked the door behind me. The cat was fed, a light was on. Everything would be fine and I'd be home soon.

We drove silently. I hoped that a bridge would be up, anything to delay our arrival, but within fifteen minutes we were parked and in the lobby. Miss Priss appeared out of nowhere. She pointedly looked at Marcie and asked her to walk with us to the unit, as if I was going to make a break for it.

We rode the elevator in silence to the third floor. Marcie hovered for a few minutes and then left with a brief hug as I was escorted to a room. There were two beds but neither was occupied. It looked like a regular hospital room.

"Most of your preliminary paperwork has already been done," Miss Priss told me. "This is a detox room. Because you have been using so extensively, we will want to monitor your vital signs for a couple of days. The doctor will order some Librium to help you sleep."

I didn't like pills, but at that point I was open to anything. Miss Priss Robot Woman handed me a hospital gown and told me to disrobe and get in bed. A nurse would be in shortly to get my blood pressure and labs.

I laughed. "I should have brought my notebook. I've got a blood pressure cuff at home and sometimes we take our pressure after we do a hit of speed."

Her lips got thin. "The nurse will be in."

This woman had no sense of humor. The blood pressure thing was fun. One time mine topped out at 190/90. Another time, Daniel shot heroin into one of his arms while I shot speed into the other, and then we took his pressure. We were going to measure it after an orgasm but never remembered until later.

I undressed, leaving on my panties under the flimsy gown tied in back as directed. I climbed into the hospital bed, noting the metal railings. I tried to raise or lower the head with the various levers and buttons, but nothing moved. I sat for only a minute, then went to my overnight bag. Taking out a spiral notebook and a pen, I climbed back into bed.

My handwriting had gotten sloppy and intense. My letters had shrunk and I crammed lots of words onto one line, sort of like I talked. Daniel had recently pointed out, again, that I wasn't speaking in complete sentences. I tried to be conscious of that but sometimes felt the words floating away. I concentrated on what I was trying to write.

Dear Mom and Dad,

I am writing this from the hospital, from the detox unit. Jamil and Marcie have sent me here to take care of a problem with drugs, which has gotten worse since Jamil got married. John will take care of my cat and the house. I'll call you when I can, but I don't expect to be here long. I love you both and I'm sorry if I'm a disappointment to you.

Love, Annette

I crawled back out of the tall bed for an envelope and stamp from my bag, addressing and sealing it before I had time to think. I knew this would shock my mother.

Heaving myself back on to the bed, my foot twitched as I waited for the nurse. I was still amped from the hit I'd done before leaving the house, though I yawned as a woman with glasses and a brown suit walked in.

"I'm June, from the business office," she said, pulling up a chair. She had a clipboard with a stack of papers on top.

"Hello June," I answered. At least this was something to do.

She ran me through a stack of paper: A Consent to Treat, with an assurance that there would be no experimentation without my knowledge, and a financial responsibility form, even though I told her that I wasn't paying for this.

"It's fine," she said. "You have insurance. Now who should know that you're here?"

"Anyone who needs to know that I'm here already knows that I'm here," I answered.

"Sorry. I mean, you're protected by confidentiality laws. No one can know anything about your being here unless you give permission. Who needs to know what is going on with you while you are here?"

That was a loaded question. I didn't want them talking to anyone about me being here. I was here. Marcie signed, sealed and delivered me. What else was there to know?

I gave her my brother's name. He was the one person I knew I could still trust. The woman pointed out that without a signed release they'd have to deny I was there at all. I gave her Jamil and Marcie's names too.

After a few more forms, I lost interest and simply signed. Ms. June left, giving me a rueful little smile. *Save it,* I thought.

I wandered to the window and looked out at northwest Portland. God, here I was, just feet away from the street and access to any amount of drugs I wanted. What was I doing here? This sucked. Jamil was an asshole, and so was Marcie. God damn it anyway.

I climbed back into bed just moments before a nurse came in. She looked to be about 20, chubby and cute in pj scrubs, a perky smile on her face.

"Hi!" she bubbled. "How are you doing?"

"Great. Wonderful."

She introduced herself as Debbie and asked a bunch of questions about my medical history. I was healthy as a horse, save this minor problem and a healing abscess. I didn't smoke, had never had surgery, no major illnesses. There was nothing significant other than Dad's recent heart attack.

"I'm going to need to get some blood so we can check your liver function, among other things," she said, reaching into a brown plastic basket for a syringe and some tubing.

"Good luck," I said, watching as she perused both my arms. She tried my right arm, and then my left, going where I knew she wouldn't have any luck. She tied and untied the tubing around my arms, tracing what might've been veins but weren't.

"You know, I could probably do that a lot easier myself," I said.

"Really?" she asked. She hesitated, then handed me a fresh needle. It felt odd to have someone watching, but I went for the vein in my forearm, not quite "Old Faithful" but generally responsive, until now. I started to try again, but she stopped me.

"Maybe this isn't such a good idea," she said, taking the syringe from my hand. "I'll see if there is a phlebotomist available and come back later."

I sighed as she left the room. Within a few minutes, yet another person came in, this time a man in a white lab coat.

"Pharmacy," he announced, rolling a small cart. "Two Librium, coming up. Any allergies?"

Shaking my head, I took the small paper cup he offered and emptied the pills into my mouth. I swallowed them dry and he left, whistling.

I lay back, waiting to feel something. Please let me feel something.

I awoke to someone putting a tray of food in front of me. I was barely able to sit up but managed a few bites of bland meatloaf and mashed potatoes before lying back down and closing my eyes. The next memory is of a semi-darkened room, another nurse, more pills in a paper cup. I sat up to swallow.

There is very little like an amphetamine crash, unless it's a cocaine crash, but with speed it is deeper and with an intensity that borders on comatose. I was out for hours and hours, with only vague recall of different faces with more little white cups. The few times I did wake up, my head was like cement. I would have burned to death had there been a fire.

After days of nothingness, my head began to clear. I made it to the bathroom and sat up for a meal, devouring everything on the tray, wondering where I might get more. As I swabbed up gravy with the last bite of a dinner roll, a guy came in and pulled up a chair beside the bed.

"You're Annette?" he asked.

I looked at him.

"Sorry. I'm Mark. I'm a patient on the unit. I just came over to welcome you and invite you to come over for group."

I pushed the food tray away and fell back on the pillow.

"I can barely move," I said, surprised that I could speak. "I'm not going anywhere."

He sat a moment longer, but I'd closed my eyes.

"Well, I'll be back tomorrow," he said. "We'll see you soon."

Like hell, I thought, drifting back to sleep.

The sun was still up, or maybe it was again, when I next opened my eyes. Miss Priss herself was back.

"Hello, sleepy head," she said.

I didn't answer.

"You've been in detox for four days now. It's time for you to move over to the unit and join the program." She was smiling but in a way that didn't look at all happy.

"What program?" I asked, sitting up. I was feeling better, but didn't want her to know that.

"You'll be learning about your addiction, in group and individual therapy as we help you to explore ways to stay clean and sober. There is a group starting in forty-five minutes and I'd like you to be there."

"Do I have a choice?" I asked.

"You can't stay in this room any longer. Your period of detoxification is over. I'll send Mark and another peer over in a few minutes to help you move."

As her heels clicked out of the room, I sat up fully and swung my legs over the side of the bed. I felt weak, like my bones had turned to rubber. Sliding to the floor, I managed the two feet to the bathroom. My reflection showed matted hair and droopy eyes, despite all the sleep of the past days.

Moving slowly, I dressed in the jeans and sweatshirt that I'd left in the little closet and grabbed my overnight bag. I sat in the chair to put on my tennis shoes.

Mark and some girl with bleached white hair greeted me.

"Hi. We're here to help you move."

My chest constricted. I shut my eyes, holding on to the edge of the chair.

"I've changed my mind," I said as I stood up. "I'm not staying."

I reached for my purse on the shelf in the closet. "Thank you anyway, but I'm going home."

"Let me go get somebody," the girl said, turning quickly from the room.

"Yeah, you can't just leave," Mark said.

"Uh, I think I can," I said.

Little nurse Debbie returned with the white-haired girl. I gave her fourteen seconds to tell me why I should stay.

"Well, thanks for all you've done. I feel a lot better now. I need to leave."

Miss Priss entered the room. There were too many people in the small space. I wanted out, but she was blocking the door.

"What's going on?" she asked, looking from person to person.

"Nothing," I said. "I'm done. I'm leaving."

I don't think that she tried very hard to stop me, but she went through the motions, bringing up Jamil and Marcie and being a worry to my family.

"I can't stay," I repeated, inching my way towards the door. I didn't want to have to push past her, but I would.

"You realize that you'll be leaving against medical advice?" she said, holding up a clipboard.

"I'm fine. And I'm leaving," I said.

"Sign here."

I hadn't realized that they had my wallet for safekeeping, but it was returned as I left the floor. Miss Priss rode with me in the elevator, holding the button as I walked out into the lobby.

"Good luck," was all that she said. I didn't answer.

It was chilly as I stepped outside. October? Maybe November if I'd slept for four days. The day was closing in on evening with the kind of late fall sun that barely lights the sky. Bright red leaves on a large maple and a yellowed oak rustled in a sudden wind. What do I do? What do I do now?

I walked a block and sat at a bus stop with my eyes closed, shivering. Traveling another block to a phone booth, I pulled a dime out of my otherwise empty wallet and dialed my brother.

"Johnny? Hi. They let me out. Can you come pick me up?"

He pulled up in his rattling truck twenty minutes later.

"Thanks" was all I said as I climbed in, putting my bag on the floor at my feet. We rode in silence until we got across the Fremont Bridge.

"So what exactly is going on with you?" John asked, staring straight ahead.

I laid my head back against the seat and closed my eyes.

"What do you know?"

"Nothing I'm real thrilled about after talking to Marcie," he answered. "Are you fucking crazy?"

I laughed. "Yeah, maybe," I said, and told him at least part of what I'd been doing the last couple of years.

"How did you keep all this secret?" he asked, finally turning to look at me as he drove.

"Well, it's not like we spend a lot of time together," I said. "Speed isn't like a downer. I can function quite well, thank you very much. So, pop in, pop out, 'hi, how are you doing?' and always wear long sleeves."

He shook his head, glancing at my arms as he drove.

"God, Johnny, it's not like none of us get high or anything. You've done your share of cocaine with me. And let's not talk about Jamil and our lost weekends."

He pulled into my driveway and shifted into park, the gear vibrating as he idled.

"Get your head out of your ass, Annette. The needle is a big deal, and the dealers and the whole bit. This is huge. What will it be next time, a call to pick you up from jail, or worse?"

The veneer, which had once been a mile-thick wall I'd constructed around my drug use began to chip.

"I'm sorry I had to involve you in this," I said, reaching for the door handle.

He gripped the steering wheel, and then turned towards me.

"Annette, you're my big sister. I love you. And I'm scared for you."

I looked at him as my eyes filled with tears, then turned and got out of the truck. He'd never said, "I love you" before.

"Thanks for feeding the cat," I replied.

I went inside, feeling like a cutout character in a book of paper dolls. I sat on my couch, looked out my kitchen window, opened the refrigerator. My brain raced, pinballing from my mother to my brother to Jamil to Daniel to the bag of dope in the cupboard, to the guy at the hospital who invited me to the unit to Robert to my bank account and back again to the dope. I felt like I was shattering from the inside out. If this was four days clean, I didn't want any part of it. But I should hold out because what if Jamil came over or, worse, my mother, and it would be better to just be cool for a few more days until the dust settled from this little episode and I should go grocery shopping and fuck it.

I went to the kitchen and got the dope out of the bottom of the cereal box, then walked upstairs with intent, to the closet, to the little box in the bag in the bigger box in the back. I sat on the bed with the stash box in my lap. It's okay, it's okay, I told myself over and over. It's okay, as I walked to the bathroom and set the box on the counter, removing a fresh syringe, a bit of cotton, the scale. I sat on the closed toilet seat and measured out a hit, mixing it with water in the fit cap, rolling the cotton between my fingers to make a tight ball, drawing the thick liquid into the chamber. I balanced the outfit on the counter and took off my shirt, looking at both arms. Prolonging the seduction, I undressed and turned on the shower, stepping in to the hot spray. I turned the heat up until my skin turned pink, doing push-ups now off the opposite wall. I turned back around, clenching and unclenching my fists as the hot water beat against my arms. Be there. Be there, I said to my veins. Please let me get a vein.

189

I turned off the water, stepping out to wrap myself in an oversized towel, my reflection a blur in the foggy mirror. I cracked open the tiny window by the toilet and watched as steam escaped into the evening. Staying wrapped in the towel, I sat down and picked up the fabric belt I'd been using to tie off. I took deep breaths, then got up and drank a glass of water. Sitting back down, I tied the belt a couple of inches above my right wrist, clenching and unclenching my hand. I felt a slight bulge on the top of my thumb. More important, I saw it, straining against the skin. My vein. Waiting.

Taking a deep breath, I turned my right hand in towards my body, and positioned the syringe. Yes. I nearly cried out as I hit the vein on the first try. I pulled back on the plunger and watched the beautiful thin stream of blood enter the chamber. I twisted my hand just slightly so that I could balance the needle while I let go of it to loosen the tie, then hesitated for a second, enjoying the sight of the small river as it began to pool. I then slammed the plunger as quickly as I could, watching the thick liquid leave the syringe and enter my body.

I closed my eyes and waited the seconds that it took for the methamphetamine to travel from my hand to my heart, and did cry out as the heat exploded in my chest and then through my torso. Yes. Thank you, God. I kept my eyes closed, swaying back and forth slightly as I sat. This was good. This was what I needed. Fuck those people at the hospital. Fuck Jamil and Marcie. I'd figure out a way to make it without them, without Jamil's money. I'd be fine. I took deep breaths and reveled in the sensation. I'll be fine. I'll be fine.

With energy I hadn't felt in months, I got up from the toilet and went to my room to dress. Where was Daniel? I needed to see him.

I found him at Brandy's new place. He'd been cooking all week at Sandy's but was taking a break to market his wares. Brandy's car was gone, but the front door was unlocked as I drove up. Daniel was sitting in a dirty overstuffed chair, his own stash box on the side table along with a cluster of dime baggies. He raised he eyebrows as I came into the dark little living room.

"Out so soon?" he asked.

"I couldn't stay. It was weird," I answered, not meeting his eye. "Can I buy a bag or two?"

"You can always have whatever you want from me," he answered, "but are you sure this is what you want?"

"What do you mean?"

"I seem to recall something about Jamil and money and not wanting to be on the streets," he said.

I sat on the velvet couch, avoiding the slump in the middle.

"I don't know, Daniel. I'm tired of him ruling my life."

He chuckled as he rolled a joint. "No one rules your life but you, Annette. That's something you've never seemed to understand."

I didn't understand. I didn't understand why Jamil had gotten married. I didn't understand why Daniel was now giving me shit. I didn't understand how I could be held responsible when I'd done so much to make Jamil see that I loved him. It was his doing that I'd quit my job in the first place. And now he was going to just drop me?

I didn't say much more, other than to ask him when he might be coming over. "Soon" was his standard reply lately, which meant maybe next week, or not at all.

He walked me to my car in the dark that would soon turn to a pale dawn. It wasn't raining and the cold felt good against my sweaty skin. As I opened the door, he said, "You know Annette, it might not be a bad idea for you to go somewhere for a while. You went twenty-nine years without methamphetamine. You could probably go a month or so without it, and it might be good for you to take a break."

I started to say that I didn't need a break but just smiled as I got into the car with one of the dime baggies tucked into my pocket.

"Come by when you can," I said, driving out of the little flag lot and on to 82nd. I was home within ten minutes, followed by the November sun trying hard to rise.

The phone was ringing when I walked into the kitchen. I looked at the clock. It wasn't even 7:00.

"Annette, it's Marcie. Where in the hell did you go?"

"Well, obviously, I'm home," I answered.

"This isn't good. Jamil is pissed. He's in Cleveland but will call you later. You'd better have some answers."

Fuck this. I hung up without another word. Answers. I'd have some fucking answers.

I paced the house for the next three hours. What to do? What to do? Where could I move? What would I do for work? I waited an hour and called Joanne's office, and hung up when she answered. I called my Mom.

"Are you okay, honey?" she asked, in a voice that made me cry. "Is there anything I can do?"

"Yeah, Mom, I'm okay. I just didn't want to stay there."

I wanted to be eight and on the couch with a thermometer in my mouth. Or seven, as she sang me a lullaby, brushing the hair from my face as I fell asleep. Not thirty-one with a needle in my arm, getting backed into a corner.

We hung up, with my promise to see her the next day. I called Brandy's to talk to Daniel. Maybe he could come over today instead of later.

"Hey, Annette. No, he's not here. So how was it?" she asked.

"It was strange. I mostly slept," I answered.

"Yeah. It would seem weird to be right in town. You could walk out anytime and get anything you wanted."

She coughed, and I heard her take a long drag on a cigarette.

"You know, if you do have to go somewhere, I've heard about a place at the beach that's alright."

"I don't know what I'm going to do," I said. "Tell Daniel that I called if you see him."

The next few days passed in a fog. I did not go to my mother's. Jamil did not call. At some point, I came alert sitting on the toilet, a spent needle in my arm with no recollection of mixing the hit or shooting up. That was a day after I'd knocked the wind out of myself shooting up in the chest. With the needle still in, I lost my breath and had to gasp for air. All the while, Daniel's voice talked to me:

"Maybe it wouldn't be such a bad idea to take a break." I heard his words over and over, no matter how much I tried not to. A break. A break. Maybe a break. Someplace at the beach.

Jamil did call a week later. I was unprepared to hear him on the other end of the line as I answered the phone. His voice echoed, like I was hearing him through cables under the sea.

"Jamil? Where are you?" I asked.

"I'm in Jeddah. But never mind me. You didn't stay."

"No."

He paused and I heard the tinkling of ice cubes in a glass.

"Annette, this isn't good. You need to get some help. The insurance will pay. You need to go."

My chin trembled. It felt like the walls of my bedroom were breathing with me. The whole world seemed dark except for a glow around the phone.

"I know I do," said a tiny voice that sounded like it came from outside of my body. Part of me wanted to continue the fight, but the part of me that was talking was just plain tired.

"Good. Okay. This is good," Jamil said.

He talked so quickly that I could barely keep up, about calling Marcie and how they'd take me back and it would be better this time. I came back to my self and stopped him.

"Jamil, wait. There is a place at the coast that I've heard is good. It wouldn't work for me to just be here in town. I'll give the number to Marcie."

"Maybe," he said hesitatingly.

"Marcie will check it out. It is a good place, I'm sure," I said, as if I knew. "And Jamil? I'll go in after the New Year. This is a big decision and I want to be sure I'm ready. I want one last New Year's Eve."

Again I heard the glass tinkling, and a swallow, followed by the sound of a cigarette lighting.

"I'm not sure this is such a good idea," he said.

"I need to do this for me. I promise that I'll be there January 2."

"If you aren't, the money stops, Annette."

My voice caught. "I don't want this to just be about the money, Jamil. I love you, and I'm so sorry."

"I love you too," he sighed. "You know that I do. Tell Marcie to call me when it's arranged."

Shit, I said to myself as I hung up the phone. Now what? It was late, so instead of doing another hit, I undressed and got into bed. I was asleep within seconds.

The next day I tracked down Brandy, then gave Marcie the name of the place in Seaside. She called me back within hours. "They want to hear from you," she said.

"What do you mean?"

"They'll only set it up if the person who needs help calls them. It isn't enough that other people think you need help."

I tried to ignore the number for a couple of days, making wide circles around the piece of paper on my desk. I decided that I should go see what I was getting into before making a final, final decision. John agreed to drive me.

We got to Seaside an hour and a half before my appointment, which is a fair amount of time to kill on a rainy November day at the beach. We had lunch on the main strip, reminiscing about riding the bumper cars as kids, driving up to Ecola Park while the whoosh-whoosh of the windshield wipers lulled us to sleep in the back seat.

I laughed. "That's the time you sat up and said, 'it's pretty, but where is the scenery?'"

He stared out the window and didn't answer.

We'd spent a lot of time at the beach when we were kids. A friend of Dad's had a tiny cabin a block from the ocean and before the fighting years began, we'd fill it up with cousins and dogs and wet beach towels while the parents sat on the porch with scotch on the rocks.

"Remember when the bunks had earwigs and no one would go to bed?" I asked.

"Yeah, I remember" John answered, crumbling a packet of crackers into his bowl of chowder.

We ate in silence as the rain beat sideways against the restaurant window.

"So what do you know about this place?" John finally asked, pushing his empty bowl to the table's edge.

"That it's not a hospital," I replied.

We paid the bill and ran the few steps to the car. I had the address on a folded paper in my pocket. Seaside meant Broadway and the Promenade and cotton candy to me but we'd asked at the counter so knew we were headed a few blocks south. After navigating a one-way street, we pulled into the parking area of what must've been a hotel in a previous life

"You go ahead. I'll wait out here," John said, reaching to take a worn paperback from the glove box.

I stared at the ocean. I didn't want to go in.

"Okay," I said, pulling up the hood on my sweatshirt against the rain.

My last hit had been three hours earlier so I was getting edgy. Opening the front door of the yellow building, I was nearly backed out by a wall of cigarette smoke. There were a couple of guys on couches, and a crusty-looking older man behind what looked like a lobby counter, cigarette dangling from his lips as he looked over his glasses at a newspaper.

"Yes?" he said, looking up at me.

"I have an appointment at 2:00? For a tour?"

"Oh. You must be Annette. I'm Jim," he said, taking off the glasses and sticking out his hand. I shook it gingerly and stuck my own hands back in the pockets of my sweatshirt.

He stubbed out the cigarette as he set the paper down. "Most everybody's in group," he said, "so I won't take you over there, but here, let's start in the pantry."

He walked me through a small kitchen, with four full coffee pots on the counter, along with packets of hot cocoa and sugar and cream.

"The only vices we have left," he laughed.

I didn't smoke or drink coffee, but maybe I could learn. He walked me upstairs and showed me the men's hall and the women's, each bedroom equipped with twin beds and not much else.

"You're encouraged to stay out of your room," Jim said. "You know, addiction is a disease of isolation, so we try to keep people from hiding out. Your peers will see to that."

That guy, Mark, at the hospital, had talked like this too. Peers. Isolating. Groups. Drug of choice. I felt like I needed a dictionary.

"Can I reserve an ocean-front room?" I asked, as we passed several that faced the Pacific.

Jim laughed. "I hate to break it to you, but this isn't a vacation resort. We get a bit of a rush at the New Year, so it will likely be a matter of what's open."

I felt stupid. Of course it wasn't a vacation. I knew that.

I must've blushed, because he said, "Don't worry about it, kid. Not too many people know what to expect when they come to treatment. Unless they've done it before, and believe me, we see our share of retreads."

We walked down a different set of stairs than we'd gone up.

"There is no smoking whatsoever on the second floor or food allowed in the rooms," Jim said. "After four or five days, you'll be able to take a walk on the beach but only with another person."

"So what's to stop you from going in to town and getting a drink?" I asked.

Jim paused, and turned around to look at me.

"I guess that would show just how sick you really are, wouldn't it?"

There was a young woman behind the desk now, on the phone, chewing on the end of a pen.

"That's Mary Jo. She came through here a couple of years ago and now does the insurance. A lot of people end up staying in the area when they're done. It's safer than going home."

God, don't let this be weird. A special language, people working here after they get out, smoking and drinking coffee. Maybe the hospital was better. It was cleaner anyway.

Mary Jo put the telephone receiver to her chest.

"Jim, the insurance company says that Dale has to leave tomorrow," she said.

Jim waved his hand in the air. "Tell them to fuck off. He's not going anywhere."

Now it was my turn to laugh. Sterile or not, the hospital was not for me. I could deal with this place and these people, and if I couldn't, I'd leave.

I shook hands again with Jim, telling him I'd see him in another few weeks. He held my hand for a minute and looked at me, his other hand reaching for my shoulder.

"You take care of yourself," he said. "Get back to us in one piece."

Chapter Fifteen

I STARTLED A napping John as I climbed into the truck. "Let's go," I said.

"So?" he asked.

"It's okay. I'll be back in January."

I peeled off my sweatshirt and rolled it into a pillow, leaning against the passenger window. I dozed in and out on the way home, keeping my eyes closed so I wouldn't have to talk. An hour and a half later, John dropped me off in the street in front of my house with a simple "See ya."

I walked in to Daniel, Robert, and two guys I vaguely knew, Ted and Roy, in my basement setting up shop. We'd agreed that Daniel and friends could run a mega-reaction before I went away, sort of a last hurrah. It wasn't like I'd had some sort of "save me, God" experience. I was going into treatment to take a break, and so I wouldn't have to move. I figured I'd stay clean for a month or two to show Jamil I could do it, and then pick up where I left off, but in a more controlled manner. I didn't want to leave Daniel and his heroin habit in my house while I was gone but had told him he could work until I left.

They went at it for days, in shifts. It was like a party with all the activity in the basement and men's laughter and the Rolling Stones on the stereo. Brandy came over, and even Lorie, to wish the boys a productive batch, and to wish me well.

On one of his breaks, Daniel crept into my bed. We made love as if we never would again, his feet fluttering like flippers as he came. As we lay side by side afterwards, he looked at me and smoothed my hair.

"You know, you could do this on your own," he said. "You don't have to go away. Why not prove it to everyone by just stopping?"

I was glad it was dark in my room. I didn't want Daniel to see that, while I was scared to death, part of me wanted to go away. I wanted to be away from him and his crew, from Lorie and Brandy and the all-night visits, from the strange noises in the basement when no one was home, from the dope calling to me. I didn't think I could do all that on my own.

"It'll be fine," I whispered. "I'll be back."

"But will you really?" Daniel asked, drifting off to sleep. "Will you really?"

They were done in a week, carting out boxes of glassware under cover of darkness. Robert, who had only given me a few cursory nods while they were working, stopped in the kitchen on his final trip out.

"This is for you," he said, handing me a full prescription bottle full of off-white crystal. "Rent for the basement, and sort of a farewell gift. This should get you through the rest of the month before you go."

I smiled back at him. He wasn't really a bad guy. I'd been pretty lucky, all things considered. Daniel and his friends were good people.

"Thanks, Robert. I mean it," I said, reaching out to give him a hug.

"Oh geez," he said, stiffly hugging me back. "See you around."

Daniel was the last to leave.

"You know, you can always change your mind," he said, looking up at me from his down-turned face.

We agreed to spend New Year's together. In the meantime, it was me and my bottle of dope.

I didn't actually see my mother until Thanksgiving. I was expected for dinner, along with my brother and his family. It was early when I woke up, maybe 6:00, greeted by the muffled whiteness of a snowstorm. As I sat in my bedroom chair, watching flakes drop from the pewter sky, I thought about the day and what kind of flak I could expect from my family. In all likelihood, no one would say a word. We would talk about the weather, and the size of the bird, and remember the Thanksgiving when Grandpa snuck off and ate all the peanut brittle. My addiction would be like the drunken uncle you tried to ignore.

At 2:00, I geared up for the five-block walk. John's wife didn't want to go out in the snow, so it would be just me and my folks and lots of food. I shot up before leaving.

We ate in silence, me on one side of the table, my parents on the other, a diminishing bottle of sparkling cider in the middle. Dad hadn't had a drink for over a month. And he was watching his diet. At least that's what Mom said. He got up and began to clear the table even before we were finished eating. When he was in the kitchen, Mom set down her fork and looked at me.

"Annette, I just don't understand," she said.

"Understand what?" I asked.

"I don't know what I thought when you said 'drugs.' Marijuana, I guess, or pills. Your brother told me about the needle. I just don't understand."

The truth was that I didn't understand it myself, but I did my best to convince her that shooting speed wasn't that big a deal. Most of my friends did it, it was sterile, I was fine and just needed a break.

When I finally looked at my mother I saw that she was crying, big tears falling down her cheeks and on to her rust-colored sweater with the appliquéd turkey on the front. I caught my breath and held it to stop my own tears from flowing.

"I didn't raise you like this," she finally said, dabbing at her eyes with her napkin. "What did I do wrong?"

"Oh God, Mother. I haven't lived in this house for over ten years. This has very little to do with you."

I picked up my dishes, brushing past Dad on my way to the kitchen.

"Look, I understand that you're worried, but you don't need to be. I'm fine. I wish everyone would just stop worrying about me."

My parents looked at each other uneasily, then at me.

"We just want you to be alright," Mom said, squeezing her napkin.

"I know you do," I sighed. "I just want to go home."

I stood in the kitchen as my mother, with lips tight, packed up leftovers. Dad had gone to his place in front of the television, giving me a peck on the cheek before he sat down. He only did that when he was sober.

"You call me when you get home, so I know you're okay," Mom said, handing me the bag of small containers.

"Mom, it's five blocks. I'll be fine."

"I don't care if it's two blocks. You call me," she said, zipping up the last few inches of my jacket.

I trudged back the way I came, my footprints already filled with new snow that continued to fall.

"Mom? I'm home. Talk to you later."

She called several times a day until I went to treatment. Always it was "Just checking in honey," as if she thought I might die if I she weren't vigilant. Sometimes I let the phone ring and ring and ring. Sometimes I unplugged it.

If you're lucky as an addict, a moment comes when you realize that you need help and can't go on any more. Some people call it "hitting bottom" and honestly, I probably hit bottom sixty times before I knew it. For a long time I was able to avoid or ignore the quiet voice that said "Hey, something is wrong here." That is, until I couldn't.

My moment of truth came in those weeks leading up to the New Year. I had my bottle full of dope and had shot up in the breast a few days earlier and missed the vein. It had abscessed painfully. On a cold December evening, I balanced a lamp on the bed, and sat, naked, with a heating pad secured under one arm and across my chest in an effort to bring the abscess to a head. I held a full syringe in one hand, and a mirror in the other, searching for a viable vein. As I scrutinized my arms and upper body, I caught my face in the mirror and cringed at the wounded animal I saw looking back at me. I shuddered and closed my eyes. It felt like whatever it was that was the essence of me, Annette, was shrinking. I was afraid that I would disappear altogether.

But like the wounded animal that drags its bleeding body through the underbrush, I kept going. I kept sitting on my closed toilet with a belt around my arm, I kept listening to the whispering voices, I kept not answering the phone.

Christmas came and went with barely a ho, ho, ho. I spent an hour at Mom's annual party, moving from kitchen to living room and back again as cousins and brother and in-laws avoided me. Aunty Ruth was the only person to wish me a Merry Christmas, putting her arms around my shoulders as she whispered in my ear, "If you don't beat this thing, I'll beat you, damn it. Get better, honey."

I slipped out without saying good-bye.

Daniel came over at 11:00 on New Year's Eve. I had a good bottle of champagne that Jamil had left in the fridge all those months before, a fire in the fireplace, and the rest of the speed. As the clock neared midnight, I opened the bottle for a toast, except that Daniel was in the bathroom shooting heroin. As the neighborhood exploded with the banging of pans and the blowing of horns, I chugged from the bottle and did a shot of crystal, in a vein on the top of my foot. I waited for a jolt, from the booze or the dope, and it didn't come. I drank more and even snorted a fingernail of the speed, but I was in that limbo between fucked up and sober and couldn't move towards either one.

I stood outside the bathroom before going in. Daniel was slumped on the toilet seat. I panicked momentarily, but he was just nodding and I was able to rouse him enough to come upstairs to bed. We both passed out.

When I came to, it was dark. I sat up with my heart pounding. Shit. It was the 2nd of January, going fast, and I was supposed to be in treatment. What had happened to the 1st? I shook Daniel.

"Come on. We need to get to the beach!" I said in a panic. I wasn't packed, and it was snowing again.

I showered and shot up, and went back to find Daniel sitting on the edge of the bed smoking a joint. He went to the bathroom as I started opening drawers. What did one pack for a month away?

He found me a half hour later, packing and unpacking my bag, clothes strewn on the floor.

"Annette. It's okay. Just close the suitcase and we can leave."

My lip quivered as I started to cry. I was so scared. Maybe he was right. Maybe I could just do this on my own. Maybe I could go tomorrow.

"It's okay," he repeated. "Let's go."

And so Daniel pried me out of the house and into the little MG that he'd traded some guy a bunch of dope to get. The arched top of the Fremont Bridge was empty. With the packed snow and that falling from the sky, it looked like we were driving off the edge of the world. I closed my eyes until we got away from the city.

I made Daniel pull over just before the tiny town of Elsie in a parking lot with a cluster of overhead lights.

"I'm not going in empty," I said, pulling out the syringe I'd pre-loaded.

At first Daniel sat in the car as I poked and prodded at my arms. It was too cold to take off my shirt, and I didn't want to shoot up between the breasts in front of him. Finally he said, "I'm going to take a leak" and got out of the car.

I closed my eyes for just a second, then held my left hand tight around my right wrist. I clenched and unclenched my fist, watching as the veins on the lower thumb-pad of my palm stood out. I tied off and hit the biggest vein on the first try. It was a sad attempt, more like a gentle wave than the rush I wanted, but it was done. I was done.

Forty minutes later we pulled up outside the treatment center, across the street in front of a phone booth. I could see the old guy, Jim, at the desk, again with a cigarette dangling from his mouth and glasses perched on his nose reading a paper. A couple of guys sat writing at the dining room table, coffee mugs giving off steam, books and papers piled high. A woman reclined on one of the couches.

I looked at my watch. It was after 10:00. I should probably wait until the next day. It was probably too late. I could use a drink. I got out of the car and went into the phone booth, pulling the folded paper with the number out of my pocket.

"This is Jim. What can I do for you?" I watched as he turned away from the window and answered the phone.

I took a deep breath. "Hi. This is Annette. I met you last month? I was supposed to be there today. It's late, so I think I'm just going to go to a motel and come in tomorrow," I said, talking fast so he couldn't interrupt.

"Oh, no need for that. We've been waiting for you. Come on in."

If he had said anything else, if I had sensed even the slightest hesitation in his voice, I would have hung up the phone and gone to a bar and ordered a beer. But in that split second when I realized that Jim had been waiting for me, I was hit with the certainty that if I didn't walk through those doors at this very moment I probably never would. And I wasn't willing to sit across from my mother or Jamil again to try to explain why.

I hung up and moved to get my bag from the tiny trunk.

"I'm going in," I said to Daniel, who came around to carry my suitcase up the front steps. Jim met us at the door.

"Welcome home," he said, taking my bag, glancing over my shoulder at Daniel.

My lip trembled as I let go of Daniel's hand.

"Do you want to come in?" I asked.

"No. No. I'm going to get started back over the mountain," he said, looking at the floor. When he did look up, his eyes had that vacancy that told me there was heroin waiting for him at home, if not in the car.

We hugged on the porch and then I stood in the window and watched as he drove away. It was good that I wouldn't have a car in the lot. It would be harder to leave. Jim had me sign some paperwork, and then I sat on the couch wrapped in a blanket until the sun came up. As the seagulls began to screech on their morning rounds, I walked upstairs to my oceanfront room and went to bed.

What do you say about rehab? That it is frustrating and exhilarating and exhausting. That it is confusing and clarifying and caustic. That there is nowhere to hide. I paid attention as best I could, napped when they let me, and tried to wrap my mind around the mechanics of a substance-free life. I completed worksheets and read the required assignments and cried each time we went to group. I talked about Jamil and how badly I'd hurt him. I talked about my Dad's drinking and how badly he'd hurt my mother. I talked about how badly I hurt inside almost all of the time.

The counselors told us to pray for help. How long had I been talking to a God that I wasn't sure listened, praying for help that I couldn't articulate? And then one day it all made sense.

There was a kid who'd come in a few days earlier. He was only seventeen; a heroin-addicted punk rocker in tight black jeans with a dyed mop of coal black hair. We all knew he was an addict. It was as evident as the razored lightening bolt scar on his forearm. But he didn't know it. He thought he could control the heroin and he wanted more, so he left—just walked out in the middle of a group. We followed him down the street, fifteen straggly alcoholics and drug addicts that included the boozy fifty year old from a wealthy suburban enclave, the young gay Indian from rural Montana, and me. We stood in a circle at the Greyhound stop and chanted the Serenity Prayer like some deranged cult and then watched the kid get on the bus without a backward glance.

Going back to my upstairs room, I got on my knees, crying at the futility of knowing how much that kid needed our help and him not accepting it. And in that worrying about him, something shifted in me and I got it, really got it for the first time. I wasn't in any more control of my life or my addiction than that kid was. Something snapped way deep inside and I cried out, "Fuck it, God. I can't do this anymore. You take over."

It was the most genuine prayer of my life, before or since. With those words I felt a wave of peace like I'd never experienced. It was what I'd wanted from a piece of paper when I converted to Islam. It was what I'd hoped for when I said the Lord's Prayer at night before falling asleep. It was what I'd searched for in the bottom of a bag of methamphetamine or a bindle of cocaine. And this time I hadn't even been looking.

Exactly one month later, Joanne picked me up, pregnant belly mashed up against the steering wheel of the old Impala. We stopped at Oney's for a burger on the way home, not far from where I'd shot up for the last time. We talked as we ate, about our friendship and about healing and about what would happen next. As we prepared to leave, she reached across the table to take my hand.

"I'm so glad you're okay. I'm so glad you're coming home."

Marcie and John were at the house when we got there with their spouses and kids, along with Anthony sitting in a corner of the kitchen looking smug. Mom and Dad pulled up, lugging a big pot of spaghetti and a loaf of garlic bread. Dad took me aside and whispered, "Maybe I'll go to one of those meetings with you sometime."

A colorful bouquet from Jamil sat on the table with a card that read, "I'm proud of you," and sparkling cider filled the wine glasses. People were laughing, talking about me like I wasn't in the room. I didn't feel so proud, or as happy as everyone else seemed to be. I felt hollow, gutted out like a carcass. I felt like I might break.

That night I drove myself to "one of those" meetings, one that had been recommended by Jim, the desk guy. I sat in the corner and tried to be invisible and sucked in the energy that I felt in the room. In the coming weeks I did the same thing every day, sometimes twice a day, and slowly felt the hole in my gut begin to fill. I learned people's names and they learned mine, and soon I felt like I truly belonged somewhere for maybe the first time in my life.

It was a month before I went in to the little room under the stairs. I had studiously avoided even looking in that direction as I skirted the corner into the laundry room, not allowing even a glance. I'd seen Daniel a few times, most recently at Brandy's, but each time felt a little more foreign. It was hard to converse in Recovery language to someone who was speaking Addict.

Finally I went into the lab, intentionally choosing a sunny morning. Unlocking the door, I was greeted by a rush of cold air and the faint odor of methamphetamine. The room was empty, save for a box on the workbench, but as I stood, I could almost hear the bubbling of water in tubes, the clicking of the hot plate and the scraping of the razor that harvested the finished product.

Closing the door behind me, I carried the box of Daniel's discards to the kitchen with the intent of throwing it out. I set it on the floor near the back door and kneeled to make sure that there was nothing of mine inside, nothing worth salvaging. I pulled out an extension cord, leaving the cracked beaker and a chipped graduate. At the bottom of the box was a glass dish. I took a deep breath as I worked it free. A thin, thin layer of crystal clung to the curves of the plate; not much, but enough that I knew I could feel if I stuck it in my arm. My breath came shallow as my mind raced. Was there a syringe in the house? Joanne had cleaned out my stash, but maybe she'd missed something. My palms were wet as I wiped them on the legs of my jeans. No one would know, I thought. No one would know.

And then a voice entered my head, very gentle, very sure. "But you would know. You would know, Annette."

And for the very first time in my life, that mattered. I mattered. Standing slowly, I took the dish to the sink, rinsing it in hot water to make certain that every last bit of dope went down the drain. Dumping the contents of the box into a plastic bag, I tied the top shut and threw it outdoors in the trash.

~~~

Spring came in blazing glory that year. I felt like Dorothy when she went from sepia-toned Kansas to Oz. Everything that I did and smelled and felt and touched seemed new and exciting and just a little scary. I was alive and had been given the chance to start over.

I continued to see Daniel off and on after rehab, more off than on. His heroin use had escalated, but I thought that I could love him clean, or shout him clean or reason with him. It didn't work.

He came over one night, driving that cherry red MG that had taken me to rehab. The car died in my driveway the next day when he tried to leave. It sat there for a week before I caught up with him and told him that it had to go. It did, sometime in the night, but when I left home the next morning, I saw that the car had died again just down the street.

That little red car sat in front of a neighbor's house for weeks, on a corner, tilted just slightly down hill. I passed it morning and night on my way to and from my new job, hit with a jab of regret and anger and sadness each time.

One night I came home late, after my sociology class at the community college, and saw that the car had been broken in to. It was raining, and the contents were scattered up and down the block. From the light of the streetlamp I recognized a flannel shirt, a plastic notebook, and his box of cassette tapes. And there, one in and one out of the brown paper bag were Daniel's black wing tips. For a brief moment I thought about stopping to retrieve them.

I didn't.

CPSIA information can be obtained at www.ICGtesting.com
Printed in the USA
BVOW041701110213

312934BV00002B/173/P